W9-BSI-385

Kingfishers Catch Fire

Rumer Godden

MILKWEED EDITIONS

©1953, Text by Rumer Godden
©1994, Art by R. W. Scholes
All rights reserved
Except for brief quotations in critical articles or reviews, no part of this book may be reproduced in any
manner without prior written permission from the publisher:
Milkweed Editions, 430 First Avenue North, Suite 400, Minneapolis, MN 55401

Printed in the United States of America
Published in 1994 by Milkweed Editions
Originally published in 1953 by The Viking Press
94 95 96 97 98   5 4 3 2 1

Milkweed Editions is supproted in part by the Elmer and Eleanor Andersen Foundation; Dayton Hudson
Foundation for Dayton's and Target Stores; General Mills Foundation; Honeywell Foundation; Jerome
Foundation; John S. and James L. Knight Foundation, The McKnight Foundation; Andrew W. Mellon
Foundation; Minnesota State Arts Board through an appropriation by the Minnesota State Legislature;
Challenge and Literature Programs of the National Endowment for the Arts; I. A. O'Shaughnessy
Foundation; Piper Family Fund of the Minneapolis Foundation; Piper Jaffray Companies, Inc.; John and
Beverly Rollwagen Fund; Star Tribune/Cowles Media Foundation; Surdna Foundation; James R. Thorpe
Foundation; Unity Avenue Foundation; Lila Wallace-Reader's Digest Literary Publishers Marketing
Development Program, funded through a grant to the Council of Literary Magazines and Small Presses;
and generous individuals.

Library of Congress Cataloging-in-Publication Data
Godden, Rumer.
    Kingfishers catch fire / by Rumer Godden.
      p. cm.
    ISBN 0-915943-81-6 (alk. paper)
      1. Villages—India—Fiction.   2. British—India—Fiction.
    3. Women—India—Fiction.   I. Title.
PR6013.02K56 1994
823'.912—dc20   93-37769
                                                      CIP

75°

Kingfishers Catch Fire

Kingfishers Catch Fire

LONG AFTERWARDS—"Not so long," said <u>Toby</u>, "it's only two years"; "Ages afterwards," said <u>Sophie</u>—Toby gave Sophie another lamp with kingfishers on it; he sent for it all the way to Profit David, of whom he disapproved. "And I am a fool," he said. "You will only lose it or give it away to someone else, or leave it behind somewhere."

"No I won't," said Sophie certainly. "I am more careful now"; but Toby shook his head. He knew that Sophie was like a <u>kingfisher herself</u>, choosing some strange, unthought-of place for her nest, <u>diving relentlessly for her private fish, then flashing out of sight.</u> "Well, people must do as they must," said Sophie.

She argued defensively, but her eyes were tender, as her fingers traced the bright birds on the lamp; kingfishers always made her think of Kashmir; with the bulbul, the lotus, the iris, vine, and chenar leaf, they are the symbols of the country; over and over again they appear in carvings and embroideries and are woven in Kashmiri silks and carpets. "I am—homesick for them," said Sophie. "Homesick!"

"Even with what happened?" asked Toby.

"What happened doesn't matter," said Sophie. "Not now." And she said, "I am even glad it happened."

"Good God!" said Toby.

"Yes, glad," said Sophie softly. "My eyes will never be poor again, having seen Kashmir. I saw such <u>beauty in people and things.</u>"

"Those people?" asked Toby.

"Those people," said Sophie.

Beauty of Kashmir

Chapter 1

The real kingfishers lived down by the lake in the willows, and there was one that nested on the earth bank of the aqueduct, which the villagers called the canal, behind the house. When the kingfishers were still they hardly showed their colours, but when they plunged for a fish and opened their wings and flew there was a flash of colour and they glowed, as their little replicas glowed on the gold of Sophie's lamp.

The house was called Dhilkusha—"To make the heart glad"; that was as common a name for a house in India as "Fairview" or "Mon Repos" in Europe. Sophie would not have considered living in a house called Mon Repos, but Dhilkusha was in Kashmir, and she thought it romantic.

It was her own idea to go and live there. When Sophie had an idea her child Teresa trembled.

❧

The vale of Kashmir is a chain of lakes and rivers, set with orchards and gardens, in a ring of mountains that are always streaked with snow. Dhilkusha was twelve miles from Srinagar and was built high up on one of these mountains, above a lonely little village, and looked down on the Dāl Lake with its placid reflections, its willows and islands and spreading lotuses.

Twelve miles is not far by train or bus or motor car, but Kashmir has no trains, buses do not run to the villages, and neither Sophie nor the villagers could afford cars; the only way in and out for them was by boat across the lake or along the lakeshore by tonga, the slow little local two-wheeled carriages that had tilted roofs.

In India a woman alone does not go and live alone—not, at any rate, far from her own kind, not unless she is a saint or a great sinner. Sophie was not a saint, or a sinner, but she was undeniably a woman. "Mr. Abercrombie says it's most unusual," her Aunt Portia wrote out from England, "and he knows the country. He was chaplain in Rawalpindi, remember. He says you had far better come home." "Dear Sophie, please, please listen . . ." wrote Aunt Mamie; she added, "Rose says you will do as you like; you always have." Aunt Rose was right.

"Sophie is nice to scold because she never answers back," that same Aunt Rose had once said, "and nasty to scold because she never takes any notice." Sophie took no notice now.

"It's too far," Dr. Ruth Glenister, the head doctor at the Mission, told her.

"Your Mission ladies go farther than that," argued Sophie.

"They have the protection of the Mission," said Dr. Glenister.

"We shall protect ourselves," said Sophie confidently.

"The people won't know what to make of you," said Sister Locke, the senior Mission sister.

"They soon will," said Sophie.

It was not only the Europeans who advised against it. "You may lose everything you have," said her Kashmiri merchant friend, Profit David.

"We haven't anything," said Sophie.

But we *have*, Teresa wanted to cry. They had some precious things, doubly precious to Teresa because through all the family changes these few had endured: their books, Sophie's Chinese teapot with the wicker handle, Teresa's doll Pussy Maria, Moo's tricycle, and the red numdah floor rugs and the little gold carriage clock. Teresa could not bear the thought of losing any of them. "Don't let's go there," begged Teresa.

Even the Pundit Pramatha Kaul, who owned Dhilkusha, was worried, though he was anxious to let the house. "Am I handing you over to the hounds and thieves?" he asked.

"If we were rich," said Sophie, "if we were like most Europeans and Americans who come to Kashmir, then there might be trouble."

To the pundit, Sophie was precisely like any other European or American, only more friendly; the friendliness alarmed him. "These people are poor and simple—" he began, but Sophie interrupted him.

"We shall be poor and simple too," she said with shining eyes.

2

"But madam, the peasants are rapacious—"

To that Sophie would not listen. Like many people, she had some words about which she was sentimental; one of these was "peasant." "Peasants are simple and honest and kindly and quiet," she said. "They don't want what they don't possess. They have the wisdom to stay simple. They don't want to change." In a way that was true. Here in Kashmir the boys on the mountains with the flocks looked biblical with their dark curly hair, loose robes, and round caps; the ploughs were primitive, as were the cooking pots, the water jars, the fishing spears, the very boats— "primitive and beautiful," said Sophie. The women, like the women of old, fetched water and pounded grain and ground it in a handmill and spun their flax and wool; the men smoked the same water-pipes as their grandfathers. "How picturesque they are!" said Sophie admiringly.

"And dirty," said Teresa. It was true. They were dirty.

The village below Dhilkusha was even more primitive than most. It was shut away in the fold of the mountain, which came down to a back-water of the lake; there were women and children in the village who had not seen a white woman close—certainly not white children, though they had heard about them. Many visitors came to Kashmir, to the city, to the pleasure gardens, to the health resorts up in the mountains, and they had immeasurable amounts of money; to the lucky villages near, some of the money came in the price of vegetables and fruit, walnuts, chickens and eggs and wood. "Aie! Such prices!" said the Dhilkusha villagers longingly.

"You must remember," said the pundit, worried, to Sophie, "we have not had a visitor here before."

"All the better," said Sophie. "The people will be innocent and unspoiled." And she said firmly, "I shall not be a visitor. I shall be one of them."

The pundit still looked worried.

"What can happen to you, Pundit Sahib, if you stand on your own feet?" asked Sophie sharply.

"You can fall down," said the pundit.

෴

Sophie—Sophia Barrington Ward—was then thirty-five; afterwards she often wondered how she had managed to reach that age and remain as insouciant as she was. "Insouciant is the right word," said Sophie. "Careless and indifferent." It was not that things did not go wrong. They did, very often, though she could never see why. "But what did I *do?*" she would ask when they had. "I didn't mean it to turn out like that." And how bitter was her remorse—though of course if the remorse became too much to bear in one place she could always go somewhere else. "Poor Pussy Maria," she once heard Teresa say, "Poor Pussy Maria, having to sleep in so many different beds."

"Sophie has *not* learned the law of cause and effect," said Aunt Portia, troubled. "How strange that she escapes."

"Not strange at all," said Aunt Rose. "She skips."

"*Skips*, Rose?"

"Yes, she just omits the effect." Aunt Rose's eyes were amused; she had a fellow-feeling for Sophie; then they darkened and she said, "Don't worry, one day it will catch up with her. She will be punished. And the worst part of the punishment," said Aunt Rose bitterly, "is that probably she will punish someone else, someone near and dear."

On the rare occasions when Sophie had been caught, before she had learned to be adroit, when she was small and living with the aunts, it was Toby who rescued her. "Toby always helped me," said Sophie. "Dear Toby." But there are some things that put you outside help—for instance, if you marry another man.

Sophie had married Denzil Barrington Ward. "I was quite old," said Sophie. "I was twenty-six. I should have known what I was doing." But Denzil was so tall and good-looking that few people saw him; they looked at his handsomeness instead. Even the penetrating Aunt Rose had said, "He should go far with that face." I thought so too, Sophie could have said, but she did not say it; for a talkative person she was oddly quiet about Denzil. She did not, it was true, stay with him very much. When he first went to India she had let him go alone and, though she brought the children out to join him, in the height of the war—"By way of Africa and the Canary Islands, seven weeks in convoy," as she often told afterwards—she soon took them away again.

Denzil was working then in the little provincial town of Amorra in

Bengal, where his company had a branch office. He was not released for the Army, but no one said, "He is a key man," as Sophie would have liked; they said, "Someone must stay." That seemed derogatory to Sophie. It all seemed derogatory; it was a junior post, Amorra was hot and unhealthy, its little round of European life was arid. "There is no one for me here, no one!" said Sophie. Denzil did not say that he was there; he was silent and, when Moo had dysentery and Sophie seized the excuse to get away, he did not protest. They went to a teagarden—"And then to another," said Teresa, "and then Mother thought she ought to be a war nurse and we went to Ranchi, and then she thought she would learn Urdu and be an interpreter for the Army and we came to Rawalpindi, and then . . ." Teresa could not count how many times they had moved, but each time the small ballast of hopes and plans they had collected was thrown overboard and everyone they had known was left behind.

Moo did not care. Like a little seed that is blown and can grow any-where, on a rocky ledge, in a crack of earth, he lived in a contained, contented small life of his own, no matter where he went. To Moo it did not matter, but Teresa had roots; they were tender, soft, trailing, slightly sticky roots, and they gripped what they found, and that of course made it harder when they were torn up.

"One day we will take a little house and settle down," Sophie told her.

"In Camberley?" asked Teresa. Sometimes Teresa thought she could remember a little house they had had once in Camberley in England. "Didn't we?" she used to ask Sophie.

"Yes, when Denzil was in the London office. A horrid little house," said Sophie. As Teresa remembered it, it was not horrid at all; it was a dear little house, all in a row with others just like it, all with tiled roofs and gables, green front doors and latticed windows, nice and new—and nice and safe, thought Teresa.

"Did we have a sweeper at Camberley?" she asked when the houseboat sweeper stole.

"Of course not. It was in England."

"Was there a viper at Camberley?" she asked when they found the viper.

"Of course not. It was in England."

"It was a little horror, a villa," said Sophie. But one day, thought Teresa, I shall have a little house just like that, in Camberley. She treasured up that safe-sounding name.

Meanwhile there were so many names, so many places. "How can I remember them all?" asked Teresa, and there in Kashmir was a whole new set—new names, difficult names, new strange people, new conditions, new things. Sometimes Teresa had a pucker between her brows.

"Moo is the sensitive one," said Sophie. "He has feeling." He had. The air about Moo was constantly rent with his feelings. "Moo is highly strung," said Sophie. "Teresa is stolid."

"Is it very bad to be stolid?" Teresa asked Toby later.

Toby, who was stolid himself, said, "No," but Teresa could not help thinking it was.

She was a plump, heavy, rather slow child, while Moo and Sophie were slim and quick. She had grave grey eyes. Sophie's eyes were more green than grey; sometimes they mocked, sometimes shone—when she likes anyone or is excited, thought Teresa—and they grew bright green when she was angry, which was often. Moo was more of a baby than a little boy, but when he wanted to look at anyone he put his rather big head back on his little neck and looked up in a piercing stare. His eyes were as blue as—"those little flowers on the mountain, speedwells," said Teresa. He had the same white skin as Sophie, while Teresa's was pink and freckled.

Sophie had a story that began, "Once there was a woman who had two children, one with hair like marmalade and one with hair like honey." Teresa was the marmalade one; her hair was red, but Moo's was pale gold; it stood out round his head like a cloud—a "nimbus," Sophie called it. Sophie's hair was like honey too, but dark honey; she wore it in a knot at the back of her neck, and sometimes Teresa would look at its silkiness and at the lights in it, and then look at her own straight red locks and sigh. "Teresa, take that ugly pucker off your forehead," said Sophie.

In Teresa's short life she had seen how things and people could be gone; friends, nurses, servants, dogs, cats, ponies had gone as well as houses, but there were a few people—a few things, like the books, the Chinese teapot, Pussy Maria, the tricycle, and the carriage clock—that seemed to remain. By "people" Teresa did not mean Sophie and Moo; she took them for granted. She meant people like Denzil and the aunts and Toby.

A photograph of Denzil stood on Sophie's table; he looked out of the frame at Teresa with eyes exactly like her own. "Why not? He is your father," said Sophie.

"And Moo's father," said Teresa, jealous as always for Moo; but Moo scarcely knew who Denzil was. "I think people should live with their fathers," said Teresa.

Sophie's own father and mother had died, and the aunts had brought her up. The aunts lived in a village called Finstead in England. "Like Camberley?" asked Teresa.

"Very like Camberley!" said Sophie.

"Ah!" said Teresa, envying Sophie. The aunts were the Miss Camerons, except Aunt Rose, who lived at the Hall and was called Lady Munthe.

"Why is she?" asked Teresa.

"Because she married Sir William."

"Why did she?"

"I don't know," said Sophie slowly and she thought of the pompous, fat little figure of her Uncle William. I never called him Uncle William, always Sir William, she thought. That shows how pompous he was; and she told Teresa, "Aunt Rose was an actress; she lived in Paris; she was beautiful, with beautiful dark eyes, but she gave it all up and came home. I suppose it was for Vennie."

"Who is Vennie?"

"Vennie was her son. She married—or didn't marry," said Sophie slowly, "in Paris. She was poor and struggling but she loved it—and, after all that, Vennie ran away. He didn't like Sir William."

"So it was no good," said Teresa.

"It was no good," said Sophie sadly.

Teresa knew what the aunts were like. Sophie had a painting, by an Indian artist, of the Celestial Cows of Krishna. "The aunts are just like that," said Sophie and she called the three cows Aunt Portia, Aunt Mamie, and Aunt Rose; they were painted lying down in a field patterned with daisies; two of them were white cows and they looked out of the picture with mild firm faces, neat definite ears, gentle brows, and eyes that were faintly puzzled; the third was a brown cow and she looked away, minding her own business; that was Aunt Rose. "Aunt Rose was always different," said Sophie.

"And was Toby—that man?" asked Teresa. "The man who came to Camberley—another man, not Denzil."

"That was Toby," said Sophie.

"What was Toby like?" asked Teresa.

"He is big," said Sophie uncertainly as if she did not really know what he was like herself. "He has a red face and blue eyes and thick brown curly hair. Very short hair," said Sophie definitely as if that were one thing she did know about Toby. "Far too short."

"I don't know him," said Teresa jealously.

"Yes, you do," said Sophie. "He is your godfather. Why, he sent you Pussy Maria!"

"Did he?" asked Teresa. Pussy Maria was her greatest treasure. Pussy Maria had real hair, her eyes opened and shut. "She must have cost a *pound*," said Teresa, awed. "Toby must be kind and very, very rich."

"Quite kind and quite rich," said Sophie with a little yawn. "He was the doctor's son at Finstead. Now he is the doctor. His grandfather was the doctor too; like peas in the same pod," said Sophie impatiently. Then she relented and smiled. "Dear Toby, he was always rescuing me."

"From what?" asked Teresa, breathless.

"Oh, from scrapes," said Sophie airily.

Teresa sighed. She never got into scrapes. "She is so timid!" said Sophie. Sophie was always asking, "Why is Teresa such a little goose? Why is she so timid?"

One day Aunt Rose answered that. "You must remember," said Aunt Rose, "if you hitch your wagon to a star it must often be very uncomfortable in the wagon."

Never, with all its hitches and bumps, had it been as uncomfortable as it was that winter in Kashmir, the winter they came to Dhilkusha.

Chapter 2

"Here in Kashmir," said Ayah, "we call the winter the time of the Three Sisters—Forty Days' Death, and Twenty, and then Ten."

"Forty Days' Death, and Twenty, and then Ten," said Teresa after her.

In winter the whole vale was sealed in snow, black ice, and frost, while the passes to the mountains were blocked. The villagers shut up their houses, closing the cattle into the ground stories so that the midden, collecting through the months, steamed up to warm the rooms above. "Kashmir looks Russian in winter," Sophie wrote to the aunts, "Russian in the Eastern sense, like its old name, Scythia; the perpetual salt tea they drink here is made in a samowar, which is much the same as a samovar. It is Russia of the old days," she wrote, "of the ragged animal peasant and the prosperous merchants with their full bellies and smiling white teeth"—she was thinking of Profit David—"the separate customs and language of the ruling few"—she was thinking of the Hindus. Kashmir, then, was ruled by a Hindu rajah with Hindu administrators over a largely Mohammedan people. Sophie was used to seeing the prosperity of the Hindus against the poverty of the common people but she still did not know how poor they were. She could have seen it in the land that last grasshopper summer, if she had had eyes, but in those days she had only superficial eyes. She saw the fruitful villages, the rich fields, but she did not see how each patch of ground was humbly, carefully cultivated, irrigated, every blade of rice planted out by hand when it was thinned; each honey melon grew in its circle of weed compost dragged up from the bottom of the lake; even the weeds were not wasted, and each horse dropping was picked up and taken in; even the roofs of the houses had crops.

She and Teresa and Moo had come to Kashmir in the early summer.

They had travelled up the old military road along the red gorges of the Jhelum River, where boys threw bunches of flowers into the car. In spite of the flowers, Sophie wished she could have come by a more romantic way—by one of the caravan routes overland from China, through Manchuria and Sinkiang over the Himalayas, or through Little Tibet, over the Zoji La pass with its great double glacier, or along the almost forgotten horsepath that came from Old Delhi, the path that the Mogul Emperor Jehanghir had used. "But now tourists, not emperors, come to Kashmir," said Sophie sadly. "There are more cars than caravans."

At first she had been bitterly disappointed. Srinagar, the capital city, built in the Jhelum River like an Eastern Venice, was as surrounded by roads and cars and filling stations as any modern town; its suburbs were spread like Wimbledon or the suburbs of Cape Town or Amsterdam—"suburbs *anywhere*," wrote Sophie, disgusted. It was crowded with tourists, and the tourists had loud unbeautiful voices, cameras and radios, tartan rugs and picnic hampers. There was a plague of guides and touts, houseboat and tent agents, houseboat owners, taxi-boat men—"and this is Kashmir!" wrote Sophie. "The land of Lalla Rookh, the vale of paradise, the pearl of Hind!" She wished she had never come; then one day she took a little taxi-boat and was paddled down the Jhelum to the Old City, and away through crowded waterways, under wooden bridges by gardens and islands and villages till she came out on the Dāl Lake, and, "this is a beautiful, beautiful country," wrote Sophie. "There is a quality in the beauty here that steals you."

The vale, poets say, is set like a pearl between the mountains, a pearl of water and flowers; the water comes from the glaciers on the far snow peaks and runs through high alps and valleys where gentian and primula and edelweiss grow, through forests, down rapids, till it falls to the vale floor and flows into its lakes and river and waterways.

The lakes are fringed with willows, where the kingfishers live; the foothills are reflected in the water in green and pink and blue and white from the orchards and ricefields and mulberry gardens and fields of flax. There are villages of tall wooden-balconied houses standing in groves and orchards of chenar and walnut or fruit trees; the villages are scattered on islands in the lakes, or along the shores and foothills, with narrow hump-backed bridges and built-up roads between them.

Sophie liked the people—the boatmen, the farmers, the shepherd boys, the pony-men, the Mohammedan merchants, the Hindu pundits and their decorative women, even the poor women with their handsome faces and dirty clothes; everything she saw that summer, to her, was poetry.

Most visitors had houseboats; Sophie took one and moored it among the willows of a little island; boats passed it all day long—wood-boats, grain- and cargo-boats. The light traffic was by shikaras, small boats, slim and light, of natural wood, paddled with heart-shaped paddles; some were bare, with only a child gathering weeds or a woman in the stern or a fisherman standing with a spear, watching for fish in the lake; some were taxi-shikaras with embroidered curtains and cushions, and waggish names to attract the tourists: "Whoopee," "Here I am," "Where are you?" These shikaras were like water palanquins—"as romantic as gondolas," wrote Sophie. She hired one, and she and the children loved to go in it, moving in narrow waterways among the lotus leaves that floated on the water everywhere and held the dew, or out across the lake where the shikara floated over fish, silver in the weeds; always there were reflections of mountains and sky and cloud. Sometimes they went across the lake to the old Mogul pleasure gardens of Nishat, Chashmishai, or Shalimar, with their pavilions and fountains and water channels and tangles of roses. All the boatmen grew to know Sophie and the children and salaamed, with their paddles across their knees, as they passed.

There were merchant shikaras that flew over the water after each new tourist arrival; their paddles raced against each other, and the merchants leaned forward with glistening smiles, holding out their cards. They called themselves names like Suffering Moses, Patient Job, Long John. Sophie's friend, Profit David, had meant to be different. "I have respect for the Bible," he said, "for biblical souls. Religion is the heart, the poetry, of man." He particularly admired the Psalms and called himself after David, whom he always spoke of as a prophet. "Prophet David," he said often, with reverence, but his spelling of English was muddled, and he had "Profit David" on his cards. Sophie thought it suited him much better.

He dealt in carpets, precious stones, embroideries, and wood carvings, and was as richly handsome as the things he sold. He wore a grey pheran—the loose robe that most Kashmiri men and women wear—of wool so soft and fine that it looked like silk; he carried a darker grey paschmina shawl and wore a white turban of folded muslin. His face looked like that of the David he admired; his skin was olive, and he had a fine nose, fine brown eyes, and a brown beard, beautifully combed. "I call him my Persian Humbug," Sophie wrote home, but he was not such a humbug as some. Most of the merchants sold sham papier-mâché, cheap walnut carvings, machine-spun shawls, and Persian carpets made in Kidderminster. "That is your fault," said Profit David. "By your own greed you tourists have debased the very things you want."

Sophie did not like "you tourists." "I am not a tourist," she said with asperity.

"You are a different kind of tourist," said Profit David in a voice of honey and oil. "You at least, lady sahib, are prepared to pay genuine prices for genuine things." That sounded so expensive that it silenced even Sophie. The whole summer was expensive. She bought a desk, trays, a shawl, and a lamp from Profit David; and she could not resist those merchant boats.

The confectioners had their cakes in bright red chests that reflected tulip red in the water; the children liked those best, but Sophie liked the flower-boats. In the early morning the flower-boats came, laden to the gunwales with fresh flowers that made lilac and yellow and green reflections in panels on the water. Sophie spent far too much money on flowers.

It was odd that it was in this beautiful poetical land that she first began to think about money. Perhaps, though she did not know it, the poorness of the people touched her. Sometimes, even in this last grasshopper summer, looking out from the curtains of her taxi-boat as it was sent flying across the lake—four boatmen to paddle one woman, two children—she would see a particular little house standing in a ring of trees on the mountain, and she would wish that she did not live extravagantly, carelessly—selfishly, thought Sophie. She wished she could live frugally, without guilt, in just such a little house.

Then, in the autumn, Denzil died and the winter came.

≈

Under the windows of the Mission Hospital was a Mohammedan grave-yard. In winter the funerals went on all day long. There was one coffin for a village; the body was tipped out onto a side shelf cut into the grave, which itself could not be dug more than two feet in the frozen ground. Babies were brought in bathtowels, but the towel, like the coffin, was taken away because a towel cost a great deal of money. "One can't bury a good towel," said Ayah. The relations, if they were careful, piled stones on the place after the grave was closed, and set a stone at the head and at the foot, but when the snow turned to slush the earth was often washed out and the bodies showed. The graves were planted with irises; Sophie had heard a legend that the iris meant money and was planted so that Raschid or Ramzan or Taja would have money to buy bread and rice and tea—all the tea they wanted—and apricots and kidflesh, and wood and shawls and robes and jewellery and carpets in the next world, even if they had starved to death in this. As Sophie grew delirious she cried, "I must get irises. I must get irises." The cries from the graveyard, the sound of the maulvi's voice chanting the prayers for the dead, mingled with her cries.

It was the poor who died in winter, when the price of rice was high and the allowance of wood sank to two small logs a day for each person, and that at prohibitive prices. If the peasants were not barefoot they had only homemade straw sandals; perhaps they had no woollen shawls, only cotton cloths and cotton pherans. As the winter wore on men and women grew more and more haggard and thin; the children were hollow-eyed and played their hopping games with feeble little hops.

"Before that winter I did not understand about living," said Sophie afterwards. "I did not know it was so hard to live."

"It's the last sister, the Ten Days' Death, who takes the most," said Ayah with relish. "Though she is small she is fiercest, because then the people are weak."

"Weak!" said Teresa.

➴

"You must not go in to Mother; she is too weak," Sister Locke told Teresa. Sister Locke was a pale little woman with colourless hair and a sharp face and a small spare figure; her eyes and her voice were sharp too, and she had, as she said, no patience with children. "Children!" said Sister Locke. "As if we hadn't enough to do!"

"Children!" said the junior sister, Sister Pilkington. "Little English children!" she said softly, and when she could she stole away from her work to play with Teresa and Moo. Ayah was supposed to look after them; she smoothed the counterpanes over their crumpled beds, washed Moo's face and hands when he would let her, and told them fearful stories as she sat over her firepot till it was time to go down again to the kitchen for tea.

"Ayah! Moo's vest is dirty," said Teresa.

"He shall have a clean one in the spring," said Ayah.

"Ayah, Moo Baba ought to go *out*," said Teresa with longing.

"No one should go out in winter," said Ayah. "Do you want to get like the memsahib? Get ill and die?"

"Die?" Teresa quailed. "This is a hospital; people come here to get well," she said.

"Na, na, they die like flies!" said Ayah cheerfully.

"Who will look after us if Mother dies?" Teresa asked Sister Locke. "Who will buy us things and choose our clothes?"

"Well, you are a nice selfish child, I must say!" said Sister Locke.

Sister Pilkington gave kind soothing answers, and Dr. Glenister said sadly but truthfully, "While there is life there is hope." Dr. Lochinvar said with his lips set, "I shall pull her through," but Ayah was more downright. "The memsahib has that look on her face," said Ayah. "I remember when I saw two sahibs dug out of an avalanche that had come down on the rest house at Kanghan." Ayah rocked cheerfully with her firepot. "Aie! their faces were white and frightened, frozen like that! They still had their hats on, but they were dead!"

"They still had their hats on, but they were dead," said Teresa with a fascinated shudder. She was not really of Ayah's kidney; Ayah's tales were like the chili juice that the drivers squirt into the eyes of a wounded elephant; the smart of the juice diverts the elephant's attention from its wound.

In the graveyard a hand had come up, and there had been the skeleton of a baby under the window for days. Sister Pilkington told Teresa not to look at it, but who could help looking at that?

"You have to remember," said Sister Pilkington, "they are not dead, but sleeping." The baby looked very dead to Teresa, and she began to have that ugly pucker always on her forehead between her eyes.

"That child needs glasses," said Sister Locke.

Teresa did not think she did. "I—I want mother," said Teresa.

"You may stand at the door and call 'Good night' to her," said sister Locke as she left each night after her evening visit. "But don't expect her to answer. She is too weak."

Teresa did expect Sophie to answer. Every night she stood at the door and called firmly and persistently, "Moth-er. Mother. Good night. Good night, Mother," until from the bed came a sound that was not like Sophie at all, a fluttering sound that seemed as if it came from a long way off. "Good-night."

⁊❧

Denzil had died of a cold.

"But people don't die of colds!" Sophie had said, stunned.

"There was an old infection; the cold stirred it up, and he hadn't any resistance," said Mr. Kirkpatrick, the company manager, who, up on leave in Srinagar, had had to break the news to Sophie. "To give him his due," said Mr. Kirkpatrick, "he had been trying to do two men's work with very little leave. He was run down and he had no resistance."

Sophie had a sudden and cool little thought that it was just like Denzil to have no resistance. She was immediately shocked at herself. I loved him once, she thought, or I thought I did; and she could have cried, I would have loved him if he had made me. I—was ready to love. Her tears, when she shed them, were for having failed.

"There is no happiness in a house," Aunt Portia had once said, "if the man of it isn't the head."

"Then why doesn't he make himself the head?" Sophie had snapped out, annoyed.

"You should have married Toby," said Aunt Mamie. "Though Denzil is a charming boy, of course."

"He isn't a boy, he is a man," said Sophie, but Aunt Portia shook her head.

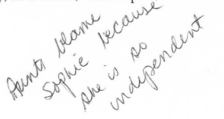

Aunt blame Sophie because she is so independent

15

"You are too strong for Denzil."

"A little slip of a woman too strong for a six-foot man?" said Sophie scornfully.

"You are not a little slip of a woman, you are a little whip of a woman, like me," said Aunt Rose. "We should be careful. We can sting." And Sophie remembered Denzil's silence when she had a new plan, a new enthusiasm, a new idea—silences that she now heard echoed in Teresa.

Then is it wrong, thought Sophie in these unhappy nights, lying awake in the dark—is it wrong to have ideas? "What are you to do," she asked Aunt Rose when she saw her again, "if you are the kind of person who has them?"

"You have to learn to temper them," said Aunt Rose. "Temper them with discretion," said Aunt Rose, and she gave a little yawn. "Discretion is very, very dull," said Aunt Rose.

❧

"Mrs. Ward, did you know anything about your husband's private affairs?" That sentence was to burn in Sophie's memory forever. Denzil had died intestate; there were debts, old bills, new bills. "They will have to be paid," said Mr. Kirkpatrick. He looked as if he hated to say it.

At first Sophie was not dismayed. "There are trust funds from his mother's estate," she said confidently.

"He made those over long ago," said Mr. Kirkpatrick.

"There are insurances," said Sophie. "At least we had sense enough for that."

"He called those in," said Mr. Kirkpatrick.

There was nothing left, nothing but Sophie's own small capital that had come to her from her father.

"We must have been very extravagant," said Sophie slowly. Mr. Kirkpatrick said nothing, and, Oh, Denzil! Why didn't you tell me? Sophie could have cried. She was to think that over and over again in the days that followed. Why didn't you warn me? Was I such a little shrew as that?

Mr. Kirkpatrick could not soften facts, even though he tried. The company, he had to tell her, had lost a great deal of money through Denzil one way and another. "He—he wasn't very able," said Mr. Kirkpatrick as kindly as he could, and he said reluctantly, "The directors feel they can't give you the usual death gratuity and passages home—nor pension, I am afraid—as they will have to pay his debts."

"I shall pay his debts," said Sophie, lifting her chin. "*Our* debts." And she said, "If you will tell me what they come to I shall give you a cheque."

Mr. Kirkpatrick blew his nose suddenly. "You are so—gallant," he said.

"It's not gallant, it's sense," said Sophie. "If I pay his debts they will have to give me his pension, and a pension goes on until you die. I may live till I am ninety." But Mr. Kirkpatrick persisted in thinking her gallant.

He came to see her very often; he brought flowers for her, chocolates for the children.

"Isn't there anything I can do?" he asked when his leave was over and he had to go back to Delhi.

"Yes. Find me some work," said Sophie.

In those days she had been prickly and proud. Her only idea was to work. When the debts were paid she had little money left, and though the directors paid her pension it was very small—"a pittance," said Sophie.

"I don't like to think of you working," said Mr. Kirkpatrick, troubled.

"Why not? We are poor whites now," she said, her chin in the air.

She decided to teach—"English to Hindu and Mohammedan ladies, and Urdu to English people," said Sophie.

"But you were not qualified to teach Urdu," said Toby afterwards.

"Well, I could speak it faster than most people," said Sophie. "I learned to write it in three months."

"But how well?" asked Toby.

"Well enough," said Sophie. She could always give an impression of knowing more than she did. She was skilful in keeping it up. Soon she had more work than she could do.

Ayah, the old woman, came to look after the children, and Sophie worked fanatically. "I won't let the children suffer," she had said. "They shall have what they had before"; and she worked all day and far into the night; but "Even if you are successful you can't charge much for teaching," she said. "Even if you teach with your whole heart—your heart and your brains," and she came to the depressing thought that her heart and brains were not worth very much. She had not told the aunts; she tried to hide what had happened from everyone; but every month she spent more than she earned, and every day she grew more tired and nervous and cross.

"Poor Mother, she worked too hard," said Dr. Glenister.

"Well, why did she? Why didn't she just work?" said Teresa.

If Sophie thought of Denzil then, it was only to think, It's easy to be dead. She tried not to neglect the children, to read to them and play with them, but she could not find enough time.

Teresa felt it bitterly. "Mother, today I—"

"Teresa, *please!* Go and keep Moo quiet."

More than ever Teresa was struck by the injustice of grown-ups. Could Sophie keep Moo quiet? No, she knew very well she could not. Teresa could, but only at dreadful expense to herself. Her lip trembled, and she had one of her rare rebellions.

"Everything is horrid now, horrid!" cried Teresa. "Why do you have to work and work? Why do we live in this horrid houseboat? Why do we have Ayah and not a proper nurse like Margaret Robinson?" Margaret Robinson was a little girl Teresa particularly admired. "Oh, why can't we be like proper people?" And she burst into loud wails.

Sophie had always kept away from what Teresa called "proper people." Sophie specialized in friends who were not of her own kind. Srinagar had a large European community that was hospitable and friendly, but "When I go to a country I like to meet the people of that country," Sophie had said and she refused to join the Club. "I can meet Lady Andersons and Mrs. Robinsons *anywhere!*" said Sophie and was coldly ungrateful for their kindness.

"But I want to go to tea with Margaret Robinson," said Teresa tearfully.

"We are going down to the Third Bridge to see Profit David's collection of agates," said Sophie. Soon Margaret Robinson stopped asking Teresa to tea.

"Have you no friends who would take the children?" Dr. Glenister asked Sophie in the Mission. "People are so kind. Some nice English friend?"

"I have no English friends," Sophie had to say, and her lips quivered. "Please try and keep the children here," she whispered to Dr. Glenister. "I—will pay you back. I promise."

There had come a day when Sophie could not get up. Teresa had to dress Moo when he would not allow Ayah to do it. Sophie had purple circles under her eyes, and her voice was a croak, not a voice, as she said, "Teresa, write a letter to Begum Shamsher Ali and tell her I can't come today to give her lesson."

"Wha—what do I write?"

"Anything," said Sophie, lying back on the pillow with closed eyes.

Teresa wrote in a laborious round hand: "Deer Begum . . ."

"Teresa, take the keys and give out the wood." Teresa quailed. In spite of all Sophie could do she was frightened of the servants. "I can't."

"You must," said Sophie. The long day dragged on, and in the evening Sophie whispered, "Teresa, tell Ayah to get a doctor."

Ayah scolded and grumbled, and in the end Teresa had to write another note. Of them all—Ayah, the servants, the boatmen, Teresa— Teresa was the only one who could write. Her note was terse. "Deer Doctor. Please cum." The only doctors Ayah knew of were the Mission Hospital doctors. Dr. Glenister was not on duty. Teresa's note was given to little Dr. Lochinvar, the surgeon, and it was he who came.

"You had a crimson shawl on the bed," he told Sophie afterwards, "and you were wearing something white."

"My old shawl and an old bed-jacket," said Sophie.

"You were like snow and rubies," said Little Lochinvar. "Your hair was lying over the pillow. I don't remember having seen a woman's hair loose like that," said little Lochinvar.

"As a doctor, you must have done," said Sophie. That was true, but then he had seen as a doctor. Now he saw Sophie's hair as a man; this was one of the painful things that Sophie did to him, turned him from a doctor to a man.

If Sophie's hair was a wonder to him, he was a wonder to Teresa She stood watching him while he used his stethoscope, took Sophie's temperature and pulse, dealing quietly and firmly with this terrifying thing that had come to them. When he left to make arrangements to take them to the hospital, Teresa followed him to the houseboat door and stood on the prow, looking adoringly after him. She waved steadily till he was out of sight, but, thinking of Sophie, he did not see her.

*

In the winter the Hutchinson wing of the Mission Hospital was usually empty.

"But it's for our own people. It was endowed for the use of missionaries. Mrs. Ward should go to the European nursing home," Sister Locke had said indignantly when Dr. Lochinvar brought Sophie in.

"She hasn't any money," said Little Lochinvar. He was so daring and dauntlessly fierce in his opinions that everyone called him Little Lochinvar. "We can't turn her away," he said. Sister Locke folded in her lips. Little Lochinvar set his.

"I can hardly put her in the wards," said Dr. Glenister, torn between them.

"And there are the little children!" said Sister Pilkington, who took Little Lochinvar's side even though, looking at Sophie, she felt her own rosy prettiness to be suddenly ordinary and childish. Little Lochinvar took no notice of Sister Pilkington. He meant to have his way, and Sophie went into one room of the Hutchinson Wing, the children into the other.

*

Day after day the snow fell steadily past the window. Sometimes Sophie saw it; sometimes it was blotted out. "You have typhoid fever and pneumonia," said Dr. Glenister. "You must lie still. You are not very well."

Sophie thought that an understatement; the Mission had few expensive drugs, her illness had to take its full, weary course as in the old days; but, as she lay there, she came to understand that Dr. Glenister did not mean to be unsympathetic; Sophie's case was trivial compared with most that came; the only diseases they had room to isolate in the Mission

Hospital were leprosy and smallpox, and the state hospitals were more crowded still. The people came in every extremity, and many of them died, as Ayah had said.

The voices in the graveyard came up to Sophie's window, with the sound of shuffling feet and of digging and of the maulvi's voice. "There is no one except one God . . . He is the only One. He only is worthy of praise. There is no one . . ." but now the voice was lost in the snow; the snow was silent, and it silenced, and, as it muffled the sounds in the graveyard and the hospital and the lane outside, it muffled the thoughts of the children in the next room, of Denzil, of the unpaid bills and bills to come. Irises, thought Sophie, but she was too weary to say it.

"Why didn't she come before?" asked Dr. Glenister. "Why leave things so late?"

"She was anxious not to be a nuisance." That was the gentle Sister Pilkington.

"And she was more nuisance in the end," said Sister Locke. For a moment Sophie had come back to life indignantly. She had thought life was warm, but it was cold—white; the hard white light pressed in on her when she opened her eyes. Life is the pain in my head and my eyes, Sister Locke's sharpness, the voices crying under the window, the children, the bills. "I must get irises," cried Sophie to Dr. Glenister and the fervid little Dr. Lochinvar. "We need—money. I must get up. What do the children do all day? And who pays Ayah's wages? And the houseboat rent?"

"Don't worry," said Dr. Glenister. Sophie could not help worrying. She asked Sister Locke over and over again, "How much—does all this cost?"

"Well, illness is expensive," said the sister.

When you are ill, thought Sophie, people are kind, they make allowances for you. Now, suddenly, she saw a starker world where to be ill was a tragedy. She had lost her work, she might never get it back; and after this she would be weak. No one could wait months for a sick teacher. The little sister was stating a fact. No one knew better than she the cost of illness. She had seen people die, not of their illness, but from the poverty and starvation after it. For every hour she spent on Sophie, every drug that she gave her, someone else went without. Every day at the

Mission people were turned away, every day things went undone. "You should have gone to the European nursing home," said Sister Locke.

"I haven't any money," said Sophie, and that started it again. "No money. I should be working. What can I do? Irises. Irises."

Little Lochinvar bent down. He took her plucking, worrying hands into his own firm, young, clean, disinfectant-smelling grasp.

"You must thole it," he said, and Sophie lay still.

"She is the kind that is better with a man," remarked Sister Locke acidly.

"Well, she is a woman," said Little Lochinvar.

When Dr. Lochinvar's hand closed on her, Sophie had the feeling that it was Toby's.

The snow began to fall close round her, covering the irises, and she was quiet and warm. An inertia was creeping up her knees; like snow-sleepiness, it lapped her, and she was taken under the snow that said, "Rest . . . drift." The snow changed into a tide that was taking her away, and she went, peacefully . . . restfully . . . still.

"Mother."

I am deaf, said Sophie silently. I am gone.

"Moth-er."

"I can't," said Sophie and drifted away.

"Moth-er. Good night, Moth-er."

Teresa always was a tiresome child, thought Sophie angrily.

"Moth-er."

Sophie made a supreme effort so that the sweat broke out on her skin. "Good night—you little—nuisance. Good night."

❧

There came a night when Teresa called at Sophie's door and there was no answer.

Teresa waited a long time, then slowly went back into her room. Long after Moo had gone to sleep she kept creeping back to the door and listening. At last she went and lay curled in her bed in a cold stiff little knot, her eyes wide open and staring into the dark.

With her hand she rubbed the edge of the bed; its iron was rough and cold. I suppose now I shall have to bring Moo up, she thought. She did not know how she could do it. Outside the window she could see stars, like Christmas-card stars, bright and frosty and she remembered how Sophie had told her they were other worlds bigger than this world.

"The world is a pinpoint in the sky," Sophie had said. "And each of us is a tiny pinprick on it." Teresa felt she must be bigger than a pinprick to feel so much. She felt a whole world of tears inside her; then they overflowed; the stars swam together into a blur; she put her head down on the edge of her bed and wept.

All at once she heard voices—Sister Locke's voice, Sister Pilkington's, the gentle softness of Dr. Glenister's, Dr. Lochinvar's Scots burr; they were coming up the stairs and they seemed to walk through her despair. She heard the light snap on in Sophie's room. She heard firm steps; she waited, listening and straining.

What were they doing to Sophie? She crept out of bed to listen, but all she could hear were quiet movements, quiet voices. She crept round the other way, out onto the landing, and stood there for what seemed to her to be hours.

Suddenly the door opened, and Dr. Glenister and Dr. Lochinvar came out. Dr. Glenister was in her white coat, Dr. Lochinvar was rolling down his shirt sleeves; Teresa shrank back against the wall, and they went downstairs together without noticing her. After a moment Teresa tip-toed to the open door and looked into Sophie's room. Sophie was lying in the bed just as usual, a shaded light burning beside her. Sister Pilkington was tucking in the bedclothes; she had her back to Teresa, but, as Teresa looked, round the door, wheeling a glass trolley, came Sister Locke. Teresa shrank back again, but she was too late, the sister saw her as she came out onto the landing. "Good gracious, child! What are you doing here?" said Sister Locke.

"Is—Mother dead?" asked Teresa.

"Of course not. She is sleeping."

That was what Sister Pilkington had said about the baby. "Then she *is* dead!" said Teresa and she opened her mouth to give a tremendous wail. Sister Locke let go of the trolley and clapped a hand over her mouth and, with the other hand, shut the door. "Don't you dare to make a noise," said Sister Locke, taking her hand away. "And don't talk nonsense," she said sharply. The sharpness was balm to Teresa. "She isn't going to die," said Sister Locke. "We have been giving her a blood transfusion, that is all."

"A—blood transfusion?"

"Yes."

"How?" asked Teresa.

"I can't stay here, this time of night, giving explanations to you, miss," said Sister Locke. "What next, I should like to know? You get back to bed."

"Oh, please. Please," begged Teresa, and she dared to take hold of the sister's white overall. "*Please!*"

The sharp little sister looked down at her and she did not shake Teresa's fingers away; instead, slowly and precisely, she began to tell Teresa about a blood transfusion. Teresa's eyes stretched in surprise, but her terror oozed away. These were facts, not ideas; she found them infinitely soothing.

A blood transfusion! Over and over again in her head she head something they sang in the chapel to which Sister Pilkington took her. "Whom Thou has redeemed by Thy most precious blood."

"And that redeemed—stopped Mother being dead?" she asked.

"Yes," said Sister Locke. "If you can do that for people, you can stop them dying of weakness."

"The Third Sister takes the most because then the people are weak." Ayah had been sure of that. Teresa seemed to see the Third Sister, the Ten Days' Death, a dark figure, little now, slinking away. "Then— Mother will get well?"

"She should get well," said Sister Locke judiciously.

Teresa looked at the trolley and the bottle and funnel, a tube with a big needle—her eyes widened—the syringe, all stained with blood, as if they were revelations. People, tiny pinprick people, had this power to save! Though awed, Teresa was an exact child. She had one more question.

"Where did you get the blood?" she asked.

"Doctor Lochinvar gave his blood," said Sister Locke. She sounded cross again, but Teresa was too rapt to pay attention.

"Doctor Lochinvar!" Her eyes glowed, and when, a few days later, Sister Pilkington came to her and said, "Teresa, you can come into the chapel now and thank God for saving your dear mother," Teresa said, "I think I should go into the surgery and thank Doctor Lochinvar."

Chapter 3

Aunt Rose sent Moo a little doll from England.

"A doll for a boy?" asked Aunt Portia.

"Yes," said Aunt Rose.

Moo loved it. It was so small it could go in a matchbox, and it had one peculiar quality—it was weighted with lead so that, no matter how you laid it down or knocked it over, it sprang up again. This was what Moo—and Aunt Rose—liked. Sophie thought there was something in her that made her do the same; sooner than anyone had thought possible she was out of bed and able to sit up in a chair.

Little Lochinvar cautioned her. "You have taken a big toll of yourself," said Little Lochinvar.

"But I must work," said Sophie.

The little doctor shook his head. "You will have to go very carefully. You certainly won't be able to work for a long time."

That was dismaying. How shall we live, then? thought Sophie. What can we do? We can't live on Denzil's pension.

It was deep winter; Sophie was so cold that Ayah brought her a fire-pot. In Kashmir a firepot is the poor man's fire, a small earthenware pot in a wickerwork container like a basket; it is filled with live charcoal and held pressed to the stomach; every poor man, woman, and child carries one under his robe in winter, so that they all look pregnant; sometimes they burn themselves terribly, but the firepots save them at least from death by cold. Sophie held hers on her knee; its warmth kept her from shivering; she seemed to have no warmth of her own. When she looked at the graveyard she felt colder still, but beyond it she could see one of the city lanes; the lane was full of life and people.

In the afternoons, when there was a gleam of sun, men well muffled in thick shawls came out for half an hour to sit on their balconies and smoke their water-pipes; after months in Kashmir, Sophie was familiar with that hookah stench and the soothing gurgling noise. Down below in the street the women worked all day; they did so many of their household tasks out in the cold, and Sophie could watch them pounding corn with wooden poles in a great wooden mortar, using the poles like flails while their jewellery clanged and the earrings hit their cheeks; they sifted the grain in flat baskets and ground it on a stone handmill that was cruelly hard to work; they fetched water and chopped wood. The women had no shawls, and under their cotton robes their bare legs and feet were mottled with cold and chaps and sores. They were filthy, their veils grey with smoke, their robes greasy.

Sometimes Hindu women would come down the lane to the cake shop that was kept by a Brahmin. Hindu women in Kashmir wear dresses like a medieval painting: a long kilted gown of brilliant colour, kingfisher blue or green, or pink or mustard yellow, edged with bands of scarlet braid, with a pocket outlined in scarlet low down on the hem; their cuffs are turned back over wide sleeves, and each gown is girdled with scarlet at the waist. On their heads, falling over their shoulders and necks, they wear wimples of snowy white muslin. In the snow and grey, among the dulled filth of the Mohammedan women, Sophie thought, they shone with a jewel cleanliness. They bought honey cakes or kulchas and then picked their way, on wooden pattens, down the lane among the mud and chickens.

The state officials, the schoolmasters and clerks, were chiefly Hindus; the agencies were staffed by them; they held senior posts in the palace and hotels; a few were confectioners, tailors, but all were privileged among the Mohammedans, making a separate society. Sophie watched with her firepot on her knee, and new thoughts seemed to come to her from it. I belong to the poor now, she thought. She almost felt that she was glad that it was so and that she did not want to be privileged again. She thought that, with her illness, the last scales of her old life had fallen away. I'm like a snake that has cast its skin, she thought. The skin splits, but the snake wriggles out. I thought I was going to die; well, I expect for a moment the snake thinks, This is death; but it's the old skin that is dead; the snake is alive in a fresh new skin.

"When I am well," she said to Teresa, "I shall be quite different. Everything will be quite different."

28

"How?" asked Teresa cautiously.

"I was insouciant—careless and indifferent," explained Sophie. "Now I shall live and work for other people—like the missionaries do."

"You have to train to be a missionary, Sister Locke says so," said Teresa dampeningly, but Sophie was not listening.

"We shall be poor like the Kashmiris," said Sophie, and her eyes began to shine. "We shall be poor and frugal. We shall toil."

"What is toil?" asked Teresa.

"Work very, very hard," said Sophie. "Like that." She pointed to the working women, and Teresa looked down at them with fear and distaste.

Sophie watched the life in the houses in the lane. She could see the herbs and onions hung to dry from the third-floor balconies, cloths and shawls hung out on the railings, red chilis spread on a cloth. I wish I had a little house, thought Sophie suddenly; these homely things touched her; I want a home, thought Sophie. She needed a home in which to be poor and frugal, a home in which to toil. How can I do it without? she asked. She had never wanted a home before. How like life that she should need one now when there was no chance at all of getting one! Srinagar rents were high; a house such as Europeans live in would cost each month more than her whole pension, and it would be some time before she could work. I shall have to write to the aunts, she thought, plead with the company for passages. I shall have to go home to Finstead. Her heart was heavy as she thought it.

She looked farther down the lane to where there was a gateway, an arch of old red bricks with the winter sunlight striking on them. Two boys walked up the lane with a length of turban muslin between them; it was diaphanous, dyed bright orange, and they were drying it in the wind for the dyer; a little Mohammedan girl in tunic and trousers, carrying a satchel of books, stopped to watch them; she had a scarf-veil of parrot green. An old man sold sweets and nuts and apples from a wicker tray, and a donkey, with its front legs hobbled together, hopped on the snowy verges of the graves. The colour and life and the bargaining, the chatter and splashing of water, the pounding of the grain, the cries and shuffling of feet and pony hooves and all the smells rose up to Sophie's window. The lane felt alive and, in spite of the poverty, happy; above all, it was strange, fascinating, adventurous. She had had the blows of Denzil's death, her poverty, her illness, but was she, then, to forsake her life and end in Finstead? Aunt Rose did, she thought. She admired Aunt Rose, but she, Sophie, was herself—and I won't go home, thought Sophie, though I don't see how not to. But I shall see, she thought. I shall think of some way to get round this; and she told Teresa, "I am sure I shall have an idea."

"Are you well enough yet to have an idea?" asked Teresa apprehensively.

&

The lane was one through which the peasants came to the city. With all their wretchedness they were different from the city people; the women and children had more pink in the olive of their cheeks, they were fatter, and the men were sturdy and big under their rags.

"These people are not really poor," Dr. Lochinvar had told Sophie. It was surprising how often he found time to drop in for a few words with her. "They are not like the peasants in India. How could they be, with land like theirs? They have only to scratch it for crops to grow; the land is rich, and, for all their taxes, they don't starve." Of course, to the little doctor, to be really poor was to be starving.

Now Sophie watched those country people.

"How much," she asked Ayah, "would a peasant like that need to live?" She pointed to an old man in straw sandals, driving a pack-pony laden with wood.

"Country people are fools," said Ayah. "They don't know cinemas, they don't know shops," she said in great scorn. "What do they need? Suppose he had a house and a field that has rice in it, and a patch to plant with sāg"—sāg was the Kashmiri spinach. He has some badam—almond—trees or a walnut, and some apples; he will have a few hens and perhaps he has a goat," said Ayah with more respect in her voice. "The goat has kids. If one is a billy they can eat it or sell it; if a nanny they have more milk. He has a fishing spear, he catches fish. He burns his wood for charcoal. He sells his nuts for salt and tea, for a new firepot or tobacco for the hookah. If he needs some cloth he can work for a few days for someone else, or on the road, or hire out his pony. How much money does he need? None," said Ayah in great scorn.

Sophie did not of course quite believe Ayah—Ayah was not a country woman—but it was near truth. Suddenly Sophie's tiny pension, her dwindled capital seemed big. If I went and lived like a peasant in the country I should be rich, thought Sophie. If I just lived on my pension, didn't try to make it bigger by teaching or in any city ways, I should be rich by being poor. The thought tickled her, and she made up her mind at once.

"We shan't be poor whites," she announced to Teresa. "We shall be peasants."

The thought that they were not peasants did come into Sophie's mind, but she pushed it down.

"How shall we be peasants?" asked Teresa fearfully.

"I don't know how—yet," said Sophie, and it was then that she remembered the house she had seen from the lake, that speck among the faint far green of trees, the house in which she had wished that she could live.

Chapter 4

"This is a wild place," said Sultan, the little city servant, peering round.

"How can it be wild? It is only a few miles from the city," said Sophie crossly. Sophie could shorten or lengthen distances quite easily in her mind.

"A few miles can be wild," said Sultan.

They had driven, looking for the house, for three hours along the road that wound along the lake below the mountain. Sophie remembered the house but could not remember where it was. They had stopped to ask at villages, where the people stared, stupid with cold, and the middens steamed out into the road when the doors of the shut houses were opened. The horse trotted on and on beside the lake, below the frozen foothills where the ice was thick in the ricefields, the orchards bare. The driver huddled himself in his shawl; Sophie's hands and feet were numbed, and Sultan sat and shivered.

At last Sophie saw it, a house standing alone above a village. "There. There," she cried, standing up in the tonga. Sultan and the driver looked where she pointed. "*That!*" they said. "That isn't a house for a mem."

A rough track led off the road, among the ricefields with their iced stubble, to the village. The tonga was able to jolt a few hundred yards beyond it, through the orchards, out on the mountain, and then stopped. Sophie and Sultan got out and stood looking up.

"How wild it is," said Sultan, his teeth chattering. It did look wild. The village was behind the fold of the mountains, but now Sophie could see Dhilkusha above her. It looked very small, the mountain vast. Down in the lake the reflections were pale, cold, still, with no sign of life.

"Memsahib, let's go back," whispered Sultan, but Sophie's mind was made up. "You are not used to the country," she said severely to Sultan.

"The country is better than the town. All over the world there is suffering and death. In little country places those things are far away; people suffer, certainly, but from the winter, from the weather, not from one another."

Sultan opened his mouth, but Sophie swept on. "In the city there is quarrelling and avarice and filth and disease," she said. "It will be much better living in the country."

"It is very cold for living in the country this afternoon," whispered Sultan, shivering; his cotton trousers clung to his thin legs in the wind, his face looked starved with cold. He was no support to Sophie, who was still weak. Why couldn't I bring someone useful? she thought, but there had been no one. To make up her mind to go to Dhilkusha had been one thing; to get there had been another.

She had thought it wisest not to take any of the missionaries into her confidence; instinctively she felt there would be criticism. "I shall do it first and argue about it afterwards," said Sophie. Ayah and Teresa would have asked questions, much too critical ones; she could have sent for Profit David and asked him to take her, but she owed Profit David money and felt she did not want to argue with him just now. She could only take Sultan. "And you are not to say a word to anyone," Sophie had said incautiously. Sultan said, "Better." Kashmiri servants say "Better" when they are given orders. Someone must once have told them that it meant "Very Good." "Better," said Sultan, but his eyes dilated with importance and Sophie could just imagine the tales he would tell when they came back.

Now she dragged herself up the mountain, leaning on a stick. Sultan followed, bowed with cold, and at last they came up through a small gully onto a knoll of cherry trees and saw the house close.

૪જ

It was the pundit's habit to go out to Dhilkusha from Srinagar four times a year. When he has last visited it that autumn he had been near despair.

Kashmiri Brahmins are called pundits, and they are well known for their sharpness of mind, their subtlety and sensitivity. The pundit was very sensitive. As he toiled up the steep stony path between the shali fields where the peasants had been reaping, the stones hurt his tender small feet and spoiled his pointed city shoes; the reaping songs that the villagers sang sounded as if they were mocking him. The songs had spoiled the beauty of the clear autumn day, and he had begun to worry. "How has everything been?" he asked the caretaker, a young man called Nabir Dār, who came from the village. "How has it been?"

"Very well," said Nabir, but the pundit saw at once it was not very well. As soon as he had come up the gully to the garden he had seen that some of his fruit trees had had their branches lopped; now he saw that stones had been tumbled off the wall, a Peshawar apricot tree had been broken, and some of his new young peach trees were missing—he had paid for ten, and there were only eight. "I paid for ten. There were ten," said the pundit. He was right; two new peach trees were in the garden of Nabir Dār's uncle; Nabir Dār had not stolen them, but he knew who had and he felt uncomfortable. The pundit saw more. There were holes dug in the vegetable beds, on which precious manure had been spent.

"What is this?" asked the pundit.

"Bears," said Nabir sullenly.

"Two-legged bears!" said the pundit.

In the house banisters were missing from the staircase, and the legs were off the only chair. "My father's chair," said the pundit. He felt like weeping.

"They break in and steal wood for firewood," said Nabir.

"You should lock the house."

"If I do they force the windows."

The pundit, though he despised the big young Mohammedan bulk of Nabir Dār, was afraid of him. Nabir Dār had brothers as big as he, and a virago of a mother. The pundit should have beaten Nabir—it was normal for an employer to beat his employed—but he was afraid of beginning; anyway, if he did—or if he did not—he knew that next time he came to Dhilkusha, after the next long absence, there would be even more trees out, more peaches gone, more wood taken away.

He had taken refuge in threats. "I shall complain to the police," he had said.

"The Pundit Sahib should live here at Dhilkusha," said Nabir smoothly. "Then none of these things could happen."

"Live here?" cried the pundit in alarm. "What? Far from my business? And what about the winter?" asked the pundit.

The pundit was like a small woodland creature with bright eyes and a pointing nose. With his shoes he wore neat socks; he had clean white cotton pantaloons, a black quilted waistcoat, a brown overcoat, a neat, small, intricately wound turban of butter-yellow muslin, and a large watch with a silver chain. He smelled a little of cardamom seeds, which he always took against indigestion and ground with his teeth. He was very delicate; he suffered from cramps and nerves; though he could be waspish, he had to gird himself up to make his sting, and this left him exhausted.

Now he gave way to panic. "My father built this house," he cried. "And what am I do to with it? I can let it in the summer as a garden house, but to put it in order costs much money, and in the winter it is all torn up again. You—you are devils!" cried the pundit. "Wolves! Beasts! Devils!"

He was not quite fair. The young Nabir Dār looked after the house and garden as well as he could; no Sheikh—the rival family in the village —was allowed near it, and his own clan made only the mildest depre- dations; only someone as exact as the pundit would have noticed them.

"You should have taken half the peach trees and told him they had died. Half would have been quite fair," said Nabir's brother Amdhoo, who had had his eye on those peach trees.

If he had known it, the pundit might have been worse off than he was in having Nabir; he might, for instance, have had Amdhoo—but "Wolf! Beast! Devil!" shouted the pundit.

Nabir shrugged. He had the most insolent shrug in the world. "Someone should live here," said Nabir.

"I shall pray to the gods to send me someone," cried the pundit fer- vently.

Nabir was not impressed. He had seen many Hindu gods and smiled at them. He knew there was only one God—Allah. It did not occur to him that a little of Allah might be in every god.

᠄ⷮ

36

"There is an English mem up at Dhilkusha," cried Nabir's small brother Mahomet, running into the Dār's house.

There were two chief families in the village, the Dārs and the Sheikhs; almost every villager bore one of those names, and there was bitter rivalry between them. Nabir, the young caretaker, and his four brothers, Raschid, Amdhoo, Samdhoo, and Mahomet, were Dārs. Their father had been the village headman, and Raschid was one of the village elders. They were all said to be *shaitans*—devils—though Raschid, who was a little simple, was in reality quite gentle. Most *shaitani* of all was the mother. Nabir's mother was as handsome as her sons; she had a beautiful aquiline face, fine black eyes, and hair that was still raven black, not grey; she wore a filthy green pheran and a dirty white veil, but her jewellery, like her voice, was second to none in the village.

The brothers had good chosen posts as gardeners in the pleasure garden of Nishat not far away. Nabir could have worked in the garden too, in comfortable fellowship with his brothers and the score of gardeners there; but, for some reason that he could not name himself, he liked better to work alone at Dhilkusha. He liked to be alone; even as a boy, when he had driven the herds as the young Mahomet did now, he had liked to take his goats higher than the others, even above where the charcoal-burners lit their fires; he had not liked to stay down and fraternize but to be up there alone with the clear air that seemed to spin in the gorges, with the streams that tumbled from the ice; he had found things that he spoke about to no one—an eagle's nest, the rare pink saxifrage, once the track of a mahkhor. He had found a cave that was really a half-tumbled-down kiln, and he had made a bed of furze in it and lit a fire and slept there.

Nabir could be gay and sociable but he grew tired of the intimacy of the village, the gossip, the feuds and the emotion, especially of the women. Young men of Nabir's age were lordly; they had been taught that women were unimportant, but Nabir knew that women had penetrating voices, their jewellery clinked as they fidgeted, they had small quick hands that went into everything, their eyes were quick too, and their instincts acute. It was difficult to be lordly with them. Nabir had no wife, but Amdhoo, Samdhoo, and Raschid had wives; Raschid had two girl children and Samdhoo a girl baby. Nabir had never heard of a kindle of kittens, but that is what his house was filled with, and every day he was glad to take his bundle of food, his shawl and his spade, his firepot in winter, and go up to Dhilkusha.

"He works, and there is no one to see him!" said his mother. "He is a very queer boy."

ॐ

The air at Dhilkusha always seemed more clear than the air down in the village. In winter there was silence there except for the splash of the stream where it broke through the ice and an occasional high bird-call like an eagle's, and a shadow sound, carried up from the lake, of paddles and splashes from the nets and fish spears; in summer it was busy with the noise of fruit-pickers, of the herd children, of field-workers, of cows lowing and the bleating of flocks, and of birds that drowned the many noises from the lake; but even then, in the evenings it was still.

The path ran up onto the knoll of cherry trees, where a gap in the wall served as a front gate; inside a rough wall spread a garden of terraces and fruit trees. The house was built on the second terrace; it was like a small chalet, the lower half of stone and wood, with a veranda; the upper story was pink, earth- plastered, the roof of wooden shingles. There were four rooms, two up and two down, separated by a small hall with a flight of stairs. The house was dilapidated, but the wood was sound; the earth floors were not damp, though very dirty. There were no ceilings, only crossbeams stuffed with dried furze, as in most Kashmiri peasant houses. There was no glass in the windows, only hanging wooden shutters; no water system of course; no lighting; but it was a rarely beautiful little house. In summer it was hung with vines and honeysuckle and white scented roses and all round it were flowering trees. On the terrace below the house was a rough lawn; there were flowerbeds tangled with roses, and the whole garden was ringed with poplars. At the back of the house was a courtyard; the stream splashed there in a little waterfall, and a servants' hut stood under the apple trees. Above it all the mountain reared its head, while below lay the lake and its reflections, and, far, the horizon of snow peaks.

That afternoon Nabir had just come down from Dhilkusha and was sitting comfortably with his firepot, waiting for his mother to bring him some tea, when Mahomet ran in. "An English mem!" cried Mahomet shrilly.

"Owl!" said Nabir. "It's winter." In winter people stayed where they lived, and English ladies lived in Srinagar. Anyway they never came to the village; they came to Nishat or drove along the lake road in parties on their way to trek in the far mountains.

"Little fool," said Nabir to Mahomet and settled into his shawl.

"There *is* an English lady," cried Mahomet. His voice was shrill, and it went through Nabir's head so that it almost hurt. "Go and see!" cried Mahomet.

The village had an intelligence department in its children; they knew all the news long before it happened. If it had been summer the children would have been up on the mountain with the herds, but now they were all in the village, getting into trouble, hiding from school, and gambling over their eternal hopscotch and the game of Teenka they played with pebbles.

"I tell you there is an English lady. Go and see for yourself," shrilled Mahomet.

"Was I born yesterday?" asked Nabir tolerantly and gave Mahomet a cuff, but Mahomet still insisted that the lady was there. "She came in a tonga and made it drive high up the hill; and she had a servant, and she walks with a stick. She can't walk properly, she is walking very slowly, but she is walking to Dhilkusha," cried Mahomet. "Hurry or she will be there. Go and see."

At last Nabir half believed him and cursed and went.

≥●

The sun came out as Sophie stood at the top of the gully, under the cherry trees, looking.

It was getting late, but now she had forgotten that she was tired and cold, that her legs and back ached with the struggle of getting up the mountain, that her heart was pounding. A new strength had come to her.

"It's wonderful how strong Sophie is when it is anything she wants," the aunts often said. As soon as she saw Dhilkusha, Sophie knew she wanted it. Her instinct had been right. She looked at the pink walls, the wooden shingled roof, the brown tangle of creepers, and her heart swelled. It's beautiful, thought Sophie and drew a long breath.

The afternoon was beautiful too, with the sheen of snow under the dark branches of the trees, the pale shapes of poplars. She heard the tinkle-splashing of the stream; a fall of snow, sliding off a branch, made her jump. She stood, taking in breaths of the pure air, thinking of getting Teresa and Moo into it, out of the fetid city. She thought of Moo's wan cheeks—even Teresa's were pale. She thought of their fretful voices and the way Moo screamed in his sleep. I shall bring them here, thought Sophie, and she walked up the path from the cherry trees towards the house.

It had not crossed her mind that it might not be empty, or even that it must belong to someone. Now a young Kashmiri, with a boy at his heels, came suddenly out from behind the house and stood in her way. His breast was heaving, not with indignation but because he had run so fast up the mountain, but it made him look angry. He stood in Sophie's way and said in Urdu, not Kashmiri, "Visitors are not allowed in the house."

"I am not a visitor," said Sophie. She felt as if she had been slapped in the face. She had almost been thinking that the house was hers.

"I am not a visitor," she said crushingly, but he did not give way.

He was an unusually large young man. He wore a ragged homespun shirt and dirty cotton pantaloons, and instead of being muffled in his shawl he carried it like a Highlander's plaid on his shoulder. He was like a Highlander altogether; he stood before her with dignity. He was clean-shaven and wore the skullcap of the country people instead of a turban; his skin was light, and his blue-green eyes had a slight sloe shape that made them look lazy and insolent.

Nabir knew Sophie was a visitor; all English mems were visitors. His brothers saw many of these visitor ladies, English and American, in Nishat, and they often told about them at home—how they gave orders to their husbands and how men stood while they sat down. Men carried things for them, handed them cups of tea, and lit cigarettes for them in the strangest way. Now this mem confirmed what they had said. Nabir was a man, but she gave him one hard look and walked straight past him into the house. For the first time in his life Nabir felt helpless.

Sophie went through the house at lightning speed and then stood at the back door of the little hall, making calculations on a pad. Nabir did not know a woman who could read and write; he had thought he could do both himself quite respectably, but now he watched the speed of Sophie's pencil with something like horror. She asked him questions so quickly that they made his head reel. "Have the ceilings always been like that?" asked Sophie in her quick Urdu. "Could we sell that furze? Why are so many banisters missing? Why are the floors so dirty? No glass in the windows? Only wood or—yes, paper panes? How do you see when the windows are shut?" Nabir had not thought about these questions before; he had always accepted things as they were. Now he felt as if Sophie were probing, and his answers grew shorter. "From the beginning he was uncooperative," said Sophie afterwards.

If Nabir thought Sophie dismaying, he thought Sultan, the little city servant, despicable. "Are there animals here, wild beasts?" asked Sultan, and his eyes rolled.

"Yes," said Nabir, amused. "Many."

"What sort of wild beasts?" said Sophie. She said it scornfully, and a flicker of respect woke in him. He was used to the shrill vociferations of his own women if they heard as much as a rat on the roof. He answered Sophie truthfully, which he might not have done if she had seemed in the least alarmed. "Foxes, lynx, perhaps a panther," he said. "A panther will come sometimes for goats or dogs, and in spring the bears are dangerous."

"Aie!" cried Sultan.

"But they are high up," said Sophie.

"This is high up," said Sultan.

A slight smile crossed Nabir's face. "Look at the mountain," he said. "You will see how high you are."

Sophie went out to the courtyard and stood looking up. "We are not even as high as the charcoal-burners," she said. Her voice was exact, unexcited, and Nabir felt that respect rise in him again. He had yet to learn how excited Sophie could be over inconsequential trifles.

As they stood there, there was a roar and a shaking. "What is that?" said Sophie, startled, and Sultan shrank with fear and turned even more yellow than he was already from the cold.

"It's the mountain snow coming down," said Nabir. "Now, on a warmer day, sometimes there is a thaw."

"Oh, an avalanche!" said Sophie, as if it were nothing, and Nabir smiled. But Sophie was paying no attention to him. She came back onto the veranda, thinking. Before she made up her mind she had a moment's pause.

Could I live here alone? she was asking herself. Alone with the mountain and lake, the mist and reflections and the silence? There will be no one but the children, a servant, and the village people—like this young man to whom I can't speak in his own language. Could I live here? asked Sophie. Dare I? Why, anything could happen. But already the idea was putting new life in her; she felt alive, almost strong and well. "I shan't be alone," said Sophie. "These people shall be my people. I shall be one of them."

She ignored the respectful way in which Nabir stood, and smiled in friendliness at him. Nabir did not smile back. He would have felt it to be disrespectful.

All at once Sophie saw something she had not noticed before. On the veranda floor someone had cut a cross with the four compass points— North, South, East, and West—and marked each with a star.

"Who cut that?" she asked Nabir.

"A sahib," said Nabir. "He stayed here the night. He was walking, not like proper sahibs with servants and ponies," said Nabir with disapproval. "He was by himself with a pack on his back. He went with the goat people."

Sophie knew the goat people, the nomads, gypsies. She had seen them last summer driving their flocks up to pasture in the high Himalayas and down again in autumn to the plains. They drove with wild shrilling hawk-whistles. The men rode shaggy ponies; the women walked with the cooking pots in string nets on their heads, dragging fierce big dogs, driving the goats, carrying their babies in slings. Sophie liked their height and carriage, the way their tunics and wide trousers swung, the gay impudence of their children, their piercing whistles. She never saw them without wanting to go with them. No wonder he went, she thought. She looked at the compass points and the stars. I should have made a different symbol for each, she thought. A mountain for the North, a sun for the South, a crescent for the East—but no, perhaps a star was best, a star each way you went.

"He was a sahib from the sea," said Nabir.

"A sailor," said Sophie. "Did he come back?"

"No," said Nabir.

He wouldn't, thought Sophie. No, you must go on—go on . . . And she took a deep breath and asked, "What is the landlord's name?"

"Who was the mem?" asked Amdhoo when Nabir reached home. By now the whole village knew about Sophie, her stick, the servant, and the tonga; the villagers crowded round Nabir so that he could hardly get into his own house.

"Who was she?"

"I don't know," said Nabir. He felt tired out.

"But what did she want?" asked his mother. "At least you know that."

"I think she wants to live in Dhilkusha," said Nabir miserably.

"She won't," said Amdhoo certainly. "English ladies have to have electricity." In his early years, before he had become a gardener at Nishat, Amdhoo had been one of the flower-boat boys. Now Nabir listened intently as Amdhoo told how he had seen every houseboat connected with the electric supply as soon as it was moored. "The electricity," said Amdhoo sagely, "is one of the things they have to have."

Nabir was a little comforted—but not for long. In a week the news was all over the village. Amdhoo was wrong. Though it had no electricity, the English mem had taken Dhilkusha for five years.

Chapter 5

Sophie always hoped that one day someone would say of her, "That little woman has a good head on her shoulders." No one had said it yet, but she drove a shrewd bargain for Dhilkusha with the pundit. In India it takes a long time to make a bargain.

"It's very upsetting, all these people coming in and out," complained Sister Locke. This choosing and making of a home was something strange to the missionaries; a missionary goes where she is sent, to the house and furniture allotted her. The Mission seemed full of Sophie's plans, and there was a disturbed look—sometimes Sophie thought it was of envy—in Sister Locke's and Sister Pilkington's eyes.

From the very beginning Sophie had disturbed them. "You read poetry," Sister Pilkington had said, picking up a book from the table by Sophie's bed. "So does he. That is a great bond"—and she sighed. Sophie had no need to ask who "he" was; she had seen the pretty sister gaze at Little Lochinvar with a deep soft look in her eyes.

"The hair generally falls out after typhoid," said Sister Locke as she carefully brushed Sophie's hair. "I can spare it," said Sophie wickedly as its lengths spread over the pillow; she knew that Sister Locke had thin patches under her veil. Sophie's smooth white skin made the sister look sallow and freckled. "You must spend a nice sum on creams!" said Sister Locke. "Not at all," said the aggravating Sophie. "I don't have to bother with creams; my skin stays white like this by itself."

When Sophie was ill she had been quiet, but now, into the Mission, she brought this stream of life, of rents and contracts, home and gardens, furniture, china. The Mission was for sick people, and now there was a coming and going of lively ones, landlords and lawyers, carpenters, masons, painters. "And that carpet-seller, Profit David," said Sister Locke indignantly. "What has he to do with it, I should like to know?"

"Oh, Profit David always hopes to pull a plum out of the smallest pie," said Sophie.

"He is the worst rogue in Srinagar," said Sister Locke sourly.

"He has the best cook in Srinagar," said Sophie. "I am going to eat a Persian dinner with him tomorrow."

"Well, you can't get typhoid again so soon, I suppose," said Sister Locke.

To have a meal away from the Mission, to feast her eyes on the carpets Profit David would show her—Bokhara and Lashar, Kirman, Tabriz—to handle his agates and jades, his shawls and jewels, to talk a little wittily and drink cups of hot spiced tea would be a breath of life, thought Sophie.

"Last time I went," she said dreamily, "we had honey-rice and mutton balls stuffed with spices, and apricots stuffed with mutton, and pilaf and fish coconut."

"How *strange!*" said Sister Pilkington.

"Not as strange as for a Kashmiri cook to make a blanc-mange," said Sophie.

"Well, give me a cup of English tea, that is all I want," said Sister Locke.

"Tea isn't English," snapped Sophie, and Sister Locke was hurt.

"Dearie, the Hutchinson Wing is empty till the spring," said saintly Dr. Glenister, who did not notice any of these sparrings. "Why not stay here till the spring?" But Sophie thought the sooner she left the Mission the better, and she drove her bargain hard.

"If I put your house in order—it is in a very bad state now—can I live there rent free for five years?" was her question to the pundit.

The pundit was superstitious. Sophie was the direct answer to his prayer; she had undoubtedly come from the gods; but he hoped for a least a little rent. "Fifty rupees a month," he pleaded. "Thirty. Twenty." But Sophie spoke sternly of the cost of building materials. He had not thought that someone from the gods could be so practical.

"I feel so sorry for you, having to deal with all these people," said Sister Pilkington.

"But I like it," said Sophie. The Mission seemed to think it a little unseemly that she should like it, but as she and the pundit skirmished cautiously round the question of rent and repairs they came to like each other very much. At last, "Not rent free," said the pundit. "Let it be a nominal rent, because of what people will think—so that I can *say* you rent it."

"What is nominal?" asked Sophie cautiously.

It was finally settled at five rupees a month. "After all, no one is living there, and it is falling to pieces," said Sophie, but when he agreed to the price she could not help feeling jubilant. Rents in Srinagar for a small house were as high as three hundred rupees a month, and for five rupees—seven shillings and sixpence—she had the house, the servants' house, the stream, and ten acres of land.

The pundit was jubilant too; now his house would be put in order with no trouble and expense to himself. "How much will you spend?" he kept on asking Sophie.

A lady from the gods should have showered down money, but "I shall spend what is necessary," said Sophie.

Her contract was for the land under the trees. "But Pundit Sahib, we can have some fruit?"

"I will give you some, but"—his eyes grew big with alarm—"out of courtesy, *not* on contract."

A lawyer—a vakil—came to draw up the contract. It had a huge state stamp upon it and was written in Urdu; not only did it have to be signed, the pundit's five fingerprints were taken as well.

"Why the pundit's and not mine?" asked Sophie.

"They trust you because you are British," said Sister Locke, and she said complacently, "It's a part of British prestige."

"But—it isn't manners," said Sophie, troubled, and she insisted on having her fingerprints taken as well.

"Well, really!" said Sister Locke.

Sophie had thought it a good gesture, but the missionaries were angry. Even Dr. Glenister said, "Dearie, surely that wasn't necessary."

"You should be what you are, British," said Sister Locke. The vakil said the same; he and the pundit were embarrassed. "And I didn't mind," said the pundit. "It's customary."

"It's a horrid custom," said Sophie. "One should trust people."

"Never!" said the vakil. "Never."

47

The vakil was very stern with Sophie and the pundit. He modified Sophie's offer. "It is the landlord," he said, "who must keep the roof weathertight."

"Weather is very expensive," said the pundit dismally. Sophie, on the other hand, had to undertake to let the bird-scarers and the fruit-pickers come and go; she had to give the pundit the right to make charcoal on his land, and promise to cultivate and keep the flower and vegetable gardens; she was not to pick almonds and not to burn for firing any of the wood of which the house was made. "But I wouldn't," said Sophie indignantly.

"If you were very cold you might," said the vakil. "Tenants have been known to take the shingles off the roof. You may be cold," said the vakil. "Already your circumstances have altered. You have become poor, and all your requirements you must provide yourself."

"Yes," said Sophie and sighed.

꿋

"How will you do it? How will you live?" asked Profit David.

"We shall live by spending little."

"How miserable!" said Profit David crossly. "Like a beggar."

"A beggar's bowl is filled," said Sophie.

"Only a lucky beggar," said Profit David, but Sophie was in love with her idea and would not be disturbed.

"Poverty need not be mean and ugly," she said to Sister Locke. "It can be 'the Lady Poverty.'"

Sister Locke sniffed. "The two don't go together," she said.

"They can," said Sophie. "They shall."

"There are a good few things you will have to do—and do without," said Sister Locke, and she asked unkindly, "What about smoking?"

For a moment Sophie was silent. She was remembering that even in those days of teaching and worry she still had managed cigarettes—too many cigarettes. Then, "I shall go without," said Sophie.

"You asked to smoke even when you were ill," Sister Locke reminded her.

"I shall go without," said Sophie more firmly. "I shall go without most things."

"It's easy to say," said Sister Locke.

But Sophie was very firm. "Pickles," pleaded Sultan when she ruthlessly cut down his stores list. "All sahibs have pickles."

"We shall make our own pickles," said Sophie. "We shall grow our own vegetables and keep hens and bees." It sounded idyllic. "We shall even grow our own toothbrushes," she said, laughing. Kashmiris use willow twigs to clean their teeth; the juice keeps them sound and white. "We shall use willow twigs," said Sophie. "Think," she told Teresa, "think of picking your toothbrushes off a tree." But Teresa and Sultan plainly thought it all beneath their dignity. "Can't we have a proper house?" asked Teresa.

The pundit and the workmen wanted to wait till the spring. "No one works in winter," said the pundit.

"We will," said Sophie.

"Plaster will freeze, paint will spoil, the men won't work. Don't do it now. Wait till spring," said the pundit.

"Now," said Sophie.

"It will be very expensive."

"*Now*," said Sophie. She felt she had to get away from all these criticisms and cares.

Profit David was worrying her with his bill:

One walnut wood writing desk	Rs. 160.
One set of walnut wood trays	75.
One embroidered shawl	115.
One papier-mâché lamp with kingfishers	170.
Total	Rs. 520.

Paid Rs. 200.   Rs. 320. still unpaid.

"*Still unpaid*," said Profit David.

The lamp was golden, painted with kingfishers and flowers in deep rich colours. "But what is the difference in it, to cost all that money?" asked Sister Pilkington, and she looked at the lamp and then at a papier-mâché box she had bought for three rupees in the bazaar.

"That box is made of newspaper and painted with cheap Japanese colours. It will crack in a few months. While this," said Sophie reverently, touching the lamp, "this is made of handmade paper from a village outside Srinagar that has made it for generations—generations!" said Sophie. "It's pulped and moulded by hand and painted with stone colours that come from Tibet. The blue is real lapis lazuli, the gold, real gold; its painting and design take weeks, and the patterns are tradition-al, and after it's painted it's lacquered with a lacquer of amber and oil. If you can't see the difference I can only be sorry for you," said Sophie bitingly.

Sophie had tried to resist buying the lamp. "It's very expensive," she had said weakly.

"Shall I sell you what everybody buys?" asked Profit David severely.

"No! Oh no!" cried Sophie.

That shawl was woven in paschmina, taffeta twist, of the softest goat-tip wool, and could go through a ring; its border was so finely embroi-dered that a magnifying glass was needed to see the stitches. The desk and the trays, too, were handmade, beautiful and plain. "One day I shall sell you a carpet," said Profit David to Sophie. She had a feeling that one day he would, but—how did all this extravagance go with her vow of frugality? asked Sophie, ashamed. And yet, in a way, she felt she and Profit David were more two of a kind than she and the Lady Poverty. "You—and a Kashmiri carpet-seller!" Toby was to say later, and Sophie had to answer, "Yes."

"I shall pay you, little by little, every month," she said now to Profit David.

"Little! Little! Little!" said Profit David testily. "You, lady sahib, are big. Then be big!" said Profit David. "These missionaries are making you small." He and the missionaries looked on one another with mutual hos-tility and suspicion. Little Lochinvar hovered near Sophie each time Profit David came.

"Don't let him dun you," said Little Lochinvar.

"He won't, except most charmingly," said Sophie.

Sophie could see Little Lochinvar felt she should not have been charmed, but he would not criticize. He had even kept out of the criti-cism that had broken round her when she announced her plan.

"Mr. Abercrombie is *most* distressed," wrote Aunt Portia, "and so are

Mamie and I. Rose washes her hands of it, as usual, but we *beg* you to come home."

"Toby came in to lance a swelling on Portia's finger," wrote Aunt Mamie. "We read your letter to him. He said nothing, but you should have seen his face."

"I'm convinced you should go home," wrote Mr. Kirkpatrick. "I have been trying to find work that is fit for you, but meanwhile have seen the directors, and the company will pay your passages home."

"I am going to Dhilkusha," said Sophie.

"It's too far," said Dr. Glenister again and again.

"I am going to Dhilkusha," said Sophie.

"It's too lonely a place for Teresa and Moo," said Sister Pilkington.

"Mrs. Ward is not the kind who is lonely for long," said Sister Locke.

All this broke round Sophie and did not touch her, but when she told Little Lochinvar he said, "I shall go out of my mind thinking of you there."

"Doctor Lochinvar," said Sophie gently, "I shouldn't be in your mind." But it was too late to say that.

"Why not?" he asked, ominously quiet.

"Because it isn't suitable," said Sophie. That was the aunts' word, and she took refuge behind it.

"It isn't suitable," said Little Lochinvar with great bitterness. "I quite agree. A medical missionary shouldn't be haunted—by violets, for instance."

"Violets?"

"Yes."

"Nobody knows," said Sophie thoughtfully, "what is suitable for anyone else. Why shouldn't you think of them?"

"You have a condition following on your illness and malnutrition. I have seen it in tuberculosis—a discolouration round the eyes. I know what it is, but it makes me think of violets." And he said, looking past Sophie, his eyes rapt behind his glasses, his face lit, "'Violets dim and sweeter than the lids of Juno's eyes.'"

"We are waiting for you in the theatre, Doctor," said Sister Locke in the doorway. "Please hurry. It's an incomplete abortion." The ugly words blotted out the sound of the violets, and Little Lochinvar blushed and went.

"Now I suppose you are pleased with yourself," said Sister Locke as she turned to follow him.

"No, I am not," said Sophie truthfully and sadly.

Little Lochinvar touched her. His face had the peaked look of a delicate child, his hair was like soft fur on his head, he wore glasses, and his ears and his teeth stuck out, but sometimes he looked almost incandescent with tiredness and enthusiasm, and he did not care how he drove and used his fragile small body. "So daring in love and so dauntless in war," thought Sophie. He isn't badly named.

His admiration had come at a time when she felt cold and old, and it warmed the cockles of her heart when they needed warming. "But do hearts have cockles?" asked Sophie, and she looked it up in her dictionary and found they were the heart itself. And that won't do, thought Sophie. "You know it won't do," she told herself.

It was odd for her to have fallen among the missionaries. She had often been very witty and sarcastic about them in the old days; now all those words came back to her, two-edged. Everything you do comes back to you, thought Sophie. That discovery was one of the discouragements of the these days.

She had come to love and revere Dr. Glenister; Sister Pilkington had poured herself out for them—even though Sister Pilkington might very well have been jealous, thought Sophie. She and Sister Locke had come to appreciate each other, if only as adversaries; Sophie had come to appreciate them all, and she tried to see only their toil and zeal, to have the single eye of a child.

Teresa, she thought, sees nothing wrong. Peter and James and John were probably horny-handed and bearded and smelled of fish, thought Sophie sensibly. "But they were peasants," she cried. "It's the gentility that irks me."

"Teresa hasn't been taught to say, 'Pardon,' or cough off the table," said Sister Pilkington. Sister Locke was particular that the servants put crocheted doilies under the cake plates. Religion should be beautiful and spacious, thought Sophie, and she thought of the beauty and simplicity of a nun's dress, or the red robes of a Buddhist priest.

"The missionaries are *narrow!*" cried Sophie. "They don't know anything about the customs of the people they live and work among. They—they work for the people but they don't respect them," said Sophie.

Little Lochinvar had tracts in his pocket as well as his stethoscope; he would press them on a devout clean-living Mohammedan, a Hindu sage, a Buddhist, as he would have on a savage. "But a Hindu or a Buddhist has a religion of his own," said Sophie.

"They are not religions," said Little Lochinvar.

❧

Sister Pilkington was cross because she could not sweep up the little figure of the Goddess Shakti, with her garlands and flowers, that a young Hindu husband had placed over his wife's bed in the maternity ward. "Such rubbish," said Sister Pilkington.

"It was his prayer to keep her safe in childbirth," Sophie felt impelled to say. "Shakti is an aspect of God."

"An idol," said Sister Pilkington shortly.

"What a nuisance this Ramzan is," said Sister Locke, speaking of the Mohammedan month of fast that comes once a year. "The people may not eat or drink from sunrise to sunset. How can we diet them?" asked Sister Locke. "It's hard to make the servants work properly when they fast."

"You fast in Lent," Sophie pointed out.

"That is different," said Sister Locke indignantly.

As she had lain in bed in the Hutchinson Wing, Sophie could see an old temple on the hill that hid the city from the lake. It was the Hindu temple of the Tahkt-el-Sulei-man; its foundations had been there for more than two thousand years; at night it was lit and shone like a beacon over the lake and country on one side, over the narrow streets and huddle of bridges and houses on the other. It had always seemed to Sophie like a symbol of this country—the temple, wrapped in the antiquity and beauty of its Hinduism, standing high, its light tended and powerful, while below, herded, teeming, alive in their narrow houses, dead in their narrow graves, were the Mohammedans. Beside the graveyard the

Mission Hospital stood, and the missionaries tried to tend and care for the people, Mohammedans and Hindus alike; Sophie had always accepted that that was admirable but, as she lay those long days in bed, she had begun to think. "Tong-tong-tong," went the Mission bell, with the Maulvi's voice, the temple gong; but, "It's not *with* them; it's trying to shut them out," said Sophie. That persistent little bell sounded militant.

"Why do religions have edges?" asked Teresa. Sophie felt those edges now. She went into the Mission chapel. It was a small whitewashed room with deal pews, a strip of blue carpet, a carved lectern, and an altar; on the altar were brass vases filled with holly, and, between them, a brass cross. It was a little refuge of holiness and quiet in the press and hurry and alarms of the hospital.

"God is here," said the printed text on the wall. "Yes," said Sophie. "But," she asked, "isn't He everywhere? Then why do they make Him little?" And she thought of those edges, pressing against each other, hurting, jarring, offending, barring one human being from another, shutting away their understanding and their souls.

Yet if you have no edges, thought Sophie, how lonely, how drifting, you must consent to be.

She looked at the cross, and it reminded her of another—the North, South, East, and West of the compass cross at Dhilkusha. Both are His, she thought.

Chapter 6

When the village heard that Sophie had rented Dhilkusha it was stunned.

"But why? Why?" everyone asked Nabir.

"How do I know why?" said Nabir crossly.

"Perhaps she wants to live in it," the eldest Dār brother, Raschid, had said, but no one paid any attention to him.

"And she will live there in winter!" said the village.

"All the year round," said Nabir gloomily. He had a strong instinct that he should give notice, but, when he suggested it, the family cried him down. "An Englishwoman!" cried Amdhoo, his eyes flashing. "They spend money without knowing!" Without knowing on what, he might have added; indeed it would have surprised Sophie to know what strange things her money was to buy in the next few months. She had given up smoking, and certainly she had never smoked a hookah, yet she bought a great deal of hookah tobacco; she wore no jewellery, yet bought silver anklets—they were for Samdhoo's daughter; she did not drink salt tea but bought endless samovars of it; she had no cow and yet she bought fodder; she even bought charras. It was all done by tea money, squeeze or commission on every penny she spent.

"What a pity she isn't American," said Amdhoo. "Americans are richer, but never mind. I expect there will be plenty of money!" Everything that Sophie did seemed to bear this out.

If she had been asked what she did to make the house habitable she would have said that she did the merest necessities, but to the village these preparations were fabulous.

"A cookstove in the kitchen and stoves in both the rooms upstairs!" They could not believe it. "Think of the wood!" groaned Nabir's mother. She had never heard of such extravagance. Perfectly adequate heating came into a house from the midden below, which cost nothing and was thrown in with the cows as it were; or else there were firepots and, for cooking, the earth oven on the floor, from which the smoke went up into the room. Sophie's kitchen had a clay stove like a cookshop, and a chimney built of bricks; the stovepipes went through the windows in especially fitted panes. "Aie! She is rich!" said Nabir's mother.

Nothing, not a hole or a chink, was left unmended at Dhilkusha; panes of glass were put in the windows, not paper or wood, and when everything else was done the walls, beautiful smooth new-plastered walls, were coloured.

Sophie herself came out and put patches on the walls to get the right colours; she seemed to think it was important; she had bought packets of native dye and put them in the whitewash. She drove out with the pundit and a friend of his, a goldsmith. "And she sat alone in front," said the village. "The men had to sit at the back." That was all in piece with what Amdhoo had told them, but they had not really believed it. "And a goldsmith isn't a nobody," said Nabir's mother.

The colours Sophie had chosen were the exact colours of the turbans the pundit and the goldsmith had worn that day—butter-cream in the bedroom and pale jade green in the sitting room. She was glad they had put her in mind of them. The colours looked well with the light unvarnished wood. "It will be nice when it is sweeped," said the pundit, whose English was of the endearing kind.

But the pundit had been right in his gloomy prognostications. The plaster froze; the workmen worked for an hour and stopped to smoke a hookah and drink tea; there was a heavy snowfall, and supplies could not be got up to the house. The work went at a snail's pace, but even in this unnatural season it did get done, and the village watched, amazed at Sophie's power. Nabir was amazed too. He watched her as she made the carpenters take emery paper and rub the banister rail smooth and then wax it till it shone, made them mend the banisters and paint them, made them put up bookshelves and paint them white and yellow.

"But why does she do all this?" Nabir asked the pundit.

"So that it will look nice," said the pundit. Nabir had never heard of a house being required to do that, and, though the pundit was charmed, Nabir resented it. He soon saw that he had reason; with the beauty and cleanliness came all sorts of taboos. There was clean matting on the floor; he must not come in and out with his dirty feet. No one must smoke a hookah in the kitchen; to Nabir a hookah smelled good, but, "It smells nasty," said Sophie. For a man not to be able to smoke where he wished seemed derogatory to Nabir, and his peace was shattered.

It was shattered in several directions. All day long there was a frieze of villagers hanging over the Dhilkusha wall, their eyes staring, their voices whispering. The herd children came up; they had no excuse, the herds did not come out until the spring; in the winter it was the custom for the boys to attend the village school; the sing-song of the multiplication tables should now have been sounding out into the road. But the schoolroom was strangely quiet; the boys were up on the mountain, but you could not blame them; the schoolmaster was there too. Sophie saw the heads bobbing over the wall, heads with veils and caps and turbans; she saw the dark eyes, and an occasional pair of bluegrey ones like Nabir's; she heard the whispering. Nabir came out to drive the children away, but she stopped him. "I like to be friendly," she said.

"But they are not your friends," said Nabir. "You don't know them."

"Respect first," Nabir would have said if he could have explained, "friendship after." But Sophie was determined to be friends at once. Soon she had made some of the boys so bold that they came over the wall. Nabir was in despair.

The furniture arrived. It was simple furniture. The beds had no springs; they were wood frames with webbing across them. "We can only afford country beds," said Sophie, but, "A bed each!" said the village, marvelling. "A bed even for the children!" There were also a little dressing chest of unstained wood for Sophie, made by the carpenter as cheaply and as badly as the ceilings, and a single cupboard built into the bedroom wall. In the sitting room opposite were a table and three dining chairs, a small easy chair for Teresa, a smaller one for Moo, and two full-sized wicker ones that Sophie cushioned herself with printed khuddah, the native cotton. "One for me, one for a guest," said Sophie, though who the guest could be she did not know.

Profit David's writing desk stood under the window, and on it the lamp with the kingfishers. Sophie looked at them and sighed, but when she saw how the kingfishers glowed and how inviting was the desk she could not regret them, though they looked far too splendid for

opposite reactions

everything else. Downstairs in the kitchen were a wooden table and a safe for food and some shelves and hooks for pans and china. "That is all," said Sophie, pitying herself. "All!" said the village, dazzled.

Nabir Dār had to enumerate these wonderful things every night when he reached home. "I'm tired of them; I don't want to talk about them," he said but his mother and sisters-in-law dragged it all out of him, and every night their house was packed with listeners. Things that Sophie took for granted were marvellous to them—bathtowels, blankets, sheets, pillows, the row of new cooking pans. "Get brass," the pundit told Sophie. "They will last you all your life, and three times a year a man will come and line them with alloy for you, but on no account pay him more than one rupee eight annas for the set." Sophie was glad to have them instead of the aluminum sold nowadays in Indian shops; the brass was indigenous, and she liked to see its scrubbed gold shining; but the pans might have been made of gold from the way the village people looked at them. For china she had been to the pottery shop, where she had chosen blue cups and saucers and dishes of the cheap Kashmiri pottery that was blue or yellow or brown or green in strong native colours. She had chosen blue—"The colour of Mary's robe!" said Sophie.

"Mary has different colours in different pictures," said Teresa. "Sometimes her robe is red." What, wondered Sophie, roused Teresa to trip her up with horrid prim little observations like that?

When Nabir told his family about the spoons and forks they did not believe him.

"What are fingers for?" asked his mother.

"It's a good idea," said Nabir. "If the food is hot you don't burn your fingers."

"But you burn your mouth," said Raschid.

The wooden pepper pot and salt cellar puzzled Nabir until Sophie told him what they were for. Nabir's mother had a rock of salt on a string hanging on the wall; if she needed salt she chipped a bit off the rock with a knife. Then there was a clock that chimed. How did it chime? Nabir was afraid of it, and he did not like the cow picture; he tried not to look at it. To a Mohammedan, a face should not be delineated, and those cows had faces; two of them watched him whenever he came into the room.

Sophie's red rugs were on the floor. They were made of yak wool and were coarse, like felt. She had bought them the year before in the Srinagar bazaar. "At least let me lend you some Persian rugs," said Profit David when he saw them. "No one has country-made things in their houses like these," he said, curling his nostrils.

"It's a bare simple little house," said Sophie. "Simple rugs will do"; but she looked at them, thinking of the melting colours of Profit David's carpets, and the red seemed harsh.

"Rugs, not kept on the beds," Nabir told in the village, "not spread for sitting, but *walked* on."

"With *feet?*" asked his mother.

"With shoes." That seemed almost unbelievable treatment to the village. Were shoes, then, worn in the house? They began to think that Sophie was dirty.

"We have no curtains," said Sophie to Profit David, showing him the windows. She wanted to emphasize how plainly they meant to live, because Profit David was tempting her.

"Let me sell you some furniture, all in walnut wood, hand-made," said Profit David. He brought her two small tables, low and round, of good proportions. "This is Brother, this is Sister," said Profit David. "They shouldn't be separated. Buy them both."

"But I haven't paid you for the last things," said Sophie.

"Lady sahib, you will pay me," said Profit David quite confidently. He insisted on treating the house as a little Trianon. "Never mind to pay me," he said. "Think instead, What beautiful little tables. Lady sahib, you need a table." With an effort Sophie was firm. "Not even curtains."

She wondered why Profit David, who liked his comforts, should have driven all this way in the cold. Of course there are no visitors in winter, she thought, and he wanted to sell me those tables, but how did he think I could buy them? I have told him I am poor.

The truth was that Profit David did not believe her. Certain rumours were in the bazaar. Profit David would have been disappointed to know they had been started by Sultan.

"My mem is a first-class political mem," said Sultan. Sophie had once shown him a picture of the tea-garden where she and the children had lived. "She owns a tea-garden," Sultan said lightly. He added that she had a gold mine in Calcutta. Profit David knew perfectly well there were no gold mines in Calcutta, but "There is no smoke without a fire," said Profit David. He felt Sophie was rich and Dhilkusha was a whim. He sympathized; he had whims himself and he liked them very much; other people's whims were a golden opportunity to make good money.

Sophie arranged the whole house before she moved in. She wanted the children to see it complete. But would it be complete? The pundit worried about that. Would the village be able to resist these treasures?

"You are thinking of city people," said Sophie severely. "Peasants don't steal." By now the pundit was too much taken with Sophie to think of contradicting her. "One must trust, Pundit Sahib," said Sophie severely.

"Of course," said the pundit. "You are sure you have the storeroom key?"

Nabir Dār also had this distressing lack of trust. "Please to lock everything," he said to Sophie in agony and he thought he would make Aziz Dār, his cousin, the big tonga-man, come up and sleep with him in the house. Amdhoo had offered, but Nabir thought it better not to let Amdhoo see all these things—nor any of his brothers. "He is afraid of the Sheikhs. Afraid of the Sheikhs!" Amdhoo and Samdhoo taunted him. Nabir was not afraid of the Sheikhs but he was bitterly afraid, in this case, of his own relations. When Sophie and the pundit went back to Srinagar he quickly locked the house.

"What? When she has gone you are not going to let us in to look!" cried his mother and sisters-in-law, who had come up on purpose.

"The orders are no one is to come into the house," said Nabir desperately and, to lend himself a little authority, he said, "The Pundit Sahib has spoken to the waterworks policeman."

The waterworks policeman had his lodgings in the village in the schoolmaster's house, and he worked guarding the water shed that stood a quarter of a mile from Dhilkusha on the canal. From the shed the policeman could see into the garden, watch the house, and even Nabir's mother was nonplussed. Where the policeman moved there was a little cold circle that kept him apart from the village; the police had boots, staves, pocket books, telephones, and, behind each man, a dreadful authority. Now to Nabir's misery was added the thought of being tinged with the police. "I shall leave," he said.

"And let Guffar Sheikh have your place!" said Amdhoo. Guffar Sheikh was Nabir's personal enemy. Nabir said nothing more but he had a prescience of trouble; as his brothers became more and more light-hearted and jubilant at each of Sophie's extravagances, he became more and more melancholy.

Chapter 7

A little while ago Sophie had thought she could never be happy again, but she had found surprising happiness in arranging the house; she was happy with the pundit and his goldsmith friend, with Profit David, with her glimpse of the villagers. On the whole she was happy with Nabir, but he had moments of—blocking me, thought Sophie irritably; blocking her with a hard little impact of truth that reminded her of Teresa. At times, too, the compass points seemed to mock her; here she was settling down for five years, perhaps forever, and they still pointed to stars—north, south, east and west. "I am chasing no more stars," said Sophie. "I am being simple and quiet." She put a rug over them and she dealt with Nabir by being exceedingly authoritative.

Then into this happiness came the children and Ayah.

When the tonga put them out they stood—Teresa, Ayah, Moo—in a forlorn little group at the foot of the rocky path. As Sophie went down to meet them the wind blew cold from the mountain, the sky was dark with snow.

"This is a wild place," said Ayah, as Sultan had said, but far more crossly. "I can't stay here." Sophie did not mean her to stay long but she needed Ayah until she herself was strong; the move, the effort of all these arrangements had tired her. "I can't stay," said Ayah, and Moo clung to the tonga like a limpet and had to be torn away from it. Even Teresa turned away her face so that no one would see her; that meant she was crying. A village boy sent by Nabir Dār shouldered the luggage, and they began to climb. Moo would not walk, and Ayah had to carry him, grumbling under her breath, then aloud. Teresa climbed without a word. Sophie, looking at her solid little figure patiently toiling upwards to this new, unknown, and alarming place, was smitten with remorse. She went and took Teresa's hand.

"You can make a home anywhere, Terry."

Teresa did not believer her. The size of the mountain was over-whelmingly big and desolate to her; the house looked frighteningly alone, not at all a safe place for their treasures, their books, the Chinese teapot, Pussy Maria, Moo's tricycle, the carriage clock, Moo himself, and Sophie. "I shall look after you," said Sophie. You got ill and you couldn't look after us, Teresa thought. You might get ill here, and then . . . She continued to turn away her head.

As they came up on the knoll and saw Dhilkusha, Sophie stopped, hoping Teresa at least would say, "What a dear little house," but she said nothing until they came to the gap in the wall. Then, "In Camberley we had a gate," said Teresa.

ॐ

Teresa had known something was in the wind since the day when she heard the tonga drive away with Sophie and Sultan. "Your mother is up and about again," one of the old hospital dressers had said as he came through the garden where Teresa was standing. "What happiness!"

Teresa had answered, "Yes," with a sinking heart.

Then, a few days after, Sophie had told her. "We are going away to a little house of our own."

For a moment Teresa's face had lit up; then she had known it was silly even to hope. One of Denzil's silences settled on her. It had made Sophie uneasy. "I believe you don't want to leave the Mission," she said.

She said it as if that were incomprehensible, but to Teresa the Mission had been safe. When Sophie was up and about again and Ayah had been made to work properly, it was better than any place Teresa could remember—except Camberley, thought Teresa with a pang. At the Mission she had grown, not only on the outside but in the inside as well; there had been something in the Mission that pushed her forward.

"You are always busy!" she had once complained to Sister Locke. An alliance had sprung up between Teresa and the sharp little sister. "Always busy!" said Teresa.

"Of course we are. We haven't enough hands," Sister Locke had said. "Think, Teresa, a hundred and fifty beds and only two nurses."

"Then why don't you get more hands?" asked Teresa.

"Not enough people care for the work," said Sister Locke dryly.

Sophie called Teresa's hands "butter-pat hands" because they were so small and square. Sophie's hands were small too, but slim, and she had nails shaped like those stones in her brooch—opals, thought Teresa (she had not seen that brooch for a long long time)—but Sophie was careless about her hands, not like other children's mothers, who used creams and scented soap. Teresa had always thought she would have hands like those mothers', ladies' hands, but now she was not sure; she almost thought she would rather have hands like Sister Locke's, though Sister Locke's smelled of disinfectant and today they were scratched. "Who scratched you?" asked Teresa.

"A girl having an operation," said Dr. Glenister, who had been listening. "The girl was frightened of the anaesthetic, and Sister had to hold her."

Looking at the scratches, Teresa asked Sister Locke, "Didn't you mind?"

"It was a good operation!" said Sister Locke and she explained it to Teresa. "She was a Mahmoud girl come up with some camel-drivers. She had been bitten by a camel long ago, and her arm was shrivelled and useless. Doctor Lochinvar cut the scar tissue, the dead flesh, out."

"Ugh!" said Teresa.

"And took a little bit from her thigh and grafted it in—that means joined it—and it has begun to heal."

"What is heal?" asked Teresa.

"It is to make whole," said Dr. Glenister. "Our Lord touched the lepers and blind men and made them whole. Sometimes He gives it to us to do this, Teresa, to make something live again, like that girl's arm."

That conversation had stayed in Teresa's mind. Sister Locke had taken her to see the camel girl in the ward where all the ill people were sitting up in bed. They always sat up, no matter how ill they were, and, round their beds on the floor, their relations camped with cooking pots and samowars and firepots and babies. Teresa had noticed how angry and bewildered the very ill ones looked, as if they did not understand why they were ill—like that ox that Sophie tried to rescue on the road when it fell down under its yoke and its driver was hitting it, thought Teresa. These people's eyes were like the eyes of that ox; they made her heart swell with pity; but when the people were better, like the camel girl, their faces looked alive and pleased. The operation had healed the camel girl; frightening words like "dead flesh" and "shrivelled" became interesting when you were told about an operation like that. To heal, thought Teresa, pondering. Dimly into her mind had come the beginnings of a certainty that she, Teresa, would know what to do with her hands, and "If we can't go to Camberley," she had said with a new courage to Sophie, "I would like to stay here."

"Teresa, do you know what our new house is called?" Sophie had said, trying to win her.

"No," said Teresa stonily.

"Dhilkusha. That means 'to make the heart glad,'" said Sophie.

"Oh," said Teresa stonily.

The house looked fresh and gay with its colours, pale walls, golden wood, and red rugs. The air smelled of new wood and mountain snow and a little of woodsmoke; Sophie had put chips of apple wood in the stoves to make their first fires fragrant, and tea was ready. Still Teresa said nothing, while Ayah was loud in saying this was not a memsahib's house. "This is a *peasant's* house," said Ayah. Her rendering of the word "peasant" was very different from Sophie's.

As they sat down to tea Sophie thought of the Mission sitting room, the varnished furniture, the indigo chintzes and orange curtains, the thick white china, the doilies and tablecloth with its crocheted edging, and she looked at her table of waxed wood, the blue pottery and the hot Kashmiri bread, kulchas sprinkled with sesame seeds, the honey and good country milk; even for that safety and kindness she would not have exchanged it; even a child, she thought—and Teresa is *my* child—must see the difference; but, after a silence, "Sister Locke wouldn't let us eat kulchas," said Teresa, looking at them with puzzled eyes. What was Sophie coming to? she thought. Kulchas were Kashmiri food. "Sister Locke said they were dirty," said Teresa.

"Kashmiris are your brothers," said Sophie, "and you mustn't eat your brothers' dirty bread!" Teresa did not understand; she looked more puzzled. "You will make a good missionary when you grow up, Teresa," said Sophie bitingly.

That was what Teresa hoped, but the edge in Sophie's voice made her

66

flinch. Didn't Sophie like missionaries, then? She dared not ask.

Miserable and puzzled, she put out a hand and took a kulcha. It sat on her plate like a hard little doughnut; it was the poor Kashmiri's bread. A hot tear slid down Teresa's face. Sophie felt like crying too.

In the kitchen below she could hear Ayah's voice uplifted. Sultan did not come to clear away the tea; the house looked untidy with the luggage put down anywhere; and the small sweeper boy had gone away to the village, leaving the bathroom dirty.

It would have been odd in England or America for someone with as little money as Sophie to have a servant at all, but in India there are some things a woman cannot do. Sophie, a junior assistant's wife, had been accustomed to seven or eight servants; now she had decided that she could afford two, a sweeper and a cook-houseboy. She did not count Nabir Dār, as he would be paid partly by the pundit, nor Ayah, who would presently go away. Sophie sighed. No good well-trained servant would have come out to Dhilkusha, and Sultan was not good or well trained. He had been with her the summer before, and she had sent him away after two days. He had been eager to come back because he could not get work anywhere else. "Take me, take me, please," he had begged.

"What is the use?" Ayah had yelled at him. "You have been kicked out of every place you have had."

"But of all the places," said Sultan earnestly to Sophie, "I liked being kicked out of yours the best."

Sophie knew he was a thief and a little liar, a braggart, a poor cook, and lazy, but she thought there was something disarming about him. His references showed he had never held a place for more than a few weeks, but they were disarming too. There was one of which he was enormously proud. It began, "I can recommend Sultan Mohamet as a perfectly useless servant."

Sultan could read and write English words, though he did not understand what the words meant. "I sat for junior school exam," he told Sophie.

"You didn't pass," said Sophie.

"I had an exam-taker," he said proudly. "I hired him. He did the papers for me." His ambitions had taken all his money, and now he was an unsuccessful servant—"But still ambitious," he might have said. He was a little man with a pale gold skin and curious lashless lids to his eyes. His eyes were brown and soft; they could easily grow moist with pleading, but when he dropped his lids down he looked deceitful and secretive, which he was. He wore dirty cotton trousers and the tweed tunic-coat Sophie had given him, socks and slippers edged with fur, and a red fez. He longed for a real uniform, green with brass buttons, and a white coat for serving food. "Good servants wear white coats," he said.

"I know," said Sophie.

"Some servants wear white gloves."

"Those are rajahs' and governors' servants," said Sophie.

"Yes," said Sultan and sighed.

Ayah was already saying loudly that she would leave before the end of the month.

Few Kashmiri women were ayahs; almost all the high-born ones were veiled, in purdah, and the low-born ones, who could have been servants, were too ignorant and debased. Ayah was exceptional, and even she was dirty and lazy; she wore a soiled white pheran and a white veil and a great deal of dirty silver jewellery. Once I should not have tolerated her coming near the children, thought Sophie miserably.

There was a sullen little village boy, Habib, as sweeper. "They are the kind of servants poor whites have," said Sophie. "Perhaps we are still poor whites, not peasants." It was a miserable thought.

Soon, outside, snow began to fall, and the sky grew blind with it. The children went to the window to look. The trees were blurred, the flakes whirled down, shutting the house into a world of its own. It seemed a strange, cold, lonely little world.

Chapter 8

Sophie told Teresa to take Moo out.

"Out?" said Teresa, her eyes big with fright. "Where?"

"Anywhere," said Sophie carelessly.

Ayah, grumbling and scolding, got them ready, and they went out on the veranda and stood at the head of the steps. At first Moo shrank from the cold, the whiteness, and the space, then he stretched out his hands with a fluttering movement like a bird's; it was a movement more alive than any he had made that winter, and he had a smile just touching the edge of his lips. "Look, Moo wants to go out," said Sophie.

Teresa looked up at the mountain. "There might be—bears," she said.

"Bears are asleep in winter."

"Then there really are bears," said Teresa, shaking. And on mountains like this there were avalanches. Even Sophie said there were avalanches. Ayah had seen the men dug out. "They still had their hats on, but they were dead." Sophie said there was a canal at the back of the house that carried water along the mountain to Srinagar. "Moo Baba might fall in," said Ayah. "If he goes across those log bridges he will fall in," said Ayah. It made Teresa's head swirl to think of it. And there were the strange people, the strange villagers. "*Badmashes*, villains," said Ayah. Worst of all were the children who haunted the house wall; Teresa had heard their whistles and seen them throw stones from their slings.

"Suppose they sling a stone at us," said Teresa.

"They are *children*, Teresa!"

Sophie had been a child. Had she forgotten what children are like to children? A mob of children with a strange child? Teresa quailed. "Can't you come with us?"

"Oh, don't be such a baby, Teresa! I'm tired."

"Ayah—"

"You will have to get used to doing without Ayah. Teresa, you must not be such a coward," said Sophie sharply, but Teresa still quailed.

Sophie tried to talk her out of it. "They taught us at the Mission that all men are our brothers," said Sophie.

But you should take a good look at your brother! Teresa might have said. They had taught that at the Mission too. Cain was Abel's brother and he killed him. But eight years old cannot argue with thirty-five, and an answer like that was years away from Teresa. Sophie was kind. She put her arm around Teresa and held her close.

"A child should be friendly and confiding," said Sophie. Teresa stood in the circle of Sophie's arm and yearned to be confiding, but she could not. Instead a blank helplessness fell on her.

"When you were born," said Sophie in her beautiful speaking voice that always melted Teresa's heart, "they brought you in to me; you had a feather of red-gold on your forehead and you made a funny little noise like sparrows in the chimney."

"Did I?" said Teresa, entranced. She had heard this story many times before, but it always entranced her. Her stiffness went; she leaned against Sophie.

"It seemed impossible that I had made you and that you were mine," said Sophie. "I—I hoped so much of my little girl."

Tears pricked Teresa's throat and her eyes; she was smitten with such jealousy and envy that she threw her arms round Sophie's neck and broke into tears, her heart too full to speak.

"Don't let me be disappointed in you, Teresa," said Sophie.

"Oh, no! Oh, no!" Teresa wept. "I will go out." And she took Moo into the garden; they went, falling down in the snow and getting up again, the colour of their bonnets dazzling against the white. "We will go as far as the wall," said Teresa to Moo. "No farther." But on the edge of the garden by the wall was Nabir Dār, digging a pit.

"What is that for?" asked Teresa.

"God knows! I don't," said Nabir Dār. He seemed out of temper. It was for the sweeper boy, Habib, to empty the pots into. "Why?" Habib had asked. Nabir could not tell him.

Everyone Nabir knew, everyone he had ever known, when he had need, stepped aside and did what he wanted where it was natural to do it, on the ground; but now in the house was this bathroom, and in it were pots, and Habib had to climb up a dangerous steep stair that had cost much money to build, taking a basket in which he had to bring down those same pots and carry them here and empty them. "And not on the ground," Sophie had said as if that were a dreadful unheard-of thing to do. "In the pit"; and she said to Nabir, "You must dig a proper pit."

He dug one a foot deep.

"It must be four feet deep."

"In frozen ground?" asked Nabir darkly.

"In frozen ground," said Sophie. "And Habib must put in lime."

Did she think she would get Habib to do that? Nabir shrugged. It seemed completely senseless to him. It seemed equally senseless to send two small children out into a strange place without showing them round. "Come," said Nabir, laying down his spade and holding out his hand to Teresa. "I will show you where you can go and where you must not go."

Teresa went with him gratefully, with Moo trotting behind. Nabir made it as clear and definite as even she would like. "This," he said, planting a stick on the mountain when he had taken them over the canal, "is as high as you must go. You *must not* go any higher."

"You hear that, Moo," said Teresa.

"Sometimes," said Nabir, "the great stones get loose and rumble down. They shouldn't come here, but if one does, then don't run, stand still as you see it coming, and then you can step out of the way."

"Do you hear that, Moo!" said Teresa.

"Bears," said Nabir, "are very dangerous, but they stay up high, and if you don't go beyond this stick you are safe. In spring," he said, "when the ice melts, the canal is deep; in summer it is shallow. Except in summer you must always cross by the good wide bridge; if you try to go over the logs you might get giddy and fall in. If *you* try," he said to Moo, "I shall cuff you."

Moo put back his head to look at him. No one had ever spoken to Moo like that before. He looked at Nabir with his blue eyes and nodded. Teresa had a feeling that he would do as he was told. "Keep away from the herd children until they know you," Nabir told Teresa. "They are rough and mischievous. Soon the Dār herd children will know you, but always keep away from the Sheikhs."

In spring, summer, and autumn most of the older village children went up with the herds and stayed out all day on the mountain. The Dār children took the Dār herds, the Sheikhs took theirs and kept apart, and there was usually no trouble between them. Occasionally a Dār boy fought a Sheikh, or a Sheikh girl met with a Dār girl and pulled her hair or threw a stone at her goat; then the two clans would rally to their sides and there would be a bloody fight up on the mountain. The herd children, for all their rags and dirt, were as fierce and proud as little cockerels or wild cats. Even Nabir, whom they respected, had difficulty in controlling them, and now they were all round the garden, swarming on the walls.

Teresa decided to be firmly on the Dārs' side. Nabir had a gentle face; his hands were big and gentle too; when he had swung her and Moo over the stream she could feel how strong he was. He had a funny smell, but she liked the colour of his skin and the warm wool coat he wore and his old pink cap; she liked his teeth that were even and strong and white. She had been afraid of the houseboat servants; she did not like Ayah or Sultan; but she thought, I shouldn't mind if Nabir Dār were my brother.

❧

Sophie herself was beginning to find out that she had some curious brothers. It was difficult for her to believe to what lengths these people would go—"and for so pitifully little," said Sophie. That it was because they had so pitifully little, she did not yet understand. Some of it was almost funny; there was the day of the nails.

The three carpenters had stayed behind the other workmen to reshingle the roof.

"Carpenters are good people," Sophie often said. She said this to the pundit when he tried to warn her about these three. "Good and simple," insisted Sophie.

"Ye-es," said the pundit.

"Christ was a carpenter," said Sophie, her eyes soft.

"Ye-es," said the pundit. "But," he said timidly, "other carpenters will not all be like Christ."

The three working at Dhilkusha were all called Abdul—Abdul One, Abdul Two, and the headman, who figured on Sophie's bills as Hed

Abdul. Sophie tried to watch them because the roof was the pundit's charge; it came under the clause of weather, and he had begged her to take care. It was cold work nailing the shingles, and Hed Abdul and Abdul One came down every half-hour for tea, leaving Abdul Two on the roof, nailing. Every now and then Hed Abdul would open the kitchen window and put his head out to shout at him.

The pundit had given Sophie strict advice on how to deal with Kashmiri workmen. First, for the work on the roof, the number of nails needed should be estimated; then the nails given out should be weighed; and then, when the work was done, she should count the nailheads to make sure they were all in.

"*Count* them?" asked Sophie.

"Certainly. If you don't, where a shingle needs four nails they will use one."

"Then the shingle will fall off," said Sophie.

"Exactly," said the pundit. "It's the same with the hinges of your windows and doors. Each hinge should have four screws. Be sure they are all in," said the pundit.

Sophie tested this. When the widows were fitted she went round to see. Sure enough, the hinges, where they were bored for three screws, had one, at most two. Very reluctantly Hed Abdul produced the others. "They pocket the rest and sell them," said the pundit.

"But—I am a busy person," said Sophie. "Life is too short for this."

"Then your doors and windows will fall out, your shingles will fall off, and don't ask me for more," said the pundit waspishly.

Sophie thought she had weighed enough nails for the shingles but, presently, Hed Abdul came to her and told her they had no more.

"But I gave you enough."

"The memsahib should come up on the roof and count them," said Hed Abdul smoothly. "She will see they are all there—and still they are not enough." Sophie hesitated. "Come up and see," said Hed Abdul. The roof was high, the ladders rickety, and Sophie was still weak. Besides, it was very cold. She felt helpless, and at last she said, "Go and get some more."

"To go to Srinagar will take half a day. May I buy village nails?" asked Hed Abdul.

"Why not?" said Sophie.

"You mayn't like them," said Hed Abdul.

Sophie should have been warned by this, but she was busy with letters and could not pay much attention to Hed Abdul.

"If village nails will hold the shingles, village nails will do," she said. "Here is one rupee eight annas. Get them and bring them and show them to me, and I will weigh them." Surely that must be all right, thought Sophie.

Hed Abdul went away. There was a long silence. The quiet was too long, but Sophie was immersed in her writing. Presently Hed Abdul came back and showed her what looked like a heap of petrified worms with no points and no heads. "They look very queer," said Sophie. "Village nails always look like that," said Hed Abdul.

Sophie supposed they would do and weighed them and went back to her desk. She heard Abdul Two hammering away; when she went out she noticed that he had rags tied round his hands, and the rags were bloody. Presently Hed Abdul appeared and said the last shingle was on and, with her permission and their pay, they would go back to Srinagar. She paid them on behalf of the pundit, and they rode away on their bicycles with their tools and firepots.

After they had gone peace settled until the pundit came. "Where is my barbed-wire fence?" asked the angrily pundit. "Memsahib, you said you would watchdog for me, and now I find this! This!"

"But how could I know? How could I think?" asked Sophie. "For one rupee eight annas—twenty pennies—who would think they would take all the trouble and pain to cut up a fence?" She remembered Abdul Two's hands. "Think of unwinding all those cruel little barbs!"

"It wasn't only one rupee eight annas," said the accurate pundit. "They had the nails they stole as well. And it's not much work to unwind a fence," he said.

❧

Some of it was not funny; those same carpenters were not all like Christ. Hed Abdul was a tall black-bearded jovial man with bright black eyes. In spite of his villainy, Sophie liked him; she found him quick and amusing until they came back to mend the servants' house, which was leaking on Sultan's bed. "Must I mend another roof?" asked the pundit in agony. "Yes, you must," said the cruel Sophie.

The first day the humble Abdul Two took leave and, being kept by a snowstorm, stayed away an extra day. Hed Abdul beat him, and Abdul Two was knocked more stupid than ever. "He was away for a whole day!" said Hed Abdul when Sophie remonstrated with him, and he said in a shocked voice, "I had to *work!*" The day after his beating, Abdul Two fell on his face on the ridgepole of the roof. He had fainted. Sophie made the men bring him down and lay him in the kitchen and she saw for the first time how emaciated he was; his face was all bones, his legs and arms as thin as sticks. He had beautiful green eyes, as startling in his poor brown face as if they had been real aquamarines. Sophie could not forget his eyes. He had worked for Hed Abdul for fifteen years. He was so simple that he worked without wages; Hed Abdul clothed and fed him and gave him a little money now and then. Sophie looked at his ragged cotton trousers and thin coat; he had no shawl, no shoes. She looked at his poor body. "You don't feed him properly," she said stern-ly to Hed Abdul.

There was little she could do, but she broke into the last of her capi-tal to give Abdul Two a shawl and a pair of socks. That started trouble, and soon the only one who had asked for nothing was Nabir.

"The mem should give *you* a coat," his mother said to him.

"I have a coat," said Nabir.

"You haven't socks."

"I don't want socks," said Nabir. Nor did he; when he saw Sultan in his socks and furred house slippers he said the Kashmiri word for "sissy."

Sultan was beginning to look fatter in Sophie's service; he was devel-oping a soft little belly and a sense of importance—he would have felt really important but for Nabir. Sultan began to hate Nabir.

"Servant troubles!" Sophie had always dismissed them as trivial noth-ings but now she began to find out how important they could be.

"Nabir Dār charges double the right price for butter," Sultan whis-pered in Sophie's ear.

"Each time he comes into the room to bring wood," said Ayah, who was Sultan's accomplice, "Nabir steals a piece and puts it under his coat."

The backbiting and quarrelling wore Sophie down. "But these are grown-up men," she said. "They are behaving like peculiarly beastly children!"

"All men are children," said Ayah.

Ayah at least was another woman, and Sophie kept her on, though she knew she could not afford her and Ayah was very little use; like most Kashmiri women she could not knit or sew or mend, not as much as sew on a button. She tried to instill better habits into Sophie: that underclothes should not be changed in winter, that windows should never opened and stoves kept roaring—never mind the cost of wood—that fruit gives cold and should not be eaten, and that honey is very, very bad for children, who should be given quantities of pure white sugar—with plenty for their poor old Ayah. She seemed to have settled down to scolding and managing them, but then, all in a few hours, she went. It began with Jessica May, the nanny-goat kid.

Dhilkusha was so high on the mountain and had been so quiet that the wild animals had treated it as a part of the mountain. Sophie had seen a wildcat on the top terrace, and two king-foxes had a den in the wall. The wildcat had been frightened away, but the foxes seemed not to understand that the house was now filled, and Sophie used to see them trotting across the lawn, trailing their heavy dark brushes in the snow. "We must get some animals of our own," said Sophie.

"Well, we had Kim," began Teresa, thinking of the spaniel she had not ceased to mourn. "His ears hung down big and soft, and he would let only *me* give him his milk. I don't want another animal," said Teresa, but Sophie was talking happily of pigeons and cats, and soon she had bought a goat kid, a little grey, precociously early nanny-kid that she and the children saw in the village. She had bought it there and then.

"How much?" asked Nabir.

"Seven rupees," said Sophie. Nabir was so angry that he could not speak. Seven rupees for a kid worth three, and that had gone to a Sheikh!

"Owl! *You* should have bought her the little goat," said Nabir's mother.

"How was I to know she wanted one?" said Nabir. He could not keep pace with Sophie's wants. "It's too early," he growled. "I have told her if she keeps it there, so high, a wildcat will get it." But Sophie was too delighted with the kid to listen, and Teresa and Moo were entranced. They named it Jessica May, and it went into the little storeroom next to the servants' house, from whence its bleating filled the garden and sounded up the mountain. "It will bring the wildcat back," said Nabir, but Sophie did not hear.

A few mornings later Ayah came early downstairs to go outside and relieve herself as was the custom. When she pushed the kitchen door she felt something heavy leaning against it. Thinking it was a fall of snow, she pushed harder. The door opened, and a panther fell away from it into the snow. At Ayah's cries it ran away.

"It had come for the kid, not for you," Sophie tried to tell her, but Ayah did not care what it had come for; it had come. There were its pug marks in the snow. She had seen its shape, which every moment grew bigger and bigger; she had smelled its smell; and she was senseless with terror. Sophie had to send her back to Srinagar with Aziz, the tonga-man. Now she and Teresa were the only two females in a world of men—Moo, Nabir, Sultan, the eggman, the milkman, the woodman, the tonga-man Aziz, the baker, the tailor. Sister Locke would not have believed how much Sophie missed another woman.

But in spite of the worries, the backbiting, and the endless demand for petty money that was eating the remnants of her capital away, eating up her month's pension far too fast—and I have to pay Profit David off, thought Sophie—in spite of Teresa's frights and her own weakness and backaches, the days at Dhilkusha began to hold joy. "There will come a time," she said to Teresa, "when the last bill will be paid, the last workman will go, and we shall be clean and at peace."

The clear pure air and the quiet were healing her. The winter colours and the wide vistas were a continual refreshment, and slowly they settled into peace. Only Little Lochinvar came faithfully, once even through a snowstorm, to see them. "But that's ridiculous," Sophie scolded him. Little Lochinvar set his lips.

The post came twice a week, on Tuesdays and Fridays. "That's how I tell the days," said Sophie. The postman toiled, cursing, up the hill, in high boots, a shawl, and a muffler tied over his blue tasselled turban to shield his ears. Sophie put up a box on a tree in the gully, and sometimes he put the letters in it but usually her preferred to come grumbling up to the house, where he knew he would get hot tea. It was hard on him; no one had ever had letters at Dhilkusha in winter before, and Sophie let Sultan make him a fresh brew of tea each time. The postman took her letters and sold stamps to her—Kashmiri stamps with a head of the Maharajah on them—and brought her newspapers; she used to put them in order and read one every day.

She could see that she would be hard put to it for books; she had no money to buy them, there was no library in Srinagar except at the Club—"And I wouldn't be a member even when I could," said Sophie. Already she knew her shelf of books almost by heart—though no one could know the Bible or Shakespeare by heart, she thought, nor the Gita, nor the Koran. There were not enough books for the children either, and Sophie swallowed her pride and wrote to the aunts.

She set about teaching Teresa. "One day I must send you to school," said Sophie and she took a terrifying peep into the future.

"And Moo too," said Teresa. The thought of Moo and school was somehow fantastic; but "Yes, he will grow," said Sophie, "and you must have professions." And Teresa will need a husband, she thought; Moo, a wife. How would they meet husbands and wives? She did not know how any of it could be managed, but "One day you shall go to school," she said.

"At Forteviot House?" asked Teresa. That was where Sophie had been at school, and to Teresa its humdrum happenings, as told by Sophie, were enthralling. "When you go to school it will be to a French convent," said Sophie grandly.

"But I don't speak French," said Teresa, alarmed.

"Or to a modern co-educational school with boys."

"I don't like boys," said Teresa, more alarmed still.

Sophie had not known what to do for Teresa's lessons at Dhilkusha. Then she had a thought, She is only eight and she can read and write. I shall teach her myself. The next time she went to the Bunde in Srinagar, where the shops were, she looked for books, though she could not afford them. There was one called *The Wise Teacher*, and she bought it.

Teresa liked very much to learn columns of spelling and tables, write neat copies, and sew cross-stitch kettle-holders, but *The Wise Teacher* upset all this. It was full of ideas.

"It says you can learn arithmetic in a new way, by clapping and hopping," said Sophie, charmed.

"Can't we learn it the old way by writing it in sums?" asked Teresa.

"It says you can do writing as patterns."

"Can't we do writing as writing?" said Teresa. Sophie found her very dull.

"One of the greatest pleasures for mother and child is reading aloud," said *The Wise Teacher*, but to read to Teresa was disappointing. When Sophie read from *King Arthur's Knights* of the colours and the chivalry, the Holy Grail, Teresa only said, "If I were a man I wouldn't be a knight, always fighting. I should be an engineer."

Sophie thought she did it on purpose. "My peace I give unto you," read Sophie from the Bible with shining eyes.

"Piece of what?" asked Teresa.

Sophie sent her to bed.

Chapter 9

"Now we know the village, and the village knows us," wrote Sophie to the aunts. That was an overstatement. They had, at most, learned to know the look of each other.

The village was the usual huddle of wood and earth houses built on the mountain, with high mud walls round its gardens and orchards, and little mud walls to hold the water in its fields, and the usual poplar and chenar trees. It had a central square, and the road below it ran along the lake. On the lakeshore fishing boats bumped their prows as the small lake waves lifted them, and fishing nets, glittering with fish-scales, were hung on poles to dry. The light caught the scales and turned them to silver. It glinted on other things too—on a woman's earrings as she stood in a doorway to look at Sophie when Sophie and the children passed through on their walks; on a metal samowar filled at the tap, the water overflowing as Sophie was watched down the road. She herself paused to watch the children at hopscotch, and they immediately stopped and looked at her and Teresa and Moo with wide eyes. A caravan of ponies was allowed to wander while the driver stared. A woman throwing a bucket of cess from a window into the road let it tip and trickle down the wall instead as she stood and looked.

Sophie would have been astonished to know that her quiet afternoon walks were like a royal progress to the village. "I have to do something. I may as well walk," said Sophie, but, for the villagers, to go walking was a luxury, something that was done very occasionally on a holiday, when one might go in a picnic-boat to walk in Shalimar or Nishat, but even then the women were generally left behind. Some of the village women had not gone walking since they were little girls, and the mem, Nabir Dār said, walked every day.

"Then the clothes!" said the villagers. "The beautiful clothes!" Sophie was worried about the children's growing shabbiness, but the villagers saw sumptuous woollen clothes, without a gap or rent in them. And the pony the boy-child—if it was a boy—rode! Men rose ponies as part of their work, but who ever heard of a child on a pony! "They must be *rich!*" said the villagers in awe. In summer the pony-men hired their ponies out in Srinagar or the hill resort, Gulmarg, but in winter there were no visitors to ride them, and the pony-men could hardly keep them. Sophie arranged with one of these pony-men that she should keep a small pony, "Bulbul," free of charge for its feed until spring, so that she could take Moo on her walks. "It won't cost anything," she said. "It can eat the dried furze and hay that was in the roof." She did not know, when she arranged this, that the furze had mysteriously disappeared and she would have to buy some more; nor that what she bought was shared between the pony and the Dār family's cows. Nabir bought the furze through Samdhoo—he had, after all, to buy it through somebody—and Samdhoo took out a little on the way. Sophie thought she was being both economical and wise, but "To be *able* to keep a *pony* in *winter!*" cried the women. Each innovation raised Sophie one pitch higher.

The villagers did not admire the family. To Sophie, Teresa looked pink-cheeked and healthy, but to the village women she was horridly pale. And their hair! The village children's hair had the sturdy colour of the lambs, black and auburn; the women could not admire the red and flaxen of Sophie's children, nor their light eyes. "The boy looks like a ghost," they said, "if it is a boy."

They had heard extraordinary tales of Sophie's children's upbringing: she washed them every day in hot water; no wonder they were pale.

"How many of your children have died?" one woman asked Sophie, and they were most astonished when Sophie answered, through the barber as interpreter, "None."

She came to be on speaking terms with some of the people: the barber, the pir or Mohammedan priest, the young Hindu schoolmaster, the headman and the four other elders who, with him, made up the village council. She sent to them first when she wanted to mend Dhilkusha's garden walls, but soon she was always sending about this and that— "About strange things," said the elders. Once she objected to a dog left lying where it had died in the road. "You should take it away," said Sophie. "But it will rot where it is in time," said the elders, surprised. She sent to them about the dirty habits of the people with the canal; the women washed their wool in it, the herd children washed their feet, the flocks forded it instead of using the bridge, she had even seen men piss into it. "And it is the city water supply," she had said, horrified. "But it's not *her* water supply," said the elders to one another after she had gone. They were mystified as to why she should worry. She sent about the cruelty of the young Mustaph Sheikh to his father's wood-pony. "But it is not *her* pony," said the elders. This altruism made them uneasy.

Teresa did not like these expeditions to the village. She would rather have stayed safely in Dhilkusha garden, behind the walls, out of the village; but Sophie took her to the cobbler's shop, where the cobbler mended their shoes, to the honey-man, to the barber when she stopped by to tell him to come and cut Moo's hair. Teresa was very afraid of the barber. His pitch was in the village square; it was a flat stone on which his customers squatted, and by it he kept a dirty towel, a tin mug, and a razor. These were ordinary things, but the barber had another and more important trade. He was the village doctor and he could make spells. "He put a spell on Ramzan's cow, and the cow died," Nabir told Teresa. If this had been said to Teresa in any other country she would have known the teller was pretending, but here in Kashmir these things did happen. Teresa looked at the little dark-faced barber with the big nose and small eyes, the thick warm coat and violet-coloured turban, and she stepped closer to Moo as Moo sat on Bulbul. "We can cut Moo's hair ourselves," she whispered urgently to Sophie.

Sophie went on talking, and Teresa turned and saw a half-ring of children staring at them. A little girl bit the corner of her veil, a boy wiped his nose on his sleeve, but the rest of them stood motionless, gazing with big black eyes. They whispered remarks to one another. Like royal children, Teresa and Moo had to get used to going out among stares.

"Those babas eat three times a day," whispered one of the girls.

"What do they eat?" whispered a little boy.

"Aie! Sugar and rice, wonderful things."

"Sugar!" The little boy's mouth watered, and the children looked at Teresa and Moo, thinking of the marvels with which they were stuffed.

When Sophie turned and saw the children she smiled benevolently at them. "They want to be friends," she said.

"We don't," said Teresa hastily, speaking for herself and Moo. Nor, she thought, did they; once two of the little boys stole forward and nipped Bulbul. He kicked, and Moo slipped in the saddle and hit his nose and cried. The children laughed.

At the invitation of the schoolmaster they visited the school. Sophie looked at the boys sitting on the floor with their flimsy textbooks and slates, and she asked why there were no girls. The schoolmaster did not say he had enough trouble with the boys; instead he murmured, "This is a backward village. No one would think of sending their girls."

"They should," said Sophie. "My little daughter learns the same as any boy," and Teresa was thrust into unwilling prominence. All the boys looked at her with dislike; she made them feel belittled but Sophie was unaware of any feeling. She gave five rupees to the school and Teresa's box of chalks. "Their need is greater than ours," she said and was thanked for her distinguished patronage.

"But they were my chalks," said Teresa.

❧

"Do you know what you remind me of?" said Profit David to Sophie. He had come out in a tonga along the lake road, in the frozen cold, to collect her small interest himself. "You remind me of an emperor. You have made a little palace," he said, looking round Dhilkusha's sitting room.

With its stove crackling, its well-kept floor and furniture, its book and the cow picture, the colour of the rugs, and a pot of jonquils that Sophie had forced flowering in the window, the sitting room looked inviting enough; but "A funny kind of palace," said Sophie.

"A palace," said Profit David firmly. "And now you are gathering your court."

"Nonsense," said Sophie, laughing. But "She takes Aziz Dār's tonga," said the Sheikhs. "Ramzan Dār supplies the milk. Hakim Dār has the contract for wood!"

"With my own eyes I saw her pay ten annas for a fish!" said Guffar Sheikh, brooding on how that ten annas had gone to the Dārs.

"She paid seven rupees for that nanny-kid!" said Nabir's mother, and she brooded on how that seven rupees had gone to the Sheikhs.

Chapter 10

The winter was long. It seemed to Sophie that she and Teresa and Moo had been sealed away for always in this circle of the house, the village, the snow. These last weeks were severe. "Sister Ten Days' Death," said Sophie, and Teresa shivered. There were snowstorms after which not even Little Lochinvar could get to them; not even the postman came. With Bulbul they ploughed their way out, when they could, for a walk down to the lake road or along the canal path or through frozen fields and orchards to the village; but they could go no farther than that, often not so far. Sometimes, to get out of the house, Sophie stood out on the balcony, looking. She wrapped herself in her old crimson shawl, the shawl Little Lochinvar had said was like rubies, and hugged its colour and warmth. As she looked, the mountains were hidden, the lake was a still Japanese grey; hardly a sound came up from it, not the jump of a fish nor the splash of a paddle. The shapes of trees and willows showed against a dead white sky; as far as she could see were grey water, white hill and mist, white sky and darkened trees. The little house felt high, cut off from the world, encircled with loneliness, one warm spot that it was her business to keep alive, and she turned back to her stove fires, her teaching of lessons to Teresa, of cooking to Sultan, her playing with Moo. She tried to keep an orderliness and worked hard herself, washing and mending and ironing, sewing, writing, reading aloud, and, what she found the hardest of all, keeping herself refreshed.

It was the evenings. At first, when she was still feeling weak, Sophie had been glad to go to bed with the children, but if she did that now she did not sleep, and to lie awake thinking was worse than sitting up alone. In the night she would think about money—irises, thought Sophie wryly; she understood even more about irises now. She would worry about those schools for Teresa and Moo, about how impossible it was that she should be able to train them for any professions, or how she could not get friends and interests for them—Margaret Robinsons, thought Sophie. That she had never worried about Margaret Robinsons before did not occur to her. In the daytime Sophie had plenty of faith in herself, in luck—in God? She did not know how to put it, but at night she was craven, and—I won't go to bed till I am tired and sleepy, thought Sophie.

Every night she would trim the lamp and settle down to spend the evening. The children were asleep; Sultan had taken her supper tray and salaamed his good night; the day's work was done, there were hours till bedtime. She had no radio, only her few books. She read them, she wrote letters, she sewed, she did crossword puzzles. Sometimes she sang or learned whole scenes of plays, or poems or chapters of the Bible, and said them aloud, but the sound of her voice in the silent house was startling. Sometimes she even danced, but the flimsy floors and walls shook, and she stopped, afraid of waking the children. It was in the evenings that, as Sister Locke has predicted, she missed things.

She thought of other evenings—that I took for granted, thought Sophie. Evenings with Denzil, and she saw herself bathed and dressed in a diaphanous dress, with Denzil waiting on her, bringing her a drink, lighting her cigarette.

"Do they sell cigarettes in the village?" One night she gave in and asked Sultan that, but Sultan shook his head. "Here they smoke water-pipe, hubble-bubble, hookah," he said and added helpfully, "Memsahib get cigarettes in Srinagar."

"I know," said Sophie crossly; but it was as well they were twelve miles away. "You have no money for cigarettes. You can have only necessities," said Sophie to Sophie. She remembered despised evenings at Finstead, Aunt Portia reading aloud—and I didn't listen! thought Sophie. Toby dropping in—and I thought nothing of it. Dear Toby! But it was better not to think of Toby, and she passed hurriedly to thinking of more stately evenings at the Hall, of Aunt Rose playing, and of the excellence of Sir William's sherry; but Sir William's sherry was almost as upsetting as Toby. If only I had one little cigarette, thought Sophie. If only there were someone to talk to who wasn't a servant or a child! But there was no one, and she wearily picked up her book again.

It was only slowly that Sophie realized that she was reading in a new way. It was as if the book had found a voice—no, the voice was there all the time, but I didn't listen. Now it is as if I were being spoken to, thought Sophie. Every word impressed her, and what she read in the evening she pondered over the next day. She felt her mind stretch and deepen, grow rich; sometimes an evening had passed before she noticed. She had read these books before, but—I have never read like this before, she thought, I have never had the time, the quiet, the—the realization.

The first time it happened she looked at the clock with astonishment. Ten o'clock, and I have scarcely begun to read. After that there were bad evenings, days when she felt restless or melancholy—but I believe I have learned, thought Sophie, learned solitude. It had been a hard struggle— and I never even knew that it had to be learned!

Just when she felt that she could go on forever, if need be, in this winter, on a cold afternoon in February, in one of the small hill orchards, they found an almond tree in flower.

"Flowering in the snow!" said Teresa, marvelling, and Moo could not take his eyes off the pink buds. Sophie picked two sprays to take into the house, but as they came through the garden Nabir pounced on them. "You must not pick that, it's badam—almond," he said, shocked.

"I know it's almond," said Sophie.

"You *know* and you picked it!" Nabir stared at her incredulously. Then he shrugged and took up his spade. "The memsahib doesn't know what it is to be poor," he said. That curiously annoyed Sophie. It made her feel as if she were acting—like Marie Antoinette in the Trianon, she thought angrily. That was what Profit David had implied. But soon she forgot Nabir, and even herself, because the spring came.

It began slowly, but soon in every orchard, between the mountain and the lake, the almond blossom broke; it was strange in the snow to see the trees blossoming serenely with their exquisite hardy flowers. Then the sky cleared and the snow began to melt, and there came a time that Sophie was always to look back on as days that were dropped into her life and were as valuable to her as jewels would be to a woman who loved jewels—only I don't, thought Sophie. She might have said she loved moments, and she had never known moments like these. "I had them, and no one can take them from me," she said afterwards.

In the gully, where the sun lay warm, the water began to run quickly in the stream; there were patches of moss and grass where the snow had gone, and the willow branches were deep red. The children found crocuses, tips of yellow that had come through the snow. "Then is the winter over?" asked Teresa.

There were days and days of rain. The lake was hidden, but the mountain was grand in the wild wet weather, with the mists that blew up into the clouds and lay across the rocks, which took the colours of purple slate. Every day there were avalanches among the high peaks, and streams began to run all over the mountain; they were swollen with mud and spume and broken ice. The lake looked windy and deep, broken into waves; no fishing boats were out. Then suddenly it cleared, the sun came out, the mountain and orchards were scattered with flowers—crocuses and anemones, primulas and gentian.

Men came to pick the anemones. "Why?" asked Sophie, grieved.

"They are for medicine," said Nabir.

"Why, yes," said Sophie. "They are a herb."

In spite of her being a rolling stone, small bits of her life, like moss, clung to Sophie. Once, long ago, she had the idea of working on a herb farm; she had been enthusiastic; she still remembered a little of what she had learned and still had her books of plants and recipes. As the spring went on she found many little familiar plants. "But in such quantities!" said Sophie. "In England violets scatter the woods; here there are pools of them."

"Do you use violets for medicine?" asked Teresa.

"You make a syrup of violets for coughs," said Sophie, and she read to Teresa from an old recipe book:

"First make of clarified sugar, by boiling, a simple syrup of a meane thickness, whereunto put the flowers, cleane picked from filth and the white endes nipped away; let them infuse or steepe for twenty-four hours and set upon warm embers; then strain and put more violets in the same syrup; thus do three or fower times, the oftener the better; then set upon a gentle fire to simmer, but no to boil in anywise. So have you a syrup made of a most perfect purple colour, and of the smell of the flowers themselves. Some do add a little of the juice of

88

the flowers in boiling, which make of it a better force and vertue. Likewise some do put a little quantitie of the juice of lemons in the boiling which do greatly increase the beauty thereof but nothing at all the vertue. For cough, and phlegms and inflammations of the lungs."

It was lambing time. The herd children brought up the first herds to graze, and Nabir made Mahomet bring two lambs to show the children. Mahomet carried them in the pouch of his robe; one was black, the other kidney brown. "Oh, *Mother!*" cried Teresa. "Buy them." She forgot Kim. She forgot she had not wanted any more animals. "One for me and one for Moo," she begged.

"We have Jessica May," began Sophie. Lambs cost money. She had bought a cock and six hens and was thinking of buying some ducks; but "One for Moo and one for me," begged Teresa.

Extravagance was in the air, and Sophie had always been extravagant. She bought the lambs. "We can shear them in the summer," she said to ease her conscience, looking at their short curled fleeces. "Next winter we shall spin our own wool." Her eyes shone. "Think, Teresa. Our own wool from our own sheep! We might buy a loom and weave it, or I can knit it into socks."

She asked Nabir if one of the villagers would teach her to use a hand-spinner. "But you don't need to spin," said Nabir. "You can afford to buy machine-made cloth." He said "machine-made" reverently.

The lambs were called Christopher and Columbus. They were so young that Sophie had to buy their mothers too. It was an expensive business, but not as expensive as the Dārs would have liked. "You could have asked her for more," said even the small Mahomet to Nabir, and he opened his mouth to say, "She gave—"

"She gave seven rupees to Guffar Sheikh for the goat!" said Nabir, exasperated. "I know." And he cuffed Mahomet.

"Remember the manure," said Mahomet cheekily. Nabir cuffed Mahomet again. He did not like to think about the manure.

Every field round the village had a hive-shaped dump brought up from the house middens for the crops. Nabir had told Sophie she must buy manure for the neglected plots at Dhilkusha.

"I want *all* our own vegetables," she had told him. "Our own potatoes, even our own wheat." She saw Eden visions of fruitfulness. "We must look after our vine, and then we shall have grapes," she said. "We might even make our own wine. And we shall have strawberries and asparagus and melons, honey melons . . ."

"I can grow onions and carrots and peas," said Nabir, troubled, "and good pumpkins and potatoes, of course."

"We shall start with those," said Sophie condescendingly.

Nabir had sold her the manure from his own house midden, and, pushed by his brothers and mother, he had asked an exorbitant price. "Of course she won't pay it," he told his mother. "She isn't such a fool as that." To his dismay Sophie paid it without a murmur, and that same strange feeling filled Nabir, the same he had had with the pundit over the peach trees. In a bargain your opposite number was for the moment your natural enemy; Nabir, like most people, liked to have an enemy, but an enemy who was alert, who gave as good as he got, not a sitting bird like the pundit, not somebody behaving like Sophie. In these days Sophie reminded Nabir of a bird brooding, dreamy, on her nest, and he refused to charge her double for the lambs. If Sophie had only known it, for that brief period she had found a way to disarm Nabir and, through him, the village. She was protected—but Sophie was not thinking of Nabir.

Last year she had been too late to see the Kashmir spring— "and to see it, really see it, you must have lived through the winter first," she wrote to the aunts. The wind and the cold had gone. Now spring came with a rush startling in its quickness. There were lines of yellow under the almond trees, yellow of mustard; the edge of the lake was a fuzz of green from the willows. Sometimes a warm wind blew that beat the water into shallow waves, but usually the lake was still and it had blue and white reflections, pale blue from the sky, deeper blue from the mountains, and white from the clouds and from the snow that still streaked and hid the peaks. The orchards were thick with flowers, and the air was filled with the bleating of lambs and the lowing of cattle, with the herd

90

children's cries and pipings and, in the Dhilkusha garden, the song of birds.

Sophie had not thought there would be many flowers in the garden, but she had known there would be blossom, and now the cherry blossom began. From the lowest terrace of the garden, if she looked up, she could see terraces of cherry trees white against the mountain; if she looked down from the house or the canal path she saw them with the blue water of the lake below. Soon another blue came under the trees—forget-me-nots—and mixed with them was the green of turf and every colour of pansy and narcissus. "Dhilkusha. To make the heart glad!" said Sophie. Each day was more beautiful. The lawn was covered with daisies, and there were violets under the walls and in the roots of the chenar tree; by the stream the violets were yellow and white; below the gardens and orchards, in the fields, the peasants were sowing millet and wheat and planting out blades of rice.

Two villagers came from the village and asked if they could take the catkins from the willow trees at Dhilkusha. "They are good for diseases of women," they told Sophie. Sophie let them cut the catkins and take them away.

"You should have made them pay," said the pundit.

"Even for catkins?" said Sophie.

"You should treat these people as they understand," said the pundit.

"I should treat them as people," said Sophie. "I am the same as they."

But she was not. To her this was a strange spring. The blossom was not like English blossom; it had not that innocence. It seemed pristine to Sophie, as if the hard brown earth had never flowered before; and it was more exciting. After the cherry there were peach and pear and apricot, but there were unfamiliar blossoms as well—loquat and, later, pomegranate. The birds were unaccustomed birds—bulbuls, hoopoes, golden orioles, Indian doves that nested in the roof; and, when it grew hot, Nabir told her, the long-tailed paradise flycatchers would come. Yes, the spring was strange; there were the strange people everywhere, the colours, the dark skins, the veils and heavy jewellery, the quick alien tongue. To Sophie its strangeness was romance; she lost her quick ways and spent the days dreaming.

[margin annotation: never will be]

91

"We are busy with spring cleaning," wrote Aunt Portia.

"Thank goodness," Sophie wrote back, "we have no spring cleaning here." She was wrong of course. In the village, now the cattle had been let out, the lower rooms were cleared of their middens, the furze and hay were brought down from the roof and spread in the sun, windows were opened and bedding picked over. Every day screams and cries sounded from the lake, where children were having their spring bath; even their hair was washed, and the better cared-for little girls, who had their hair braided into ten or twenty plaits, had them undone and combed through for lice and plaited up again. Families who could afford it bought new caps for their children, even new pherans. Sophie noticed the bright clean colours, but they stirred her to no great effort though she told Sultan to clean the windows. She seemed to have fallen altogether out of her busy-body ways.

That suited Sultan. He cleaned the windows with a dirty rag, and the panes were smeared; but "I am getting better at my work, don't you think so, memsahib?" said Sultan.

"Well, no," said Sophie but she did not scold him.

She could not help a fellow feeling for Sultan; like her, he had good ideas. He mixed tea and milk together in the teapot to save washing up; he used the tail of his shirt instead of a dishcloth and kept the teaspoons in his pocket; but he was not really funny, he was quite insensitive and unthinking. Sophie found he had pounded up an old electric-light bulb.

"What are you doing with that?" she asked.

"It's to mix powdered glass with dough to kill rats," said Sultan.

"But that's cruel!" said Sophie. "You should use quick-killing rat-poison."

"Cruel?" asked Sultan. He did not know what that meant. His vision began and ended with himself, Sultan.

"Memsahib use Mackredt's tinned butter instead of fresh," he begged Sophie.

"Tinned instead of fresh!" said Sophie. "It's horrid. Besides, it's two rupees eight annas a tin!"

"Yes," said Sultan, "but Mackredt's give coupons with every tin, and if we use it you needn't buy me a bicycle or a watch. I can buy them with the coupons for myself."

"But Sultan, I am not going to buy you a watch or a bicycle," said Sophie.

Sultan was crestfallen. He murmured, "Better," but his eyes were resentful. Now that he had thought of the watch and the bicycle he felt defrauded. "The memsahib doesn't love me," he said.

"Love is a very big word," said Sophie. If it was big, she thought suddenly, shouldn't it hold all things? Even Sultan? Unfortunately for herself, Sophie decided it should, and she spoke very gently as she said, "Come, let us write up the accounts." As she bent her head over the book her eyes were soft, but Sultan's eyes, watching her, were determined. The kind of love Sultan wanted meant a bicycle, new socks, uniform coats, money.

"Five annas for onions?" Sophie had to ask.

"Five annas," confirmed Sultan, lying. Teresa opened her mouth, but Sophie had accepted five annas and was writing it down.

They were happy, innocent days. Innocent was the word, thought Sophie afterwards. They hired a boat from Nabir's cousin, Subhan, and went on the lake. Subhan's shikara had no cushions and curtains like a real taxi-boat—though Subhan hoped that one day he would, through Sophie, get some—but Nabir folded a rug on the seat and spread a clean mat on poles for an awning. Moo had a lotus leaf for a hat, and Nabir held him by a rope round his waist so that it did not matter if he fell in. Teresa leaned on the gunwale, looking down into the water. The only noise was the sound of Subhan's paddle. Sophie sat dreaming, and as they went, threading down waterways between flowering villages, going from sun to shade to sun under the narrow bridges, gliding out across the lake, a tight little thread seemed to unwind from Teresa's heart. It was true that she wished they could have a taxi-boat like other people, like Margaret Robinson, but she was at peace. "Do you like Dhilkusha?" If Teresa had been asked that now she could almost have said Yes.

There was so much that no child could resist; there was the garden where they played hide-and-seek and climbed the apple tree, the stream where Sophie taught them to sail walnut-shell boats, the new animals, Jessica May, Christopher and Columbus, and the hens; when Teresa put her hand into the straw and brought out a warm egg she felt each time as if a miracle had happened. Bulbul had gone of course, but last time

Sophie went to Srinagar she had brought back two cats that a shopman had given her, a sleek little female tabby called Bliss and a big white tom called Louis. "A house isn't a home without cats," said Sophie, and Teresa agreed. Dhilkusha was not Camberley but it was beginning to be a home. Tentatively she put down one, then another little root.

Just as a spinning wheel has an alive hum, now the house had a sound, a hum made of all the sounds in it; of footsteps, voices, the purr of cats, children laughing and—Moo—screaming; of Teresa reading aloud to herself on the stairs, Sophie's pen scratching, Habib sweeping with his soft broom; of water poured out and eggs beaten in a bowl; the sound of a hubble-bubble pipe, of bargaining, sometimes of quarrelling—that was Sultan and Nabir, but in those days they did not quarrel much. Sometimes from high up the mountain came a whistle like a hawk's call; it was the nomad goat people as they drove their flocks past, high up above the house. Sophie would raise her head and drop what she was doing and run out to see and stand looking after them. Reluctantly Teresa would follow, but soon the caravan disappeared round the mountain, and the garden sounds—the scrape of a spade, of wood being chopped, of running water from the stream and wind sounds in the trees—shut out their whistles. The sound of the goat people died away, the quiet hum went up from Dhilkusha, the mat was down over the compass stars.

"How is the memsahib?" the pundit asked Nabir.

"She has settled," said Nabir.

Then, in one week, the spring changed colour.

Chapter 11

The colours had been pale and fresh and clear, pink from the almonds, yellow from crocus and mustard flowers, pale blue from the sky, white from cherry blossom and clouds, green from the new willows. Now the colours deepened and grew rich. There was another green from the chenar leaves, from the growing grass, from the rice, and, round the villages, on the graves, the irises began to bud; they were in flower all along the lake, and there was a surrounding foam of purple from the lilacs, Persian and European.

These were the colours now, purple and lilac and white and deep green, with occasional splashes of scarlet from the big Himalayan tulips that were planted on the house roofs. The lake was a deep blue; on the lotuses were pale pods of buds; and it was warm, though there was snow on the mountains.

The pundit asked Sophie if she would like to go with him to the garden of Nishat to see the Spring Festival of Baisakhi.

The gardeners of all the pleasure gardens had orders to tidy the gardens and open the gates early for the big feast days—Hindu, Mohammedan, and Christian—and as, on all of them, shops, offices, and schools were closed, each religion, in some way, kept the feasts of the others.

"But Nabir says there is only one God," said Teresa.

Teresa saw all the different rituals. She saw the wife of the schoolmaster making her ritual patterns on her courtyard floor and knotting a garland for her tulsi plant that was sacred because it was dedicated to Vishnu. The schoolmaster's wife kept it indoors, warm, all winter; now she brought it out to taste the spring sun and at dusk she set a tiny oil lamp in the niche in the side of its pot; Teresa liked to see it. At dusk, too, Khadir, the Mohammedan cobbler who lived next door to the schoolmaster's house, stood up among his shoes and hanging tassels and strips of leather and turned his face towards Mecca and prayed.

Sister Pilkington had taught Teresa in the Mission to say a prayer—
"Now I lay me down to sleep." Teresa liked it as she had liked the
Mission chapel, and she felt its safety as Sophie had. She wished she lived
in a place with a chapel. There was a Hindu shrine in the village, a lingam
with a whitewashed platform and a little temple; Sophie showed the children the offerings of curd and rice and sugar put there for the gods. She
took them to the big mosque across the lake. It was a famous mosque;
every Friday, which is the Mohammedan Sunday, it was crowded. It had
a relic of Mohammed, a whisker in a bottle; if a prayer was answered the
whisker turned round and round. All this Sophie showed them. "You
see, God is everywhere," said Sophie.

Yes, but I need Him in a place of my own, Teresa might have said.
Instead she asked, "Was there a church at Camberley?"

Now everyone was getting ready for Baisakhi. The Hindus were to attend the festival, go to the temples, wear their best clothes, and feast. The
Mohammedans and the Christians were to watch, amongst them Sophie.

"Yellow is the colour of spring; you should wear yellow," said the
pundit to Sophie. "We shall go to the gardens and see the fountains
playing, and to the temple for immersion. You, of course, will not
immerse," said the pundit.

To Sophie, as to the Hindus, that day was the culmination of spring.
As she and the pundit came, in the early morning, near to Nishat, picnic-
boats in hundreds were already tied up under the willows. Each boat was
empty, swept and tidy after the night, carpets laid down in each com-
partment, quilts and pillows stacked, hookahs put ready, and bunches of
lilac hung from the roofs. The people were all ashore at the Nishat temple or in the garden itself.

On the waterfront were sweet stalls and cookshops, where earth
ovens, like Sophie's, had been built, and cauldrons were cooking over
them. Platters of sweets were arranged, pink and white coconut and
green pistachio, and sandesh, which is like toffee, and jilibis, which are
rings of clear sugar, and dark red saffron cakes hung with silver leaf.
Teresa had told Sophie they would be there—Nabir had told Teresa
about them—but for once Sophie had left the children behind. "It will
be too crowded for Moo," Sophie had said. "You must stay with him."
Tears had come into Teresa's grey eyes, but she did not protest.

The pundit took Sophie into the temple after she had taken off her shoes. Hindus were immersing their naked little boys in the water. Sophie went in to the women's pool, where women stood undressed on the steps; the shade patterns of the chenar trees moved over their soft yellow-brown bodies as they stared at her. On the grass outside the temple pundits were waiting to make the tika mark, the seal on the forehead in vermilion and sandalwood that shows the morning ritual has been done.

At the entrance to Nishat water fell through a stone lion's mouth into a roadside pool. The purple of the lilacs showed over the walls, and the people were streaming into the garden.

Sophie and the pundit went with them.

Of all the Mogul pleasure gardens Sophie loved Nishat the best, more even than Shalimar or Naseem or the tiny jewel of Chashmishai high up on the mountain. Nishat is built in seven terraces, falling from the mountain to the lake; it has old walls that have weathered rose red, and the gatehouse pavilion is matched in the pavilions on the wide top terrace, which in the days of Jehanghir was the Women's Garden. All Mogul gardens are water gardens, and the water channels in Nishat run in the heart of the garden between lawns and chenar-tree groves, falling into pools with fountains; from one terrace to another water runs over slats of fretted stone that make the famous Mogul water music. The slats are carved so that the water makes a thousand tiny splashes; some in knots like a tapestry, some in stripes and flowers, some in shapes of diamonds; and each has a different sound. Some are steeply slanted so that the water runs quickly; some are tilted so that it runs more slowly; and above each, on the edge of each of the seven terraces, thrones are built over the water, some octagonal, some big, some small and solitary. The emperors could choose the throne to suit their mood and sit and listen to the water music that tinkled or lulled, accompanied their thoughts or drowned them.

No one has ever loved Kashmir more than the Mogul Emperors, Jehanghir and Shah Jehan. In all their wars and pomp and complications they found time to make those arduous journeys through dust and desert and heat to the valley; they built the temples and pavilions, made the gardens, and everywhere they planted trees, poplars in avenues along the roads, and the chenars, like great plane trees, that spread in every village and grove and garden.

Now their gardens are old, their groves of chenar have grown high and stately, their lawns sunk into deep rich green, their marbles and stones weathered, but "Their spirit is still here," said Sophie. "In the tree shade, the flowers, the picnic-boats, the fountains and the water music, the old marbles. They stole away out of the dust and the clamour. Well, I have stolen away too," said Sophie.

As she looked up the terraces from the gate-house pavilion that day of Baisakhi, hundreds of fountains were playing like crystal plumes in the misty light under the chenars. The light lent itself peculiarly to the green; the arches of the trees and the grass made a frame for the colours of the dresses, the white veils and the fountains, and at each side of the lawns, repeating the white, was a pattern of pink and white apple blossom and daisies on the turf.

The fountains were playing too high, the water running too fast, to hear the water music; in any case the garden was too crowded, but the rushing of the water suited the movement and the laughing and talking, the sitar music and the running, screaming children. There were families of people picnicking on the grass, the women sitting with spread skirts that were green pink, blue, purple, broken by a mustard or a canary yellow or a parrot green, and, in the middle of each ring, a samowar smoked in a circle of tea bowls.

There were no birds in the garden; they had all been frightened away, and the gardeners ran up and down the channels, keeping the grids open and the fountains playing.

A policeman sat on the balustrade of the top terrace, singing. Even the police that day shared with the people; his voice, strong and sweet, floated down over the terraces, which fell one below the other, each spread with its people and fountains, its great trees and blossom and borders of flowers. Sophie felt that her happiness and well-being overflowed the garden too; it was in these happy people, the sun, the warm leaves, the sparkling water, the policeman's song; but the pundit was growing tired and a little cross. "We should go now," he said.

"Oh, not yet! Not yet!" said Sophie. "I am too happy to go, Pundit Sahib."

"Who laughs before seven cries before eleven," said the pundit crossly, "and you have been laughing all the morning." As he spoke, an old man stood up from a flowerbed and salaamed Sophie and nodded and smiled.

"Who is that?" asked the pundit in sharp surprise.

"A friend of mine," said Sophie carelessly.

"But who is he? I did not bring him to you, I think."

"He is a gardener here," said Sophie. "He comes from our village, and I have made friends with him." She did not say that she felt she should be allowed to make friends with whom she liked. "I call him St. Nicholas," she said, "because he brings me presents."

"Presents? Flowers? But you pay him for them?" said the pundit suspiciously.

"Only tea money," said Sophie. "I am getting some rose plants from him."

The pundit frowned and said she had much better get her flowers through Nabir Dār. Sophie knew that would have been etiquette.

"Etiquette is courtesy," said Aunt Portia often. "It makes for smooth living." But Sophie was too happy that morning to be meticulous, and the pundit frowned more when he saw her give the old man a rupee. "For what is that?" he asked as sharply as a wasp stings. But Sophie was accustomed to the pundit; she only smiled and said it was for happiness. "It's not his happiness," said the pundit jealously. "Today is a Hindu festival, and he is not a Hindu, and in any case, to get money for nothing is bad."

To complete the pundit's ill-temper they met Profit David. The pundit, except that he had a new yellow muslin turban, was in his usual clothes, the coat, the quilted waistcoat, the watch-chain; but Profit David was wound in a new pearl-grey shawl, he had a new ring, and he carried a spray of lilac in his hand. He had come, he said, in his picnic-boat, having left Srinagar late the night before.

"You have a picnic-boat?" asked the pundit, pouncing.

"I have two," said Profit David and went on talking to Sophie. "I am very lucky," he said. "I bought seven tolahs of turquoise yesterday. I bought it cheap at six rupees three annas a tolah."

The pundit cried out sharply. "One should not mention money business on this auspicious day."

Profit David took no notice of the pundit. "You would not care," he said wooingly to Sophie—"you would not care for me to make you a brooch, a little brooch?"

"No," said Sophie flatly, but Profit David was determined that she should buy a jewel that day. "I have something to show you," he said and took out of his shawl a folded paper. In the paper were cotton wool and some shreds of silk. "You are right to refuse turquoise. Turquoise is cheap," he said. "This, this is for you." He shook out on his palm a stone; in the morning sun it shone with a milky blue. "See the star," whispered Profit David and turned the sapphire for Sophie to see. The star seemed to gather in all the light of the gardens and fountains and sky and send them out in its beams.

"A star sapphire," said Profit David. "I think it is a symbol, a symbol for you."

Though Sophie did not want jewels she had always loved star stones. As Profit David divined, she read into them a deeper meaning, and, in this morning of happiness, the winking and glowing jewel in Profit David's palm had a message for her. She looked at it and felt her sense melting. "How much?" she asked.

"For you—only two hundred rupees." Profit David's voice was soft. "It is an investment. Only two hundred rupees."

The pundit gave a little cry of agony and fell behind.

"Put it away," said Sophie, and Profit David sighed.

"You should not," he said in a low voice to Sophie, "go about with Pundit Pramatha Kaul. He is mean."

"But I like him," said Sophie.

"A Hindu!" said Profit David in scorn. "They are poor through and through. Look how miserably they eat." He stayed to talk, smoothly, suavely, to some visitors, and Sophie went on with the pundit.

"You should not," said the pundit earnestly in Sophie's ear, his nose twitching with nerves, "go about with Profit David. He has dangerous, extravagant ideas."

"But I like him, Pundit Sahib."

"A Mohammedan," said the pundit. "They have no spiritual life at all. Look at their pots of flesh," said the pundit and shuddered.

Sophie knew that all the pundit ate was rice with vegetables, some curd, milk, and a little fresh fruit. Profit David would go back to his boat and eat pilaf and mutton stuffed with spices, and the apricots stuffed with mutton that had seemed so fabulous to Sister Pilkington, and roast kid and fish and honey rice.

This reminded her that the children would be waiting for lunch. She said good-bye to the pundit and went home.

As she climbed the path and reached the cherry trees, and the children came running to meet her, they called out something. She saw that there were chairs out on the veranda, and there, rising with smiles, in clean cotton dresses and khaki sun-helmets, were Dr. Glenister and Sister Pilkington and Sister Locke.

৯

A month ago Sophie would have welcomed the missionaries. Now, as she went across the lawn to meet them, she felt jerked out of her peace and joy. They were already disapproving.

"You have been to the *festival!*" said Sister Pilkington.

"Yes," said Sophie, and she added deliberately, "to the temple."

"You went *in!*" said Sister Locke.

"I took off my shoes and they let me in," said Sophie.

"Well, *really!*" said Sister Locke.

"But where is Doctor Lochinvar?" Sophie asked Dr. Glenister, and a stiffness fell on them all.

"One of us has to stay on duty even on a holiday," said Dr. Glenister.

"And Doctor Lochinvar has been to see you," said Sister Pilkington slowly.

"Once or twice," said Sophie gently.

"Whenever he could," said Sister Locke and she sniffed.

In spite of these small rufflings, as Sophie showed them round the whole house sprang into gaiety. "It likes to be visited," said Sophie.

That day it was at its best, and she was proud. She had been up very early and had tidied the rooms with Sultan before she went out; everything was shining and orderly. There were fresh flowers; the children's toys were tidy. At lunch there was a clean cloth on the table. She had made bread yesterday, and it had risen; there were eggs from their own hens, fried rice, the first lettuce from the garden, and, in honour of the festival, she had made a walnut cake.

"This is good," said Dr. Glenister, beaming behind her glasses. "What a wonderful cake! You spoil us."

"I love to spoil you," said Sophie, and now she meant it.

She had put on her nearest to yellow dress to please the pundit, a soft dress of grey roses with little leaves and yellow hearts on a white ground. She had seen the sisters glance at its small waist and low-cut neck, but she felt it fitted the house in this holiday mood; the yellow dress, the children, the garden full of running water and flowers and apple blossom, the cats, the lambs, the grey kid, the chickens, the nesting doves were all delightful. She could not help thinking it charming herself. I—I have succeeded, she thought, and she blushed with pleasure. She thought that even Sister Locke could find no flaw.

"Did you buy that cake?" asked Sister Locke.

"No, I made it," said Sophie. "It's an old recipe of my aunts. It's a trouble to make, but worth it if it turns out well."

"Do you say your prayers?" Sister Pilkington whispered to Teresa. "Do you say, 'Now I lay me . . .'?"

Teresa nodded. "Do you say them to Mother?" asked Sister Pilkington, pleased. Teresa shook her head. "I say them to God," she said, and Sister Pilkington had to be satisfied with that. "The children look well and happy," she said.

The only one who did not praise was Dr. Glenister. Sophie was surprised at her silence.

"Well, what do you think of it now you have seen it?" she could not help asking her when they were leaving. She asked it in triumph, but Dr. Glenister said seriously, "Dearie, isn't there anywhere else you could go?"

"Go?" said Sophie. "But—we have just come." And she demanded, "Haven't we made it good?"

"Too good," said Dr. Glenister, troubled. "It's asking for trouble."

"Too good"—and Profit David had said, "You are making a little palace." "Cry before eleven," the pundit had said.

"You are like a lot of ravens trying to frighten me," said Sophie, and she laughed and said, "Teresa wants us to go back and live at Camberley."

"You talk as if that were extraordinary instead of this," said Dr. Glenister.

Chapter 12

As if the visit of the missionaries had broken a spell, Sophie became aware of cracks in her happiness. She had been wrong; they had found flaws.

"Things are very bad in the valley this spring," Sister Locke had said, taking in the pretty sitting room, the bowls of ranunculus and lily of the valley that were scenting the air. "Do you *grow* ranunculus?" she had asked, as she had asked about the walnut cake.

"I bought them," said Sophie. Sister Locke said nothing, but Sophie knew that she was thinking with satisfaction, What selfish extravagance.

"I think flowers are important," said Sophie, and she added defiantly, "If you have a loaf, sell half and buy a lily."

At the mention of a loaf Sister Pilkington had looked up. "There have been dreadful bread riots in the city," she said.

"It's the price of rice and the price of wood," said Sister Locke, folding her lips in.

The missionaries thought Sophie unsympathetic, but she was very well acquainted with the price of rice and of wood; it was reflected in Dhilkusha. She and the children lived these days with real simplicity; it was necessary. They wore their old clothes and country shoes and ate as the Kashmiris ate, rice, lentils, and vegetables—chiefly the sāg that Sophie never wanted to see again—milk, dried apricots, eggs, the village walnuts, honey, Kashmiri bread; all these were cheap. "I haven't tasted coffee since we came here," said Sophie. "Sometimes we have fish, never meat, or even chickens in this land of chickens." She had forgotten what it was to smoke a cigarette or have a drink; she scarcely bought a book; she thought before she bought even a stamp, but everywhere she looked money was needed. Sultan's socks wore out; Nabir broke his spade; Hed Abdul's wood had been too cheap, and a corner of the ceiling came down and had to be repaired. She had had to take Moo to the dentist, and

Aziz, the tonga-man, charged an extra rupee because the price of horse grain had gone up.

"It's after the war," said Dr. Glenister and sighed.

"It's always a war or a famine or an earthquake—something," said Sophie.

"The people are dying," said Sister Locke.

"They shouldn't die now," said Sophie. "It's spring."

"Doctor Lochinvar had a baby thrown into his car," said Sister Pilkington. "The father cried, 'Take him and feed him, I can't,' and ran away weeping. The baby was a *son*, mind you—a boy, not a girl!"

"If we find babies can we keep them?" asked Teresa longingly.

"No," said Sophie hastily. She foresaw an avalanche of babies, and babies had hands that beat the air, mouths that cried, stomachs that had to be filled. "No!" cried Sophie; then she caught Sister Locke's look again and coloured. "I was selfish," she told Aunt Rose afterwards when, more and more, she talked to Aunt Rose. "Very, very, very selfish," she said.

"Were you?" asked Aunt Rose judiciously. "What had you been doing? Out of an empty derelict house you had built up a home; from a sick woman you had made a strong one. The children were well and happy."

"Yes, but we had pets, flowers," said Sophie.

"Pets and flowers are part of a home. Everyone tries to get what they need," said Aunt Rose.

"I didn't *need* them," said Sophie.

"What you need depends on who you are," said Aunt Rose, and her dark eyes flashed. "People will *not* understand that. You were not a Kashmiri nor a missionary. They had their means of refreshment." And, as Sophie still looked unconvinced, she said, "At least for once you were minding your own business."

"Yes," said Sophie.

In those lonely solitary weeks a hardihood had crept into her, a hardening that she knew was honest; it linked her with the people and brought her into her proper place with them. There was no pretence; each was what he was, each kept to what he did—and if I spent a few annas on flowers and made a walnut cake, that was my business, thought Sophie. There had begun to be mutual liking and trust, but then—

selfish extravagance, Sister Locke's look had said, and Sophie was coloured by it.

"Had you taken anything from anybody?" demanded Aunt Rose.

"No," said Sophie and, thinking, she was surprised to find "I had—in a way—given people things. The children were more secure. Sultan had a good place; Nabir was making a good vegetable garden, which was what he had always wanted. I had given Habib yeast and milk and cured him of boils. I helped the villagers when there was a real need. Everyone had fair prices, the pundit was happy, we were all happy."

"Well then?" asked Aunt Rose, and she asked, "Why couldn't you have been content with that?"

Why couldn't I? thought Sophie.

❧

"What is the mem doing now?" asked Nabir's mother. She could tell by Nabir's gloomy face that Sophie had been doing something.

It was nothing very much, but it was the beginning, and perhaps Nabir had a foreboding of that. Sophie, looking round for some way to be unselfish, thought that she would teach the women to sew. "Sew what?" asked Nabir.

"Well—they can't even sew on a button," said Sophie.

"They haven't any buttons," growled Nabir, and he said, "Sewing isn't for women."

Sophie was used to this seeming contradiction. Here sewing was a gentle skilled thing, professional work, and women were kept for rough work. But "I sew and I am a woman," argued Sophie. Nabir was silent. Sophie was someone apart, and it was part of her terrifying cleverness that she was able to sew. Sophie mistook his silence for obstinacy. "What happens when your clothes wear out?"

"We let them wear out," said Nabir.

"Exactly!" said Sophie triumphantly, but Nabir could see nothing that was not natural in that.

"They won't sew," he said when the women came. He was right; they would not. Their rough toilworn hands were not fitted for it, but Sophie felt her failure was Nabir's doing. "He balks me all the time," she said.

She tried to think of something else unselfish to do.

She called the servants, Sultan, Nabir, Habib, and told them they were each to have a day off once a week. "You work from dawn until dark every day without a holiday," she said. "Now this is to be the rule: one day off a week for each of you."

They were astounded. "But—for *what?*" they asked.

"For yourselves. To see to your own affairs," said Sophie, "To rest and enjoy yourselves."

They were still more astounded. "You pay us," said Nabir. "You should try and get all the work you can from us." Anything else made them uneasy, but Sophie was firm.

Habib, the little sweeper, was to have the first holiday. "But who will do my work?" asked Habib. "Who will bring the hens' food?"

"Teresa Baba."

"Who will cut up the cats' food?"

"I will."

"*You* will? Your *honour!*" said Habib, shocked.

"I will. Now go and don't come back till bedtime," said Sophie, but at three o'clock Habib was there as usual for the afternoon sweeping and to cut up the cats' food.

"Who told you to come?" said Sophie.

Habib looked at the floor. Then, "I thought—" he said. "And Nabir Dār thought too—"

"We don't want holidays," said Nabir. "We have them already. When the snow is bad we can't come to work, nor if we are ill, and we have Id and all the festivals. Holidays should come from *God,*" said Nabir crushingly. Sophie felt crushed. More than that, she was beginning to feel she was ringed round by something she did not understand.

It showed in little things. The old gardener from Nishat, St. Nicholas, brought the rosebushes and roots of lavender she had asked for. He was a mild old man with a pink face, pink cap, and grey shawl. She paid him for the plants and gave him tea money as well; he came back with roots of parma violet and lily of the valley corms. Sophie was touched and pleased, but "St. Nicholas can't come here," said Teresa.

"Of course he can come here," said Sophie. "Why not?" Teresa opened her mouth and shut it again. She knew why not; St. Nicholas was a Sheikh, Ghulam Sheikh, father of Nabir's best enemy, Guffar.

There was a little dell behind the house, hidden by blossoming apple trees. Sophie became aware that the children called it "the Quarrelling Place."

"Why the Quarrelling Place?" asked Sophie.

"Because it's used for quarrelling," said Teresa. Sophie thought it was a game and said, "You funny little things!" but it was not funny to Teresa. She tried not to show her alarm, but it came out.

"Let the children write poems, naturally, spontaneously," said *The Wise Teacher*. Sophie suggested Teresa should do that.

"No," said Teresa.

"Write a poem about a bulbul," said Sophie.

"I—can't," said Teresa.

"They are such dear little birds," said Sophie and insisted, but when she got the poem she did not like it.

> Two little bulbuls were sitting on a wall,
> Quarrelling and pecking, quarrelling and pecking,
> Quarrelling,
> Quarrelling,
> Pecking pecking pecking pecking.
> This is more than flesh and blood can stand.
> Now all that is left
> Is the tail of one bulbul
> And the beak of the other.

"But a child should be happy and confident," said Sophie, bewildered and dismayed.

Teresa longed to speak but could not. "I will not have you telling tales," Sophie had often told her. "This backbiting and tale-telling is horrid. You are *not* to do it." Teresa, unhappily, did not tell about the Quarrelling Place, and Sophie innocently asked St. Nicholas to bring her more flowers.

One day Amdhoo followed the old gardener from Nishat, and he and Nabir dragged St. Nicholas to the Quarrelling Place.

"If my brother sees you here again he will throw you off a rock and break your neck," said Amdhoo.

"The memsahib tells me to come, and I shall come. If you touch me I shall tell her," quavered St. Nicholas.

"Your mother was a prostitute."

"Your father was a donkey and got you on your mother." The ugly voices and ugly words filled the air.

It was a great nuisance. Amdhoo had to pay the head gardener in Nishat to get roots and plants for Sophie, and all that was no use; she still took them from Ghulam Sheikh.

"She should do everything through you," Nabir's mother told him severely.

"Yes, but she doesn't," said Nabir. The family clearly did not think much of him, but they could not know how strong-willed Sophie was. "You should be firm," they told him. When he was firm it had bad results. He reminded them about the fish.

One morning, when Sophie and Teresa and Moo were out with Subhan and Nabir on the lake, their boat had passed a flotilla of fishing boats. Two came paddling up, the men in them holding up the fish they had caught for the mem to buy. "The Sheikhs have no shame. She was with us, Dārs. What effrontery!" said Nabir.

"Six annas—four annas—two annas," called the Sheikhs.

"Don't buy from them," said Nabir.

"Why not?" said Sophie. "It looks good."

"I will get fish from the village," said Subhan.

"This fish is fresh——" But Nabir had taken things into his own hands. He shouted the fishermen off, hurling abuse. The sudden quarrel had spoiled the day. Sophie had been very angry and told Subhan to take the boat to shore.

In the village Nabir had dropped behind and hastily bought a fish from a Dār cousin and run after Sophie, his face beaming. It was a beautiful fish, laid out on a leaf, but Sophie would not look at it.

"But they give it for no money at all," said Nabir, lying.

"I don't want it," said Sophie.

"Not want it? For no money?" Nabir could not believe his ears.

"Give it back," said Sophie coldly.

Sophie remembered that fish too. In the evening, instead of kulchas and honey and milk, Sultan had brought in fish, cooked with rice.

"This," said Sultan, dropping his gold eyelids down, "is the fish Nabir Dār would not buy. Guffar Sheikh bought it for the memsahib."

"Sultan is on the Sheikhs' side," said Teresa.

"Sheikhs? What Sheikhs?" asked Sophie.

She complained to the pundit. "But if Nabir Dār will do things for you and arrange them without too much charge, what is wrong?" said the pundit.

"I want to arrange them myself," said Sophie.

ॐ

"Perhaps she likes to do as she likes," said Raschid, to whom no one ever listened. It seemed to them that Sophie was deliberately unreasonable. "She has given an order for lotus honey to Mahomet Sheikh for always," said Sam-dhoo. "She should have given it to Khaliq Dār." Lotus honey was the most expensive. They were all downcast; it was like finding Sultan's gold mine and being unable to work it.

It was not only that. To Nabir, though he could not have put it into words, there was something corrupting in Sophie's new ideas. She was determined to be unselfish. "We must all help one another," she had said when she had told him about the sewing circle, her eyes shining in a way that Nabir had come to know and that, in spite of the trouble it brought, turned him to this strange protective tenderness. "The whole village must help one another," said Sophie.

"But—if everyone helps themselves, who will need all this help?" asked Nabir. He could not put his feeling more clearly than that.

"If she helps the Dārs that is all right!" said his mother chuckling, but Nabir did not chuckle. In some mysterious way it was not all right. For instance, Sophie gave his cousin's wife, Suroya, a pair of socks for her baby. No village baby had ever had socks before; they did not need them; but Suroya had been as proud as a hoopoe and went about nettling all the other women.

"You should be careful," said the pundit to Sophie. "Please don't give so much."

"Much!" said Sophie. "It's so little, but at least what I give, I give without stint."

The pundit had never heard "stint" before, and when she explained it to him he was charmed with it. "I like stint," he said.

Then one morning Sophie said to Teresa, "I have an idea."

❧

Teresa had almost forgotten that Sophie had ideas. She was frightened, but when this idea was told it appealed even to Teresa.

"Do you remember the farmer?" asked Sophie. Teresa nodded.

Their first morning at Dhilkusha an old farmer had come and stood under the sitting-room window and put out his tongue. He was not being rude; it was for Sophie to see. He had said he was feeling very ill, and, looking at that tongue, Sophie was not surprised. She had given him some castor oil in a teacup, and he was extremely pleased. Two days later he had come shambling back, looking weak and wrapped in a blanket, but he said it had all passed away—illness, oil, everything. He had been able to eat his food for the first time in a week. "Your honour is my father and mother," he had told Sophie.

After that, every day, outside the back door, there was a little knot of people, sitting in the courtyard, waiting for her.

"But I am not a doctor," Sophie told them.

They went on sitting.

Apart from some necessary first aid and a dose or two of castor oil, Sophie had let them sit. Nabir approved of that.

"It's not your work," said Nabir. He added, "To doctor is the barber's work."

"The barber puts ink on your burns and dung on your cuts and charges you for it," Sophie said to Nabir. "It's disgraceful. It must stop."

Now her new idea was to make the empty room opposite the kitchen at Dhilkusha into a dispensary for the village.

For once Teresa thought it was a good idea. She could enter into it. She knew she was better at dressings, for instance, than Sophie; her plump little hands seemed to know what to do, and they were always steady, not like Sophie's, which trembled with excitement. Teresa still liked the word "heal." Since Sister Locke had talked to her in the Mission it had stayed in her mind, and it still seemed to pull her on, to

112

make her a bigger, bolder Teresa. "I think this is my work," she said. All the same, she remained cautious. "Don't you think," she said, "we should talk to Doctor Lochinvar and Sister Locke?" But Sophie had the same feeling about the dispensary as she had had over the taking of Dhilkusha. "Let's do it first," she said, "and tell them about it afterwards."

"But how," asked Teresa, "shall we pay for the medicines?" Teresa knew very well that Sophie had little money. Sophie had fallen into the way of talking too much to Teresa—"Far too much," said Sophie often to herself. "She is a little, little girl. She can't understand." But Teresa understood almost too much, and she was so practical and far-seeing that she became a curb on Sophie. "We can't pay for medicines," said Teresa.

"That is the second part of my idea. We shall use herbs," said Sophie. "Do you remember the anemones and violets? Do you remember the catkins?" Teresa nodded. "Why, all round your feet, as you stand here on the grass, are medicines, just for picking," and Sophie unfolded to Teresa her further plans.

"We shall have a herb garden and factory," she told Teresa. "It—it will be wonderful. All the village can be in it. This year we can collect a little and make some teas and jams and syrups—it is too late now for violet syrup—and grow culinary herbs. We shall plant and gather, and then *next* year . . ." Already Sophie was dazzled by what she would do next year.

"But now for the dispensary," urged Teresa.

"Yes, to begin with we shall use them for the people," said Sophie.

"You will have to be careful," said Teresa. "They see Doctor Lochinvar coming in and out. Will they want you to be as clever as Doctor Lochinvar? A doctor has five years' training," said Teresa.

"I shall manage," said Sophie.

"I don't like the way you do things without being qualified," Toby was to say later. "You didn't know anything about herbs."

"I did. I knew a little," said Sophie. "I found out the rest, and it was a success." Then she corrected herself. "For a while it was a success."

The people had a great faith in really bad-tasting medicines out of bottles. Sophie's herbs tasted badly enough to satisfy anyone, and she soon learned to put them in bottles. Their medicinal values were good. Mahomet had a rash; she treated him with a blood-cleansing tea, and the rash disappeared. Her poultices were wonderful for boils, and her syrups very popular among the children.

"You see, these poor people come to me," said Sophie triumphantly to Nabir.

"Of course they come," said Nabir. "The bandages and medicines are free. The barber charges." After a moment he said, "The barber is getting very angry. He says you take away his fees."

"He can say," said Sophie carelessly.

Her idea grew. She took culinary herbs as they were ready—dried mint, parsley, the first thyme—and put them into rice-paper packets which she had made and labelled, and took them to the chemist in Srinagar and asked him to sell them for her on commission. He sold them and wanted more. With the next supply she sent in some herbal teas and wrote a list of what she thought she could make: teas, syrups, oils, local remedies like rose-seed for dysentery, curd, fragrant herbs, dried verbena, and lavender as it came into season.

"Could you make pot-pourri?" asked the chemist.

"Yes," said Sophie, though she did not know how. She looked up her recipes:

⅔rd bushel of dried rose leaves

2 ozs. each of cloves, mace, cinnamon (I can get those, thought Sophie)

½ oz. each coriander, allspice, gum storax, gum benzoin (I shall have to write to the aunts for the gums)

4 ozs. violet powder

Add sweet geranium, verbena, lavender, bay leaves, shavings of cedar or sandalwood (There is plenty of sandalwood here)

"Yes, I can make pot-pourri," said Sophie to Teresa with relief. "But not yet, not till the lavender is ready."

She had more orders, and they soon came steadily. "It is a real herb factory," she told Teresa. "I knew something would come that we could do," and she said, lit by enthusiasm, "It will be a village industry."

The empty downstairs room opposite the kitchen had become a still-room, with shelves along the walls, on which stood labelled and lidded

114

earthenware jars bought in the village. There were a table and pestle and mortar. Outside in the courtyard the village mason made a cooking stove of clay for boiling syrups.

The Abduls came back—Hed Abdul with his black beard and bad ways, Abdul One, and Abdul Two, as emaciated as ever. In the warm summer weather Hed Abdul did not seem as distressing, or else Sophie was harder. She let him work without interfering, and he built a drying shed of mats on a wooden framework.

The Kashmiri climate is so dry in summer that Sophie's shed needed no heating; it had latticed racks under its mat roof, and eaves wide enough to shade it.

"People think that herbs should be dried in the sun," said Sophie. "If they are, all the strength goes out of them." Nabir, Sultan, Habib, and the Abduls stood round marvelling at the things she knew. It was a good shed. The air blew through it all day long, and the racks pulled in and out so that Sophie could shift them easily.

The Abduls made a low bench, filled with hollows, to take six wide-mouthed jars, over which were laid sheets of glass. Here she sun-cooked her flower oils, and there were low tables for cleaning and picking.

It did not take long to finish, and this time Sophie kept stern watch over the Abduls and counted the heads of the nails. I have to make this pay, thought Sophie. It was amazing what sense that thought gave. Now she treated the carpenters as the people they were known to be, and she and they did much better.

As she had said, all the village was in it. The schoolmaster had the labels printed; the potter made the pots and bottles; the tailor sewed the bags—"cheaper than paper," said Sophie—the basket workers wove the packing baskets; Aziz, the tonga-man, dispatched them; the oil man brought oil. She had pickers and cleaners from the village, men and women.

When the first picking of herbs was brought down in basket-loads from the mountain—Sophie had given samples and sent up three men—everyone in the house dropped his other work and came to clean it—the Abduls, Sultan, Nabir, Teresa and Sophie, and a Dār woman Nabir had brought up to sickle down the weeds along the wall. Everyone sat to-gether in the courtyard, stripping the flowers or leaves or roots, shaking them free of dust or pollen or earth, spreading them on clean paper. Sultan made tea, the children had biscuits, and they worked on though their fingers were sore and their backs ached. When the herbs were clean they were spread to dry, and four days later Sophie put them in jars ready for blending. Soon she had two men picking for her, several women cleaning. She packed her teas in white cloth bags, her syrups and oils in pottery bottles, and orders were sent away in osier baskets padded with hay. She spent long hours on the mountain, finding and identifying plants.

"They are selling," she told Little Lochinvar. With her small resources, it had been a strain to finance even this, but now she was making a little money and she was full of plans. "Rosemary hair rinse," said Sophie. "Camomile flowers." And she showed Little Lochinvar a telegram from Bombay, the first telegram that had ever come to Dhilkusha. It was an order for teas. "All that way away! How did they hear of me?" she asked.

"What tea is this?" asked Little Lochinvar. His voice was suspicious.

"It's a rose and borage tea for fever, an Indian recipe," said Sophie blithely, and she read it to him:

Macrotomia Benthami	I tola
Viola biflora	I tola
Aniseed	½ tola
Glycyrrhiza glabra ("That is Spanish liquorice," said Sophie)	½ tola
Rosea Kashmiriana	I tola
Bramble leaves	I tola
Zizyphus	½ tola

"Zizyphus is jujube, such a lovely name. It's a cooling and astringent tea," said Sophie.

"It may be," said Little Lochinvar. His eyes were troubled; they followed Sophie as she moved from jar to jar in her stillroom, showing him her teas, her blendings, giving him a fragrant handful to sniff or a root to guess at, a syrup to taste. Her cheeks were flushed pink with excitement; her eyes were very green. He had never seen her look prettier, but this was medicine and he had to speak. "It's quackery," he said.

If he had said "heresy" he could not have condemned it more.

"All doctors say herbs are quackery," said Sophie.

"It isn't the herbs," said Little Lochinvar. "Do you think doctors don't know about herbs? It's you," and he said it as if he were deeply disappointed. "Sophie, quackery is pretending to a skill you don't possess." He had never called her Sophie before, and he was quite unconscious that he had done it now; that showed Sophie how serious he was.

She felt rebuffed and chilled. She had not thought Little Lochinvar would speak to her like that; it was almost a rift. When two women came up, one with a badly cut arm—her sickle had hit a rock and glanced back at her—Sophie hoped he would be impressed with the way she swabbed out the cut, drew its edges together with plaster, and bandaged it up, but he watched, brooding. At last, "It's not fit work for you," he said. That made Sophie feel better.

"Doctor Lochinvar," said Sophie, "when you think of work for yourself you ask, 'Am I fit for it?' With me you ask, 'Is it fit for me?' Why?"

"Because you are you," said Little Lochinvar.

"I am doing no harm," said Sophie.

"You don't know what you are doing."

"You, a missionary, should encourage everyone to work for others," said Sophie, but he was silent.

"I believe you think I should spend my time trailing about a garden with lawns and peacocks," said Sophie, teasing him.

"I wish I had lawns and peacocks," said Little Lochinvar, but he was not himself for the rest of the afternoon and the next day he sent Dr. Glenister out with Sister Locke, to see Sophie. "I suppose he thinks they can scold me," said Sophie and tilted her chin.

"Dearie, is it wise?" Dr. Glenister asked, and Sister Locke said outright, "You don't know what you are doing."

"I do," said Sophie. It was true she had sold some sooji, the Indian fine semolina, as issuf-gool, rose-seed. "But anyone might have done that," said Sophie.

"Sooji would not have been much use for bad stomachs," said Sister Locke when, later, Sophie confessed this to her. "In fact, if it had been a case of gastro-enteritis, wheat is the worst thing."

"It was not gastro-enteritis," snapped Sophie.

"That was luck," said Sister Locke. She said now, "You will kill someone."

"That shows how little you know about it," said Sophie loftily. "A herbalist never uses poisonous herbs."

Though she had learned a little of peasants and carpenters, Sophie still had some sentimentalities left. When she thought of herbs she thought of English stillrooms, where gentle things were made—simples, balms, and teas; violet syrups, camomile tea, bouquets to put in cooking, lavender in muslin bags, pot-pourri. But the Dhilkusha stillroom was stronger and unmistakably Eastern; her most useful herb was southern-wood for worms in children; she had rose-seed for dysentery and strange mixtures for fever, from recipes the pundit brought her. The pundit took a great interest, though he was alarmed at the money she had spent. "Nothing venture, nothing win," said Sophie. The pundit thought "venture" a terrible word.

The aunts sent her several herbal books, and she had her own herb books and recipes, but she had stranger ones she learned from the herb-shops in Srinagar, where there was an age-old traffic in medicinal herbs. Mr. Kirkpatrick sent her others from Delhi, translations from Tibetan —"And some are coming to you from Benares, from the Sanskrit, and here is a book of Egyptian secrets." For her amusement he sent her some witches' "country medicine"—"For earache, the froth from a pricked snail dropped into the ear; for fits, a little of a human skull grated like ginger and mixed with the food; for whooping-cough, fried mice." "I like the fried mice best," wrote Mr. Kirkpatrick. Sophie thought his humour a little nasty; she was still sentimental about her herbs.

She was sent some spikenard. "Spikenard!" said Sophie, bewitched, and she showed Teresa the brown tuberous roots and told her what they were. "It was part of the ointment that washed the feet of Christ," she said, and "Touch it," she said reverently. "Think! It goes all the way back from your hands to Mary Magdalen's, thousands of years of perfume and fragrance."

"It isn't fragrant," said Teresa, and when Sophie came to sniff it she had to admit it had a curiously pungent smell.

There was something else that, while it amused Sophie, disturbed her.

Since she had begun her herb work the people seemed to suspect her of peculiar powers. Did peculiar powers, then, go with herbs?

Once an elegant old man came up the path, a Hindu with an exquisite pale skin and frail bones, a pale grey coat, white muslin pantaloons, and a lime-green turban; though it was a hot day he was muffled in a thick white shawl, and before he spoke to Sophie he motioned to the boatmen who had followed him to dust his shoes. "It is the Rai Sahib," Sultan whispered, awestruck, in Sophie's ear.

"I have come to consult you," said the Rai Sahib.

Sophie interrupted him. "I am not a doctor, Rai Sahib."

"I know you are not," he said testily. "You are a wise woman."

"No, I am not," said Sophie hastily. "I know a little about herbs, that is all."

"I am not interested in herbs," he said. Sophie opened her mouth, but he lifted up his hand peremptorily. "Would you, or would you not," he said, "think it prudent to take medicine that is made of *gold?*" He said "gold" as if it irritated him intensely. Sophie knew her reputation must be large to be consulted on such an expensive matter as that.

Another day, at the stillroom door, there was a big young nomad goat woman in her pleated black and red trousers, black tunic, and veil that she wore over her round blue cap.

"I want some medicine to make a son," she said.

She stayed all day because she would not believe that Sophie was not hiding such a medicine. "Isn't it this?" she said, pointing to the cough syrup; "Isn't it this?" to a rosemary hair rinse.

"If I had such a medicine would I have only one son myself?" asked Sophie, but the goat woman would not be convinced. She smelled so strongly of goat and sweat and smoke that Sophie had to keep her outside. Towards dusk she had to give it up; her clan had gone on she told Sophie, she had miles to go to catch them, but still she lingered hopefully, and always looking, gazing at Sophie.

Very often now people came just to look at her.

"Can you," asked Sultan, his eyes big, "*can* you make spells?"

"No, of course I can't," said Sophie.

"The barber can," said Sultan jealously.

"He can only because you think he can," said Sophie, but this was lost on Sultan. A little of Sophie's power had fallen on him, and he wanted more. "You help the mem with her medicines?" the villagers asked him. "I work *with* her," said Sultan airily.

"And what do you do?" jeered the barber.

"You wouldn't understand what we do," said Sultan. "It is written down, and you can't read and write."

"You are teaching them to dabble," said Profit David to Sophie, and he laughed. "The emperors were often poisoned," he said, "and their children had their ears cut off."

"Don't be horrible," said Sophie, and she demanded, "Surely herbs are innocent enough?" But afterwards she remembered Mr. Kirkpatrick's dark little recipes and she went and looked some up:

For a Felon or an Inflamed Sore

Red bolus, two spoonfuls ground; atlantis root, seventree, corns, white bolus, white-chalk, two spoonfuls ground of each; assafoetida, five pence worth; garlic, three spoonfuls ground. Pulverize and mix well together; give to a white horse mornings before feeding, in water. After this burn a live mole, powder it, and strew into the wound.

"Ugh!" said Sophie.

A Remedy for the Fever by which a Lady of Nobility has aided many people

Cut the ear of a cat, let three drops of the blood fall in some brandy, add a little pepper thereto, and give it to the patient to drink.

For Fits

Take some part of the hind leg of a calf; also part of a bone of a human body, from a graveyard . . .

Sophie turned over the page quickly.

A Good Stomach Plaster for a Bewitched Child

> Take a little of the oil of almonds, deer's tallow, as much of
> rose vinegar and one ounce of caraway seed . . .

"This is better," said Sophie and read how these should be pounded
together in a plaster and laid on the child's stomach.

> But before using the plaster, the mother must cut three pieces
> of bread thin, while sticking the knife three times through the
> bread, and put this knife under the child's back during the
> night. If the child is bewitched the knife will be rusty all over
> next morning and . . .

Sophie did not read any more of that recipe.

> That the toad may be prepared for a sympathetic remedy for
> disorders such as Chills, Epileptic Fits, etc., and that our ter-
> ror and natural hatred may be more strongly imprinted in the
> toad, hang him in the chimney by the legs and set under him
> a dish of yellow wax to receive whatever may come down and
> fall from his mouth; let him hang in this position, in our
> sight, for three or four days till he is dead, not omitting to be
> present in the sight of the animal so that his terror and hatred
> of us may increase even to death.

"Ugh! *U-ugh!*" said Sophie, shuddering.

"But those come from the dark ages," said Sophie. She looked at the
recipes fearfully. "Why is it that everything I do," she said, "but *everything*,
becomes startling?" What was this alchemy that turned the ordinary to
the extraordinary, even herbs? How do I do it? thought Sophie, and she
had a small shock. "I?" she said. "It can't be anything to do with me, and
anyway, it's nonsense," said Sophie.

Chapter 13

Ayah used to say Moo was possessed of a devil. Now he began to make his mark on everything. He was so bad, so passionate in his screams and tempers, that Teresa was afraid. Sultan suggested that the pir be called and asked to exorcise him. Profit David suggested Sophie should bind a silver leaf engraved with holy words on the inside of his arm.

"We must not think only of the body but of the soul," said Profit David. "In best silver it will cost you only eleven rupees."

"*With* the engraving?" asked the pundit sharply.

"Without the engraving," said Profit David. "Engraving will be extra," he told Sophie, ignoring the pundit's protests, "but the words will be from the Persian and they will speak directly out of old, old wisdom."

"Moo doesn't understand Persian," said Teresa. Moo put his head back on his neck and smiled.

"Leave him alone," said Nabir. "I and my brothers were *shaitans* when we were young, and look at us now. We are the richest people in the village," said Nabir. A Kashmiri could have no higher commendation than that.

"You are *shaitans* still," said Sultan under his breath.

Moo was a *shaitan*. He took his small iron spade and hit the walls of the hall, which Sophie and Nabir had just distempered. He took the scissors into the garden and cut off the heads of all the tulips. Teresa was appalled. "They were tulips, now they look like necks!" she wailed, and for once she said, "Do something to him."

"I shall do what they do to people who spoil things," said Sophie. "I shall handcuff him." She brought her red scarf and tied his hands together behind his back. "See how you like that!" said Sophie.

Moo walked away down the path. With his hands tied behind him he was not very steady, and Teresa's heart suddenly bled for him, and she rushed at Sophie and began to beat her with angry hands. "Untie him!" She sobbed. "You wicked, cruel Mother!"

"Teresa, don't be silly. Moo must learn."

"I don't want him to learn. I want him to be as he is," sobbed Teresa. Sophie sent her indoors. Even then Teresa hung about on the veranda. She could see the small figure of Moo in his dungarees, with the red scarf dangling nearly to his heels; he marched down the gully as if he were never coming back, and then along by the stream under the willow trees. Teresa imagined for Moo all the turmoil she herself would have been in had Sophie punished her, and tears of pity ran down her cheeks. Then suddenly she stopped crying and gripped the veranda post. Moo had met the herd children.

"*Mother!* Moo is with the herd children."

"Well? Why not?"

"Let me go to him, Mother!"

"Teresa! Stay there, where I put you!" And Teresa had to stay, watching in agony.

The herd children stared at Moo, and he looked back at them, at the green and brown pherans of the girls, dirty again though they had just had their spring washing, at their tattered veils and wild hair; at the boys with their ragged coats, their pink caps. Some had marks of sores on their faces; they all had bare brown feet; some of them had willow switches in their hands. They clustered round Moo. They had of course seen him before, but they never dared approach him; now here he was, alone and strangely tied up.

They closed round him and stared at him. One of girls flicked him lightly on the cheek with her willow. It did not exactly hurt but it stung like an insect bite, and made Moo furious. He was much smaller than they, but Moo never knew how small he was. He bent down sideways, clumsy with his hands tied behind him, and succeeded in picking up a stone, which he jerked at them. The jerk was a baby, angry one, and it made them laugh. Moo grew more angry; he bent to pick up another stone, and he overbalanced and fell into the stream. Teresa saw the splash and she hurtled down from the veranda. Her cries brought Sophie, Sultan, Habib, and Nabir running, but by that time the herd children had fished Moo out. They brought him up to the house, and that was the beginning of a friendship.

As if he had been a witch, his ducking exorcised Moo—or perhaps it was Sophie's handcuffing. From that day he was good, which pleased Teresa, and he was given the freedom of the mountain by the herd children, which disturbed her very much. He and Teresa and Sophie grew to know them. They were all, of course, Dār children. There was Zooni, who, with her thin face and sore eyes was very unlike her romantic name that meant "moon"; there was Salim, the bold leader of the boys; the sturdy Daveed; Taji, who was the prettiest girl of them all, and Sophie's favourite. There were many others, and among them a particular small boy, Rahim, who became Moo's especial friend. Moo loved him, and Sophie let Moo buy Rahim a new pink cap as a present. Moo had never been so happy, but still Teresa was full of fears.

"But they are *children*," said Sophie again and again. "What could they do to you?"

Teresa did not know, nor could she say why she was afraid of them. She could only say feebly, "They throw stones at us, and you say we mustn't throw them back."

"I should hope not," said Sophie. "I should hope you know better than that."

It was because she knew better that Teresa was at such a disadvantage. Sophie expected her to go out among the herd children but first took away all her defences. Teresa had no words to explain but she knew that the herd children had hard bare feet that ran and leaped over the stones, while she, by Sophie's edict, wore shoes, and as, being obedient, she did not take them off like Moo, she slipped and skidded in them, and they kept her feet soft. The herd children were quick to act because they never thought. Sophie impressed on Teresa that she must think. "*Think* of other people," said Sophie. "*Think* what you are doing," and, because Teresa thought, she was slow. All day long the herd children did happily and unconsciously the things Teresa was inhibited from doing; they threw stones, they picked their noses, scratched themselves, made water where they were instead of going to a bathroom. "Never let me catch you doing that," said Sophie.

Teresa was just the wrong age for the herd children. Moo was young

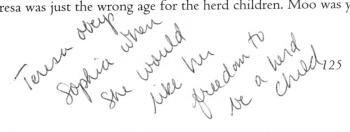

Teresa obeys Sophia when she would like her freedom to be a herd child

125

and as uninhibited as they; Sophie was old and had authority and respect. Teresa was neither young nor old, and she could not help feeling she was right to be afraid. She had seen them throw stones at one another, even at the goats they tended; they were mischievous and quick and unheeding as monkeys. Teresa knew it, but Sophie refused to know.

Soon Sophie had given them baskets and had taught them, in their long hours on the mountain, to fill the baskets with herbs from a sample plant she gave them. When they brought the flocks and cattle down in the evening they left their filled baskets in the courtyard, where a blackboard hung on which they made a tally mark. On Saturdays, Sophie paid them in pice and sugar cakes. "It is too much," said Nabir.

"A pice too much?" asked Sophie—a pice was a quarter of a penny. "A jilibi?"

"They will fight," said Nabir.

"For as little as that?" said Sophie. She should have remembered the nails.

୭

It was the middle of May, cherry time. The bird-scarers had come to watch over the cherry crop; they built themselves wickerwork huts in the garden, and all day long the air was raucous with the noise they made, jangling tins on strings, clapping wooden rattles, with cries of "Pss-ss-ss." The garden was alive with people; the traders came, the villagers came to the dispensary, the herd children ran in and out.

Then Moo's tricycle was stolen. Moo did not care, but Teresa was terribly upset and even Sophie was shaken.

"You are the caretaker, you should take care," said Sophie to Nabir.

"How can I watch everything at once?" said Nabir. "You tell the people to come and tell me not to let them come! What am I to do?" asked Nabir. It was a reasonable question, but Sophie said that he was insolent.

"When the mem speaks to you, you should say, 'Better,' and not answer back," said Sultan smartly.

"*Zinahook.* Bastard," growled Nabir. He was beginning to see clearly that Sultan was working against him, indeed against all Dārs. "What has happened to Sultan?" asked Nabir, puzzled.

126

Nabir had always dismissed Sultan as a little city rat, but lately even he had seen that Sultan could not be dismissed. Sultan entertained in Sophie's kitchen, he dispensed favours, he was treated almost as a friend by the most powerful men in the village, by the pir, the barber, the water-works policeman; and, more and more, Nabir saw him in company with the Sheikhs, even with Nabir's enemy, Guffar. While a Dār was in charge at Dhilkusha none of the household should have consorted with a Sheikh. It was not etiquette, thought Nabir again. It did not dawn upon him that Sultan thought he, Sultan, was in charge at Dhilkusha. Nabir only sensed that as Sultan came up in favour, he himself went down. "The emperors had favourites," Profit David would have said, amused. Nabir was not amused. He felt in his bones there would be trouble, and his bones were right.

꒰

Sophie found two women in the garden, lopping branches from an apricot tree. She drove them away, but next day they were there again, taking cherry branches. She scolded them violently but she felt they scarcely knew how violently this was, as she had to speak to them in Urdu, and they probably knew only Kashmiri. The next day they were there again, and she called Nabir. "They don't understand," she told him.

"They understand," said Nabir. He glared at them, and they glared back at him.

"The memsahib should not encourage people to come here," he said, and, glad to be able to act at last, he commanded Sophie, "Take away their baskets and sickles and hoes."

These were strong measures. Without her tools a woman was useless; she could not get manure or firewood, or work in the fields; if she went home without her tools probably her husband or father would beat her. Sophie hesitated, but she remembered what the pundit had said. "If you find them taking anything in the garden you must severely punish them." The pundit was always willing to be fierce through other people. "Beat them," he said.

"I don't treat people like that," Sophie had said. "These are not people," said the pundit. "They don't think; they only feel."

"All the more reason for not beating them," said Sophie, but she took away the baskets and tools. The women followed her up the path, shouting and sobbing.

"She has taken our baskets," they screamed to Sultan, who, with Habib, had run out to see what the noise was. "She has taken our sickles, our hoes."

"They have taken our wood," said Sophie, and Nabir leaned on his spade and laughed. He was laughing for pleasure. The women were the mother and sister of Guffar Sheikh, and at last the Sheikhs were being treated as they should be. Sophie told him to tell the women they could have their tools when they paid for the wood. Nabir told them with embellishments. They shrieked and screamed. Habib began to cry in sympathy.

"Memsahib, let them go," said Sultan with an angry look at Nabir, but Sophie was implacable; she weighed the wood on the kitchen wood-scales. Teresa stood watching silently.

"Tell them I shall not be unkind," Sophie told Nabir. "I shall charge government prices though it's black-market wood." It was unkind enough because Sophie's scales were doctored and the wood weighed heavy. Like Sophie, the women had to pay too much, and she had a twinge of remorse at her own hardness when at last one of them untied the money from the corner of a rag tethered deep in her robe, each small coin separately knotted for safety. They paid. Their faces were sulky as they took their tools and went, turning back to shout curses and abuse. Sophie did not like to hear the screamed invectives—nor did Teresa, who grew pale.

The next afternoon Sophie was in the garden when Sultan came, stealing on bare feet through the flowerbeds. He stood beside her and dropped his gold-seal eyelids and said, "There are two more women cutting the trees."

"Nonsense. I told Nabir—"

"Look," said Sultan.

Sophie looked. Behind a peach tree she caught sight of a green and a red pheran. She lost them, and then the sun glinted on an earring. The village women had not thought Sophie could run. She was on them before they could move; their eyes looked up at her from the grass, as frightened as does'. They have heard what I did, thought Sophie, and she shouted for Nabir.

"But these are my sisters," said Nabir as if that explained it. A sister in Urdu is not necessarily a full sister; these were his cousins, the daughters of his powerful uncle.

"Are your sisters allowed to cut the landlord's trees?" asked Sophie.

"It is understood we should pick up a little," said Nabir sulkily, but Sophie did not appear to understand it and she took away these women's tools, and they too had to pay the price of her weighted scales.

"If you can't fix things better than that, what good are you?" asked Nabir's uncle, and he slapped Nabir's face. Nabir was altogether unpopular, unpopular in the village and unpopular with Sophie. She had written and reported him to the pundit, and the pundit had answered that he was very agitated and was coming out. Nabir's character was gone in all directions; he felt as if he were being torn in half.

"But Nabira," said Teresa, laying her hand on the handle of his spade when he was digging, "why don't you tell her about the Dārs and Sheikhs?"

"Let her find out," said Nabir crossly.

It was unfortunate that St. Nicholas chose that moment to come into the garden with a bunch of yellow roses for Sophie. When Nabir saw him he scowled and laid down his spade.

St. Nicholas stopped. "The memsahib asked me to bring a bunch of roses," he said with a bleary, deprecatory smile. "I am going in to the memsahib."

Nabir did not answer. He left his spade and spat on his hands. All the vexations of these days seemed to rise up into his face. He stepped across the plot he had been digging and took St. Nicholas by the neck of his robe and marched him to the Quarrelling Place. Teresa followed.

"The memsahib ordered these roses, Nabir Dār," quavered St. Nicholas. "She will be angry if they don't come. Very, very, very angry."

"*Hehra! Zinahook!*" said Nabir, swearing at him. "You use your daughter. Bastard!"

"By your leave, Nabir Dār," cried St. Nicholas. His voice rose to a shriek, but Nabir dragged him on. "Nabir *Dār!* Nabir *Dār!*"

The stream hid the sound of his voice from the house. He began to cry and kick his legs feebly. Nabir's exasperation mounted to fury, and he shook St. Nicholas. The roses dropped to the ground. St. Nicholas wrenched himself from Nabir's grasp and stood holding up his hands to shield himself. "In God's name, Nabir Dār," he screamed. The scream tore through the garden, and Nabir knocked him down.

Teresa saw the old gardener's face as he fell backwards. His cap dropped off, in his throat were horrible cords, and his mouth opened and showed he had no teeth. As he hit the ground, his fingers scrabbled at the earth and he sobbed; he had a dribble of blood on his chin. Teresa had never imagined anything as horrible as this, and she too screamed.

The pundit had just arrived. Sophie was in the hall, explaining Nabir Dār's iniquities to him, and they came running out together.

At first Sophie saw only the mangled roses. She went forward and picked them up. Their scent came to her from the broken heads, and she was angry, angrier than she had been yet. "It is you who spoils this house," she said to Nabir. "It is you who make it impossible for us here. *Shaitan!*" said Sophie to Nabir.

He had not known her eyes could blaze like that. He too hated to see the roses, but how could he explain? He opened his lips, but "Don't say one word to me," said Sophie peremptorily.

She did not want to touch St. Nicholas but she held out her hand to him. The old man knelt up, sobbing, and came on his knees to her and touched her shoe with his forehead. Sophie flinched but she was full of pity. "A man old enough to be your grandfather!" she said to Nabir and turned away from him. "You must deal with him," she said to the pundit. "I am too angry."

The pundit was already speaking to Nabir in Kashmiri, his nose twitching in paroxysms of excitement and nerves. Nabir answered in his most insolent voice. "Aie!" cried the pundit. "He is rude!" The pundit danced about on his little legs. "There is nothing else he will understand. I must beat him, madam, with your permission."

Sophie hesitated. She had always said that no one in her service should be beaten or forced, but she looked at the blood on St. Nicholas, at her ruined roses, and she thought of all the trouble and frustration.

"Why do you give so much trouble?" she said to Nabir, and Nabir answered what to him was the truth. "You make the trouble yourself."

Sophie's face hardened. "Yes, beat him, Pundit Sahib," she said.

Neither she nor Nabir had known that he was to be beaten there and then in front of her; it was in front of them all, because by now Sultan and Habib were there. Sophie had not dreamed she would see it, but the pundit had keyed himself up and, without waiting for her and Teresa to go, he rushed at Nabir.

Like all gentle people, when he was roused to violence he was far too violent. He had a stick and shoes; he beat Nabir's head with his stick, he kicked Nabir's bare shins with his shoes.

Sophie was too shocked to speak or interfere, but Teresa behaved as she had done about Moo. She screamed with fury at Sophie and then fell upon the pundit, sobbing loudly and beating him with her fists. Moo came running out and burst into tears and stood wailing; the women in the fields ran to look over the wall; the fruit gatherers came up.

Sophie stood silent and sick until Nabir, his cheeks scarlet under the brown, put the pundit away from him and said, "That is enough." To Teresa he said in Kashmiri, "Stop your noise." He went over to the vegetable plot and picked up his spade and put it on his shoulder. "Get the old Sheikh to work for you," he said to Sophie and walked down the path.

Teresa and Moo went after him. Sophie called them back, but they paid no attention; wailing loudly, they trotted at Nabir's heels. At the wall he told them curtly to stop and stay there. They stood watching his tall figure go down through the fields until it was far out of sight. Sophie could hear their cries. "Nabir Dār! Nab-ir Dā-r!" It sounded like a chorus of woe against the silenced cookhouse, the now silenced fields.

From that silence, mysteriously, the news went from house to house. "The Dārs have fallen. Nabir Dār had gone."

Chapter 14

Sophie felt sick and shocked all day, and in the evening she took the children to Nishat. She wanted to be lulled and soothed and get out of the house.

It was late when they arrived, and most of the people had gone. Sophie had always wanted to see Nishat by moonlight, but there was a notice on the gates that said, "This garden will be closed at sunset. All visitors must pass away by then." They had not very long before it closed; the sun was low in the sky. Moo began to play on the borders of the water channels, Teresa watched him to see he did not fall in, and Sophie sat on one of the marble thrones. Now that it was hot, the gardeners let the water run every day; the bird sounds were broken by water splashes. The water on the slant below her tinkled lullingly, and the scent of roses was delicious. Close by Sophie was a hoopoe; its long beak drove into the grass for insects, and occasionally it stopped and raised its head and lifted its crest.

Slowly Sophie began to feel more at peace. Then she looked up. Teresa was watching her. Sophie knew she meant to interrupt, and soon Teresa walked across the water on the stepping stones to the throne, frightening the hoopoe away.

"What do you want?" asked Sophie.

Teresa knew she was unwelcome but she leaned her arms on the edge of the throne and looked at Sophie, her face puckered with worry. She looks ugly when she looks like that, thought Sophie, and she thought involuntarily, as she still did in moments of tenderness, My baby!

But Teresa was not a baby. She stood there like a block between Sophie and peace. Presently she said, "Are you really going to send Nabir Dār away?" Moo's head appeared beside Teresa. His chin was level with the throne; the sun caught his hair so that he seemed lit, and his eyes looked piercingly at Sophie.

"He has sent himself away," said Sophie crossly.

"We don't like St. Nicholas," said Teresa. She was speaking for herself and Moo. Moo's look never wavered, and Sophie knew they were arrayed against her. "We don't like him," said Teresa. "He dribbles." This unsentimental view of St. Nicholas was true, but Sophie did not feel that Teresa was being very endearing. "And you paid too much for his flowers," said Teresa.

"Teresa, you are absolutely unbearable," said Sophie and stood up to go home.

⁊∾

But now Sophie found herself caught in her own trap, as did St. Nicholas.

St. Nicholas liked to work a little in Nishat, to till his field in his own time, to sit in his shawl in the sun, and now Sophie, feeling she could not start again with a stranger, asked him to come in Nabir's place.

St. Nicholas did not want to come. He had heard that English ladies expected a gardener to garden all the time, and there were messages and errands that would tire his old legs. There were people to keep out of the garden, women whom St. Nicholas dreaded, and, worse than the women, the herd children with their cows and goats, all of whom ran fast. The Sheikh children would take liberties and the Dār children would make all the trouble they could, and there was all this troublesome energetic, and potent work with the herbs.

"I don't want to come," said St. Nicholas.

"Not want! To keep the Dārs out!" said Guffar, his son. His family was adamant, and he was installed. The Sheiks went about triumphant, and the Dārs had gloomy faces. The whole village was in a ferment.

"Get the barber to put a spell on her," suggested Amdhoo.

"Owl! We want her back," said his mother, and she commanded Nabir to go to Sophie and weep.

"I won't weep," said Nabir, and his mother knew he would not. "He is so proud he might be a rajah!" she said. Nabir had always been a difficult son.

"But," said the simple Raschid, who had been thinking it all out while they were talking, "the old man won't be able to do the work. Won't the memsahib find that out?"

"She will find it out," said Nabir darkly.

Sophie had known it would be difficult, but she had not known that when Nabir left a great many things would alter. There was, for instance, a new milkman.

"This isn't my milkman," said Sophie.

"This one is better," said Sultan and St. Nicholas.

"I don't want this one. I want my old milkman, Ramzan Dār. Where is he?"

"He is gone. He won't give milk here any more."

That was true. She met Ramzan. "I can't come," he said.

"But Ramzana, I tell you to come," said Sophie. He only looked at her as if he were amazed at her ignorance. "It is not the custom," said Ramzan.

Sophie bought wood. It was another woodman. "I don't buy wood from anyone but Hakim Dār." But Hakim, it seemed, had also gone. Sultan used to buy bread at the breadshop down the village, now he went to the one up the village. When Sophie needed to go to Srinagar it was a different tonga; she had liked the big Aziz Dār, and she protested, but it was in vain. The Dārs had fallen, the Sheikhs were in; like Queen Victoria and her Tory ladies, she had to accept it. "I told you, you have made a little palace," said Profit David. "You have made a little court."

All this was etiquette. In time it would have settled, but Sophie had encouraged Ramzan the milkman, and she had asked for Aziz the tonga-man, and the Dārs had always been obstreperous. They began to lose their good manners, and there was an outbreak of fighting. The old milk-man fought the new milkman; the new woodman had his ponies stopped and his wood thrown down; suppliers of honey, bread, fish, pottery, eggs, tongas, sprang up and demanded their rights. It was not only the money; by now it had become a question of pride.

The quarrel spread to the herd children; the children who drove the Sheikh goats and cows lay in wait for the Dār children and would not let them come for their herb baskets. The Dār children missed their pice and sugar cakes, and they grew angry. The Sheikh children were angry too because Sophie had not followed custom and given the herb work to them. If the milkman changed, the herb-pickers should change, and if Moo's friends, Zooni, Salim, Daveed, came near Dhilkusha, the Sheikh children drove them off with stones. They wooed Moo with presents, silkworms in a little basket woven of leaf stems, crystals from the dry stream beds; but Moo would not take them. He ran after the Dār herds when he saw them.

Moo became a fetish and a symbol; each herd tried to have him. In the end he stayed inside the garden and played with Rahim, who managed to wriggle in.

Every day Sophie missed Nabir more. St. Nicholas ambled about the garden, doing the easy things, sweeping, tidying, when a new pit should have been dug or a lavender terrace made. He could not cut wood, and she remembered how Nabir swung his axe and sent the chips flying. If she sent St. Nicholas for butter he was gone all day and came back and said he could not find any. Sophie suspected that he went down to his house and stayed there.

Everything, too, seemed to have become vicious; even the house was possessed by it, as if the barber had really made a spell. Shingles fell off the roof, the clay oven split, the stream ran dry. Teresa found a viper in the garden, and Sophie had to kill the loathsome thing herself because Sultan and St. Nicholas ran away. Some of the devilment was human. The young pomegranates were stolen off the trees, a gap was broken in the wall so that cows strayed in, and Sophie found a hole made in her attic wall; half her store of wood had disappeared.

"Nabir Dār did it," said Sultan glibly, casting down his eyelids. That seemed plausible, and yet Sophie had a strong feeling that it was not Nabir.

Sultan was very busy. Every evening he held a little reception outside the back door; the hookah passed round, and salt tea. Sophie had seen the pir there, the waterworks policeman, St. Nicholas's relations, and the barber. "I don't think I want the barber here," she told Sultan.

"He is my friend," said Sultan.

"It is my house, Sultan," said Sophie.

There was a silence; then, "Better," murmured Sultan at last. He was getting difficult to control. Sultan difficult! Little Sultan! thought Sophie. She would not have believed it.

"Sultan Mahomet is promising that the mem will do things I think she will not do," said Nabir's mother.

"Then he is a fool," said Nabir.

"Yes," said his mother with satisfaction.

"Can't you arrange things better?" Guffar Sheikh was beginning to ask Sultan. "Look at these herbs. To one she gives a handful of weeks, to another medicine out of a bottle and a beautiful bandage. Look at the bandage she put on Mamdhoo's baby!" In village opinion it was worth more than the baby itself.

Sultan listened and gave gracious promises; none of the promises was fulfilled.

"You said the mem would buy my peaches," said Guffar.

"She will, she will," said Sultan, but Sophie did not.

"You said she would present a carpet to my mosque," said the pir.

"She will," said Sultan, but—"I?" said Sophie. "A *carpet*? Why should I? Do you think I am made of money?"

"English ladies are very difficult," said Sultan sorrowfully to the barber. "They always do what *they* want!" That was certainly a disagreeable trait in a lady. Every day he lost face—and money, thought Sultan. Little presents of tea money had been given him; now they stopped.

"Tea money!" said the barber. "She has taken away every anna I earned!" His eyes were dark. "She doesn't like me in the house, but you are her servant, close to her. If I were you," said the barber, "I could make her do what I want." The barber whispered in Sultan's ear. Sultan's eyes opened wide as he listened, and he made alarmed little noises through his nose.

❧

It was a few days after this that Sophie found Sultan busy in her still-room. He jumped in his slippers with fright as she came in. "What are you doing?" she asked sternly.

"I want to make a drink," said Sultan. He was so taken aback that for

137

once he kept his eyes open. Sophie saw they were hazy with his thoughts. Whose eyes have I seen look like that? thought Sophie, and knew they were her own. Perhaps it was this that made her speak very kindly to Sultan.

"What kind of a drink?" asked Sophie.

For all her kindness, Sultan seemed shy and reluctant to answer. He dropped his lids, and the colour in his cheeks deepened. At last he said, "A love drink."

Sophie was amused. Katiji, the pretty young mother of the pretty child Taji, had just been widowed, and Sophie had seen several of the men looking at her as she sat modestly cleaning herbs. It must be Katiji, thought Sophie and, still amused, she took down her oldest herbal book and turned up a recipe.

"Then there *are* love drinks!" said Sultan.

"Look," said Sophie and showed the page to him. It was beyond Sultan to spell it out, and she read to him:

"'Take of pepper, paprika and nutmeg, equal parts,'" read Sophie to Sultan, "'with ginger, ground, two spoonfuls. With this put Spanish kidneys that have laine forty hours in a bath of honey.'"

Sultan listened with great attention. "Spanish kidneys?" he asked.

"Or this," she said. "'Take the tongue of a turtle-dove—'"

"But how would I get the tongue of a turtle-dove?" Sultan interrupted her.

"Or a cobweb that has lain all night in the dew of wheat is good," said Sophie. "Or asparagus, very fresh. Or dissolve a pearl in vinegar."

"A *pearl?* A pearl costs hundreds of rupees!" said Sultan.

"A pearl or any jewel," Sophie teased him. "You see, there are lots of things you can do."

"But the kidneys," Sultan persisted. "What are Spanish kidneys?"

"Ask your friend the barber," said Sophie cruelly.

Chapter 15

love drink."

Spring is supposed to be the time for love, but, Sophie thought, here in this land of water and flowers the time for love was summer. In these warm languorous days she seemed to see a great deal of the pretty Katiji with her warm skin, her great black eyes hazy with goodwill and sweetness, her sumptuous dark auburn hair loose under her veil. The shortness of Katiji's pheran showed her ankles, sturdy and brown, and her bare feet had small even toes; her veil threw a warm shadow on her cheeks, and her silver earrings trembled as she breathed. All round Katiji there seemed to be restlessness that troubled even the air. Sophie was not surprised at the men.

Now the days stretched through hot languorous hours until Sophie lost count of time. It was high summer. Everything was green and thick. In the lanes and in the village, the orchards and garden, honeysuckle and wild white dog-roses were out; their scent was heavy and sweet at night, and the mountain was covered with thyme that smelled as heady in the day. At Dhilkusha the old neglected beds were full of flowers, and there were tangles of roses, the small true Damascus roses, sweetly scented, which Sophie loved. The acacias bloomed and dropped petals on the path, and she would not let St. Nicholas sweep them up. The creepers on the house flowered, and the jasmine. At the back of the house, in the poplars along the canal path, two of the paradise flycatchers that Nabir had predicted had come and nested. Sophie often saw their plumes and the male's white ribbon tail. On the roof the young doves had fledged, and the sound of their coos came into the house. The early rice was ready in the fields; on the lower ranges they were cutting it, and the sickles flashed like mirrors in the sun. Now the mountain stood out clearly, blue and dry with purple shadows, and down on the lake, over the reflections, breaking the intense blue of the reflected sky, the lotuses were in flower, mile on mile of them, covering the lake and waterways, great pink cups resting on the water or swaying above their mammoth flat green leaves, so thick and cool that all day they held pools of dew.

The lake and road, these days, were almost empty; nearly all the visitors had gone up into the mountains. Sophie had not the money to go, to take one of the chalet mountain huts as she had last year. She had spent almost the last of her reserves in financing her herb factory, and now, though she had had some return on it, in this empty season her factory was, naturally, not doing well. "It will recover when everyone comes back," she said, and thought that she would take the children into camp in the worst heat in August. "I have enough money for that," she told Teresa. "We will hire a tent and ponies and trek up into the mountains and camp by a stream." Teresa remembered the mountains; over and over again she told Moo about them, about the ponies and the cool air, the big glaciers, the smell of pine and clover, and the taste of wild raspberries. "Mother says our campfire will shine into the tent at night, and the goat children will sell us crystals . . . When shall we go?" she asked Sophie.

"Soon," said Sophie. "It will be hotter yet."

Now, for coolness, they went into Nishat or picknicked by the water or sometimes took a boat on the lake among the lotus flowers.

The lotuses affected Sophie strangely. She thought of a legend she had heard of the lotus marriage; the male flower rose up through the water when the moment was ripe and seized the female flower as she swayed, dragged her under, and pollinated her and let her go. Sophie wondered if it were true; it stayed in her mind, and she refused all Teresa's pleas to pick even one flower and take it home. "Leave them where they are," she said. "Don't let even one of them be cheated."

It was strange that Sophie, who had withstood the lonely winter, should now, suddenly, begin to feel her solitude and isolation. She was troubled and restless; sometimes she felt exhilarated, sometimes strangely low and melancholy. She felt—strange, thought Sophie. The feeling had been made sharper by meeting, once or twice, in Nishat or on her occasional shopping trips to Srinagar, some of the friends she had known last summer. Last summer she had been one of them; now she was from another world. She was stiff, a stranger. "I can't talk to people," she said. "I have forgotten how."

"Well, we don't talk to people much," said Teresa. "There is no one here to talk to."

"The Kashmiris are people," said Sophie.

"Not our kind of people," said Teresa certainly.

Sophie knew none of the current gossip, nothing of affairs, movements, trends, new books, plays, films, artists. Life is passing, and I am getting older, thought Sophie. Each time, after one of these encounters, she was more depressed. What will happen to us? thought Sophie. Shall we stay here in Dhilkusha forever? And she turned back the mat on the veranda and looked at the compass points.

"Why are you looking at that?" asked Teresa.

"Sometimes I think it has a message for me," said Sophie slowly, and she said, "I wonder if he left it for that? Like a code."

"Can you read it?" asked Teresa.

"Yes," said Sophie.

Teresa stared down at it. She too could read that code, though she did not want to.

"I like the stars," said Sophie. Teresa mistrusted those stars. "You said we were going to stay here a long, long time," said Teresa.

"Of course; this is our home," said Sophie, but she did not sound quite convinced.

The last time the postman had come he had put a square letter with an airmail stamp into the box; in these hot days he did not bother to come up to the house for tea. When Sophie had found the letter she had stood looking at it.

"Who is it from?" asked Teresa, and when Sophie did not answer she said, "Open it!"

"It's from Toby," said Sophie. "But Toby hasn't written to me for months!"

Toby had not written to her when Denzil died. He had not written a great deal before, but there had been complete silence since. Sophie had wondered why; she had been hurt and puzzled. Now, as she turned the letter over in her fingers and looked at the round, schoolboy writing that was oddly immature for such a competent man, suddenly she knew why. She caught her breath.

Teresa said encouragingly, "It's a letter, it isn't a bill." She had come to know that Sophie was often afraid of bills. "It's only Toby," said Teresa.

"I—know," said Sophie and laughed at herself and opened it.

It said nothing particular—it would not have mattered if she had not read it—but the next week brought another, and after that Toby's letters came regularly, week by week, "Your letter from Toby," Teresa would say. Sophie put them away in her desk, but sometimes, when she was feeling forlorn, she would take one out and carry it in the pocket of her dress or in her belt and she was able to look at Katiji quite benignly. In her more thoughtful moments she would have sudden visions of Finstead; again she saw the village, the small well-known houses, the clipped hedges and picket gates leading into gardens where, in each glassed porch or little greenhouse, chrysanthemums and begonias and geraniums were grown. Finstead was garden-proud. Well, I like gardens, thought Sophie. She saw the tarmac road between the hedges where the red bus ran every hour—how often she had caught that bus! She saw the electric and telephone wires, the telephone kiosk, the shop-post-office, the garage, the church and the chapel, the rectory where the Abercrombies held sway, the aunts' house, the Hall with its big gates opening onto the village green. She saw Toby's house, square and white with a slate roof, an ugly house except for the beauty of its magnolias; there was a brass plate on the gate from which all the lettering had rubbed off. That did not matter; the whole village knew its way to the surgery door at the back of the house as they knew Toby's car and his hat, his shabby case, even his voice over the telephone. "A doctor like Doctor Lochinvar," said Teresa, and she said, her fat little voice comfortable with approval, "I *like* doctors!"

Yes, Teresa would like Toby, thought Sophie. A quiet, good, and practical man, in a quiet, practical, good home in a quiet, practical, good village. Sophie could hear Aunt Portia saying, as Dr. Glenister would say if she knew, "Security for you and your children." Security. Sophie was beginning to know how excellent a word that was. Then she thought of Dhilkusha, her mountain, her lake, and she gave a little gasp and shook herself free. "I think I shall keep that mat up," she told Teresa.

"Why?" asked Teresa.

"I—need to see those stars," said Sophie.

❧

She began to be haunted by a dream. She dreamed about the lotus flower, and all day the dream seemed to stay with her so that she was by turns exhilarated, then sleepy. In her dream the male flower was a man, and when he seized the female flower it was herself, she, Sophie. She did not know the man; he was not Denzil, nor Toby—and the idea of Toby as a lotus was so funny that she laughed. Dear Toby! The lotus was not any male she had known, and sometimes, even in the dream, she thought he was the sailor of the compass points. She felt his arms go round her, and they were strong. "It's like a housemaid's dream," said Sophie scornfully and aloud to shame herself, but she could not shake it off. In the night she would wake, throbbing, and for a long time she could not believe she was alone.

Sultan had been bringing them lotus roots to eat. Cut, they looked like minute cheeses full of holes; sliced thin and fried in butter, they were delicious. "Perhaps that is why I dream, because I have eaten lotus," said Sophie. "Lotus-eaters," she said, "were supposed to be filled with a dreamy lassitude"—but not this excitement, thought Sophie. I want to laugh and shout and sing—and then I want to cry. Why, all yesterday I spent worrying about a herb recipe and then in the night I dreamed and woke and started to laugh. Then I cried.

She tried to discipline herself. "It's nine months since Denzil died." As she said that a longing for Denzil swept over her; it was so burning and poignant that it left her dizzy, but—I never felt that for him in life, she thought. It was so strong it shocked her. She sat down at her desk and tried to puzzle this out. "It is more than a year since you lived with Denzil, nearly two years," said Sophie to Sophie, and she trembled again. "You are perhaps a little starved, and," said Sophie to Sophie, "you will have to stay starved. Your business if to forget yourself and bring up your children, not to complicate matters." It was the growing heat, the heavy flower scents, the lotus roots perhaps, Katiji's potent ripeness and its effect always before her eyes, that had woken her.

To cajole her, as he had always known how to do, in these summer evenings St. Nicholas brought up an old country musician. All St. Nicholas's friends were old, but this man seemed older than any of them; he had a white beard stronger than he and a face in which life had strained away all his flesh into an emaciation that was dark and noble. Sitting cross-legged on the ground, he played on an instrument that was like a balalaika, and sang songs in a minor key. His voice was thin and sad and strangely sweet; it haunted Sophie like the lotuses. No matter how she roused herself, the singing was sure to lead her into the dream again.

"Don't you feel well?" asked Teresa one day, studying her across the breakfast table.

Sophie hardly knew what she felt, but when she came to think about it—to try to think about it, because her head felt curiously disinclined to think—she knew she felt sick and often dizzy and she had a little dysentery.

"You are not going to be ill again, are you?" asked Teresa, that pucker between her eyes.

"Of course not," said Sophie.

In summer in Kashmir dysentery is as common as the common cold in a European winter, and Sophie thought little of it. With an effort of will she put herself onto a diet of rose-seed jelly and curd, the country cure, but she grew no better.

"You are growing so thin your face is like a stick," said Teresa critically.

"Don't be horrid," said Sophie. She was absurdly hurt; absurdly she wanted to be pretty. Am I jealous of Katiji? thought Sophie, trying to laugh at herself.

She did less and less. She scarcely worked at the herbs. She told Teresa it was too hot to do lessons, and she did not go to Srinagar, as she was used to once a month, to buy their few necessities and get money from the bank. They ran out of money and matches and tea and soap. "It doesn't matter," said Sophie, and she borrowed from the oilman. "I shall go soon."

"Subhan Sheikh, tonga-man, would take you quite quickly," Teresa pointed out. "We have only one piece of soap left, and there is no darning wool."

Still Sophie did not go. She sent Sultan, and Sultan spent far too much money and bought all the wrong things. "Scarlet wool to mend Moo's socks!" said Teresa.

"It will make them look pretty," said Sophie, but Teresa did not think it would.

"Last time you bought Lux it was one rupee two annas a packet. How could it be one-twelve?" asked Teresa, looking at the list. "And four annas for a needle! Sultan is cheating you," said Teresa.

"Oh, Teresa!" said Sophie impatiently. She knew Teresa was right, but Sultan was being unusually helpful these days. "Your work has improved," said Sophie in surprise.

"Then you should give me more pay," said Sultan promptly, and Sophie raised his wages.

"You should not have done that," said the pundit.

"But he asked me to," said Sophie.

"Do you do what he *asks?*" said the pundit, shocked. "What will he *think!*"

"He will think that I am pleased with him," said Sophie. "I am."

"You should never tell a servant you are pleased with him," said the pundit, scandalized. "That you don't scold him is enough. Now he will lie on his laurels," said the pundit. "Memsahib, you would spoil anyone!"

It was true that now Sultan was more than ever like a triumphant little cock, and his work was not really any better. He was still dirty, still careless. "How careless he is!" said Sophie.

One night while Sophie was having her supper, reading abstractedly and not noticing what she ate, Teresa woke from a bad dream.

"I dreamed the viper was in my bed. I felt it cold and slithering," she sobbed.

"That is because we found one," said Sophie soothingly.

"I know it wasn't the viper. It was my feelings," said Teresa. "But I don't like them. I don't like them."

Sophie took her into the sitting room, where the lamp threw a bright circle and there were no frightening shadows. "You shall stay with me while I eat my supper, and I will give you tidbits," she said.

On the tray was a little dish of apricot cream. Sophie had taught Sultan how to beat the fresh apricot with sugar and milk, and it was delicious. Teresa's eyes kept looking at the dish. Sophie took it up and put it in front of her.

"For me?" asked Teresa, dazzled. "Don't you want some?"

"All for you," said Sophie. Teresa's eyes shone, and she picked up the spoon. She took a mouthful, but after a moment she put it out.

"It—it's gritty," said Teresa.

"How can it be gritty?" said Sophie.

"It is."

"Nonsense."

"It *is*." Teresa was still near enough to her dream to sound tearful. Sophie took up the dish and looked. The cream had odd small specks in it, like grit, but white.

"It's dirty," said Sophie. "Don't eat it." And when Sultan came to take the tray she scolded him.

"Have you put salt in instead of sugar?" she said. "I have told you not to use rock salt in the kitchen. Or you put your spoon down on the ground. How dirty and messy you are!"

"I didn't know," said Sultan sulkily, "that the baba would eat supper."

"Am I to eat dirt, then?" asked Sophie.

Sultan said nothing. He breathed quickly through his nose, his lips pressed together, and as he carried the tray out he gave Sophie a look that was—baleful? thought Sophie. It belonged to his new importance. I believe he thinks he shouldn't be scolded now, she thought.

❧

The pundit too noticed Sophie's looks. "You are getting very thin," said the pundit. "You have glitter eyes. Are you sure you haven't fever? You are too energic. You should cease work and bask with firepot."

"In this weather?" asked Sophie.

"Yes. Then, whatever is the matter, you will sweat it out of you."

"I wish I could," said Sophie. She felt there was no peace anywhere, least of all in herself.

Even the garden was not peaceful. It was the apricot and peach harvest, and that brought the pickers back, the packers and the clerk who kept the tally, the merchants who had bought the trees. Sultan seemed to have many visitors outside the back door. The herd children clustered around the walls.

"A court will have its hangers-on," said Profit David.

Without Nabir, Sophie did not seem to be able to control them. "Oh, I wish Nabir Dār was here," said Teresa often. Sophie knew now she wished it too.

ॐ

Profit David came to see Sophie strangely often in those hot summer days.

"What do you want?" asked Sophie.

"I? Nothing," said Profit David blandly.

Sophie did not believe him. She felt so witless that she could not deal with him. "I wish you wouldn't worry me," she said.

"Worry you? Lady sahib, I only wish to give you joy."

When he called her "lady sahib" that meant he wanted something—expensive, thought Sophie. She was right. Next time he came he was followed by one of his boatmen, carrying a rug. They crossed the lawn to where Sophie was sitting, and he took the rug and dramatically unrolled it.

"Oh!" said Sophie. "Oh!"

It was a Kirman rug; a Kirman is the only Persian carpet that looks feminine. This had roses and leaves on an ivory background that glimmered and shone and took the colour of pale honey. The roses were designed from the small Damascus rose that held a near place in Sophie's heart; the borders were pale blue with flower medallions.

There was a long silence. Profit David had no need to speak. Sophie knew just how such a carpet would shine and glimmer on her floor; she knew its beautiful workmanship, the number of stitches. She had been to school over carpets with Profit David. "When I show you these," he had told her down at the Third Bridge, "you are ruined forever. Your eyes will never allow a cheap carpet again."

"To have those roses in winter will fill you a need," he said at last softly. "You are an artist, lady sahib. You have been starving your soul."

Sophie hardly heard. She had been undone directly she saw those roses, and "I will take it," she said.

The price of the rug was seven hundred rupees.

"But you didn't have seven hundred rupees," said Toby afterwards.

In the night Sophie's guilt and shame overcame her. Before, I was like a citadel. I could protect the children, thought Sophie. I was growing strong and now I have fallen. She agonized over the children. Seven hundred rupees. That is more than fifty pounds. Profit David was convinced that she had money tucked away somewhere. What would he say when he found she had not? With her scrapings and her returns on the herbs she had almost paid off his first debt. Now they would have to go on for months, years perhaps, of even stricter saving, of sāg and lentils, of wearing the same old clothes, and of living with this dearth of books. I am mad and a fool, thought Sophie, looking at the sleeping children. A wicked fool!

Worst of all, she had to tell Teresa they could not go up into the mountains. She would have to use the camping money. Oh, how could I? thought Sophie, and her heart swelled with anger against herself. She thought of taking the rug back, but she knew it was useless. Profit David would not be as easy to sell to as to buy from. He would skin me, thought Sophie. I have done it now.

When she told Teresa there would be no camp this year, Teresa was quite silent.

"If we had gone into the mountains," Sophie offered her, "the money would have been gone, spent. We can keep the rug with us for always."

"We don't keep things," said Teresa distantly. Sophie could tell by the distance in her voice how disappointed she was.

"We can keep this." And Sophie argued, "It's a small rug. I can take it under my arm," and she tried to make it better by telling Teresa how a

Mohammedan often kept his money in carpets. "A carpet is his bank-roll," said Sophie.

"We are not Mohammedans," said Teresa. "I was going to collect crystals," she said, "and I had told Moo about the raspberries and the redstarts in the streams; you remember the little birds with the scarlet on their heads that played in the spray." Her voice trembled. "And it would be cool. I'm so hot," said Teresa. "And we were going to be goat men and have our own campfire." She put her red head on the table and sobbed.

Sophie look at the rug. She felt she hated it, but, looking at the colour of the roses against the blue and ivory, the velvet richness, the tracery of flowers, and thinking of how it had been woven with infinitesimal knots in some village in Kirman, stretched on its loom in the street perhaps, woven by the whole family, perhaps for a decade, she was moved again. "It's a precious thing, Terry, a lovely, lovely thing," she pleaded. "One has to pay for precious things." But Teresa was silent.

❧

The rug lost Sophie the devotion of Little Lochinvar.

He had not been the same since Sophie started the herbs. Each time he came he seemed to be struggling with himself—as if he were trying to exorcise me, thought Sophie. He is torn in half where once he was single. Sophie had never met anyone as single—or as torn. He was so torment-ed he did not notice her looks, but as soon as he came into the sitting room he saw the rug on the wall.

He was immediately hostile. "Why on the wall?" he asked.

"It's too good to walk on," said Sophie.

"What is the use of it, then?" he asked.

"*Look* at it!" said Sophie impatiently. He looked at it, his face set. "Don't you like it?" she asked.

"Such things are outside my scope," he said. He sounded cross. After a moment he said bitingly, "I thought you were poor."

"I am," said Sophie.

"A funny kind of poorness."

Sophie hesitated. "It *is* a funny kind of poorness. I still owe money but I believe that sometimes, particularly when one is afraid, one should do something bold, even with money. After all," she pointed out, "it's what you are doing. Going without for an idea."

He was furious. "Yours is self-indulgence!" he said hotly.

"Are you sure yours isn't?" asked Sophie.

"You are unprincipled," he said.

"These *are* my principles," said Sophie.

"You are beyond me."

"Yes, I am."

She could not have believed they could have been so angry. Little Lochinvar's r's rang hard. The words went backwards and forwards in her little sitting room. It had been so peaceful. A greenish light came in from the trees outside the widow; the children's innocent things, Pussy Maria, bricks, a tea set, lay about with the small signs of everyday life, a basket of mending, books, a bowl of flowers. Until he came the room had been filled only with the sound of the running stream, of doves on the roof, of the children's voices in the garden, the distant paddles on the lake, of the herds on the mountain; the sweet hay scent of the herbs in the stillroom crept up the stairs. "This room is like heaven," Little Lochinvar had often said. Now it was like the Quarrelling Place. The hot words flew; his chest was heaving under his alpaca coat; he seemed torn by a tornado of grief and rage, and Sophie stood, her fingers cold, her cheeks hot, saying wounding and biting things.

"All this about a rug!" said Sophie.

"The rug is more than a rug," said Little Lochinvar, and suddenly they stopped.

"You break my heart," said Little Lochinvar.

He went to the window, his back turned to her, his hands clenched in his pockets. His shoulders shook.

She said softly, "Doctor Lochinvar, please. I didn't mean it to be like this."

"It is like this," he said.

Sophie stood and with her finger traced out the wickerwork in the back of her chair. The wicker strands looped in and out, a clear brown colour, and where one met another were pockets of dust.

150

That is what we are like, thought Sophie. That is what people do when they get close to each other—raise the dust. But there are a few people, to do with you, strand of your strand, who are twisted with you, and there is no dust. Moo and I? Yes, thought Sophie. Teresa? Teresa and I are learning. Where there is love you can learn. Denzil—no, not Denzil, she thought miserably. I didn't love him. Perhaps I shall never love a man unless it's someone like—that man; she meant the man of her dream who was the sailor of the compass points. The rest are strangers, thought Sophie, and you should never let them come close, not admit them. If they are not strand of your strand you are better alone, unless there is real love. Real love. People don't know how rare it is, thought Sophie. They think they love, but it isn't love.

"Not love," said Sophie aloud, and she looked at Little Lochinvar's back, his alpaca coat, his ears that showed the hooks of his glasses, the soft fur hair, as if she had not seem them before.

"I loved you," said Little Lochinvar, but she shook her head.

She put her hand on the rug and felt its richness. Love suffers extravagance and recklessness, cruelty. It suffers, it doesn't break off, she thought; and she said to Little Lochinvar, "If I were you I should go now."

"Yes," said Little Lochinvar and, without looking at her, he went.

ॐ

"Why have you put on that dress?"

It was the evening of a long hot day, the hottest, the most languorous they had had. It was still hot when Sophie called the children in for bed.

All day she had felt restless, excited. Sometimes the house, that day, had seemed to swell; the sitting room seemed as big as a ballroom, the garden as a park. Sophie had wanted to dance, to walk with big steps, swinging her arms, abandoning herself. At last, to calm herself, she had bathed and changed before she called the children. Teresa, coming in obediently, stopped at the sight of her.

"You are going out," said Teresa suspiciously.

"I'm not going anywhere, you little goose," said Sophie. "Where is there to go? I might go and walk by the canal. I can hear you if you call."

Teresa was not to be deflected. "Then someone is coming," she said.

"No one is coming," said Sophie. "Who is there to come as late as this?" And she commanded, "Now into bed with you."

Teresa was tiresome these hot nights. "Why must I go to bed so soon?"

"You know Moo won't go to sleep if you are not there," said Sophie.

"Children of my age go to bed at eight," said Teresa rebelliously.

"Eight is too late for Moo."

"Why is it worse for Moo to be up too late than for me to be too early?"

"Oh, *Teresa!*"

Teresa knew she would not have left Moo even if Sophie had allowed her. Moo made her sleep with one foot in his bed so that he knew she was there. It gave Teresa cramp in her leg, but she never took her foot away until he was asleep. By that time she was so tired and stiff that she was grateful to fall asleep herself. Reluctantly she went to bed, and Sophie went out into the garden. Now the garden did not seem so big; it was small. "Small!" said Sophie.

Her green skirts brushed the flowers as she walked. She looked down on the lake, but it was empty, as the garden was empty, the orchards and the fields and the mountain. "Empty, empty, empty," said Sophie. The words came back to her alone. She did not know where to put herself that night. In the afternoon she had had a strange attack of giddiness and nausea, and now she felt light-headed—light-headed, flirtatious, and silly, thought Sophie. Shall I go into Nishat and see if I can find some soldiers? Shall I go down to the lake and watch for a passing boat? She felt more than silly, she felt—"Brazen," said Sophie and tried to laugh.

In the flowerbeds were all the bright hot summer colours of zinnias, dianthus, marigolds. Their colours seemed to satisfy a need in her, and she hung over them. There was one clump of tall gold sun-daisies; as the sun set its flowers grew richer, and each shone like a ball of gold. The garden smelled of petunias, and there was a smell of hay-flowers from the canal fields where the villagers had been cutting the scanty late mountain hay. The smell gave Sophie a sense of nostalgia that matched the feeling she had from those old sad strange balalaika songs.

In this dress she had walked with Denzil, her hand on his arm. She could feel again the stuff of his coat, the hardness of his arm, but the voice that she heard was not his; it was Toby's, Lochinvar's—no one's she knew. It was—a man's, thought Sophie breathlessly, a—sailor's.

That made her stop. "Don't be silly," said Sophie to Sophie. "Because you have put on this dress, like a wraith—and the dress itself is faded— you let yourself dream. Be sensible," said Sophie. She left the garden and went up by the canal. Sultan and his friends stared after her as she walked past them through the courtyard, as if they had never seen her before. It's the dress, thought Sophie. How silly I am, masquerading.

By the canal, away from the sun, she felt quieter. What grounds have I for this masquerade? she asked. A little man who loved me has left me—which is right, thought Sophie. Letters have come from a man who loves me, but he is far away. And I have a message from an unknown sailor. She had to laugh. "At least I can laugh at myself, parading here by the stream, and no one to see me," she said.

The stream was white with poplar fluff that blew like cotton from the trees and floated everywhere. As she walked she could hear the servants' voices and the old man singing; his voice seemed to pierce her and stir her intolerably. She left the path and, in the thin high-heeled shoes she wore, began to climb the mountain. There was a solitary little orchard far up it, and she made towards it. She saw herself, a ridiculous small lonely figure, toiling up. She reached the orchard, and there, under the almond trees, she saw a figure sitting on the wall. It was Nabir Dār.

Sophie had a shock of almost unbearable disappointment. Whom had she expected to see?

Nabir was alone, looking out over the lake; his figure looked more lonely that Sophie's. From here they could still hear the voices, the soft singing. What was there in this Nabir that made him do as she did— most of the time at any rate, thought Sophie—choose to be lonely? He seemed to bring her into steadiness.

It was the first time she had seen him since the beating, but though he stood up when he saw her and moved aside, he looked at her without resentment.

"Don't go," said Sophie. "You were here first." Nabir looked at her. Now he was not a servant he could appreciate Sophie's courtesy. She was not like most Europeans, who spoke to the Kashmiris as if they were other creatures, not people. He stayed.

It was so quiet on the road below, two miles or more down, that they could hear the hoofbeats of the tonga-ponies going home along the lake road, the sound of calls, of paddling, of a net-splash. The gardens, Shalimar, Nishat, Chashmishai, were closing, and now the lake was dotted with a few boats going home. From the village came evening sounds, children calling the cattle, women calling the children. Smoke went up from the fires, and dusk was coming.

"Can you see your house?" asked Sophie.

Nabir pointed with his thumb. "The one at the end."

"It looks like a good house," said Sophie politely. "Do you live there with your wife?"

"I have no wife," said Nabir as he would have said, I have no furniture in my house. After a moment he said, "I have a little niece."

That is as near as they will get to him, thought Sophie, and she wondered again that he should be so—proof, thought Sophie; aloof, almost austere, like a young priest but without coldness; an angel, thought Sophie, and had to laugh. She knew Nabir was no angel. He is *shaitani*, thought Sophie—like me.

She was suddenly and deeply conscious of how she was dressed, of Teresa's suspicion, and she tingled with shame. She thought of a small pariah bitch in season she had once seen running in the moonlight. How did that fit with Nabir's conception of a woman as something with which to furnish his house? With the worship of Little Lochinvar had given her? With those gentle, balanced letters from Toby? And with more than that, thought Sophie; with the mother she would want for Teresa and Moo? With Denzil's widow? With the aunts' niece? With the high-principled follower of stars? She had a feeling that Aunt Rose would understand. From the rest she turned away, hot with shame, and yet—That little bitch is there in all of us, thought Sophie; in every woman, and she will not be denied. And if circumstances are beyond your control—? She had always said she did not believe in such circumstances, but she knew now there was something pressing on her that was stronger than herself, and she thanked God it was Nabir she had met that night.

154

She could see the house roof down below among the trees. Dhil-kusha—"Heart's Gladness." Heart's Gladness! thought Sophie. Cross-currents, crisscrosses, pricks, and little stabs—hundreds of threads fastened into me, she thought, pulling me this way and that, and these strange storms and stresses. If a heart can stay glad through that it's a strong heart, thought Sophie wryly, and suddenly she thought, startled, Is that what it means? Is that what we are meant to learn?

Nabir was speaking. "If the mem hasn't told Sultan Mahomet or Ghulam Sheikh to order winter wood," said Nabir, "it is time the mem-sahib did. Later on wood will be very expensive."

"Yes, I must think of it," said Sophie. "And I must buy some apples."

"The ones on the second terrace are best," said Nabir, and they dis-cussed these quiet things for a few moments.

When the winter comes, thought Sophie—and almost she longed for that bleak, hard time—I shall feel well again and I shall be much better. This winter we really *shall* settle, Sophie vowed silently. I shall work hard, and we shall save and pay for the rug. I shall get ready a herb stock for spring. Teresa *shall* go to the mountains next year, and I shall do as *The Wise Teacher* says and teach her steadily. Everything will settle down then, Sophie was thinking, when Nabir said, "The memsahib is cold."

Sophie looked down at her arms and saw she was goose-fleshed. At the same moment a chill went over her and she had a cramp. Then she grew giddy and began retching as she had done that morning. She saw Nabir step back as she stood up from the wall. She managed to take two steps to an almond tree and, holding to it, was sick on the stones. She had not been as sick before, and when it was over she was left limp and exhausted, holding to the little tree that kept her from falling. The orchard tilted in front of her eyes; the ground seemed to lift; and there was a singing in her ears. She thought she lost consciousness for a moment. When the orchard settled again she found that Nabir was steering her to the wall, holding his shawl between himself and her so that he should not directly touch her. She sat down, shivering, the ground swaying away from her. "Don't be frightened," she said. "I have been like this lately. It is the heat." Nabir left her. Have I sent him away? Was I rude? she thought, but presently he was back again with a napkin and a bowl of water.

"I took them from the house while they were talking," he said. "They talk and don't watch. Thieves could get in." Sophie drank a little water and wetted her face; then Nabir poured the water over her hands and handed her the napkin on which to dry them. He looked worried and concerned—sullen, thought Sophie. Why sullen? she wondered giddily.

A strange feeling was in Nabir. All his instincts, all his upbringing, told him that he ought to rejoice that the mem, who had had him disgraced, was in trouble. It revenged him, but still he could not rejoice. Why? He did not know, and this inner struggle made him sullen. No one had told Nabir to beware of pity—perhaps because no one had ever thought he would feel pity—but now he looked down on Sophie's shrinking, trembling figure and, unwillingly, he felt her trouble and he looked more and more bad-tempered.

"Do you think that I have—taken the heat?" asked Sophie. She did not know how to say "heatstroke" in Urdu. She looked up and found that Nabir's eyes were fixed on her with extraordinary concentration; she felt them examine her, probe her, search, and as they looked they grew alarmed. His cheeks went red, and he gave her the shock that had been waiting for her all evening.

"Why, Nabira," said Sophie, "what is it? Why are you looking at me like that? What do you think?"

"I think," said Nabir, "I think they are giving you charras."

Chapter 16

Charras. The word stayed in Sophie's mind. Charras. That is Indian hemp. She had been told many sinister stories of it— fantastic stories, thought Sophie. Yet, as she thought of them, she supposed that they were true. But given to me? Nonsense! thought Sophie. All the same she fetched her medical dictionary from the still-room and looked it up.

"Charras. *Cannabis indica*; Indian hemp; chang; ganja; marijuana," she read. Marijuana! That is the drug they are making such a fuss about in Europe and America. Marijuana. It's dangerous, thought Sophie.

"Produces hallucinations," she read, and smiled wryly. "Small doses give exhilaration, followed by lethargy. Increasing doses, erotic and other visceral impressions are experienced, with resulting numbness and loss of power. Finally stupor, coma, and even death."

"Nonsense," said Sophie, but she said it slowly. Nabir had given her a shock.

"A shock," said Sophie. That was it, a shock. That was why she felt suddenly so tremulous. Is it to be wondered at? she thought. I am not well and have been wandering on the mountain, dressed up. "You have eaten no lunch, no tea," she said severely to herself. "Do you wonder you feel light-headed, have hallucinations?" She wished very much that she had some brandy, something to warm and strengthen her. Perhaps I should eat a little something, she thought.

Her supper tray was on the table. Sultan's cooking was never very inviting, and now Sophie looked at it and shuddered; but there was some apple, pulped fine, in a glass. That is soft and harmless; apple is good for bad stomachs, she thought. I can eat that.

The dictionary said nothing about sickness or dysentery. And I think that is what I have, thought Sophie—a quite bad attack of dysentery. I must go on treating myself. Then she looked at the dictionary again. "If baked in food, such as bread, Cannabis indica can become strongly irritant. Sometimes mistaken, among ignorant persons, for St. Anthony's fire."

St. Anthony's fire! Wasn't there, thought Sophie, some newspaper story about a French village, when the people had suddenly run wild with fits of sickness and colic and horrible hallucinations? They said it was St. Anthony's fire. Then could a whole village have been given charras? "Now you are letting your imagination run away with you," said Sophie to herself severely. "Sit down and eat your supper." And she made herself sit down and eat.

To calm herself, drown thought, she tried to read the paper. "In the Delhi Assembly last night," read Sophie, "Mr. Asutosh Mookerjee insisted . . ." The print danced in front of her eyes. "Mr. Asutosh Mookerjee insisted . . ." But she never knew on what Mr. Asutosh Mookerjee insisted. This apple has a curious feel, thought Sophie, and she moved it on her tongue. It's gritty.

"It's gritty." For a moment she could not think who had said that before. Then Sophie sat up. It was Teresa. Teresa's apricot had been gritty.

Sophie looked at the apple, turning it over with her spoon, and there were the same grey-white specks in it. Queer, thought Sophie.

She took a little on her finger and held it towards the lamp, and one of the specks sent out a tiny gleam like a diamond. Salt doesn't do that, thought Sophie, not even rock salt. Sugar does, but sugar would melt. She tried a little on her tongue. It was tasteless—simply gritty. Then in her mouth she felt a sudden little prick, such an infinitesimal little prick that she could not be sure she had felt it, but she put the grit out. She touched her tongue with her handkerchief, and when she took the handkerchief away it had a speck of blood. Sophie looked at the blood and then again at the specks on the apple. One, which was big enough to see clearly, she took up with her finger, held it again to the light, and was sure. It was glass.

Glass. Glass ground up! Powdered glass! Sophie stared at it, alarm and bewilderment welling up in her until—I know what Sultan has been doing, she thought suddenly. He has kept that rat glass; I told him to throw it away. Kept it and muddled it up with the sugar. The careless little fool! She had started to call him when—"Twice?" asked Sophie. "Twice?" She sat down again in her chair. She was remembering the look on Sultan's face when she had spoken to him that night.

She gave herself a little shake. "You are having a bad dream," she said to herself. "You know you have been having dreams. But of course I have been having dreams if charras—Nonsense," said Sophie but it did not matter how firmly she said it; there were the little white specks. At last she picked up the apple and scraped it from the glass into a china pot she kept for sweets and put it high up on the shelf out of the children's reach. She put the empty glass back on the tray.

Sultan came in to take it. "Salaam!" said Sultan, in good night, at the door.

"Salaam," said Sophie quietly.

She sat where she was for a long time. Little words came up, scattered, broke in her mind. If—thought Sophie. Then—No. No! It couldn't be. But if—Then who? thought Sophie. Sultan? But Sultan would never dare—and why? Why? Why? *Why?* Nobody *hates* me! thought Sophie.

She took the lamp into the bedroom. The moon had come up, and moonlight was on the floor. It was so bright it showed the children's colours, Moo's blue and white pajama sleeve, their red and flaxen hair on the pillows, their cheeks flushed now with sleep; they looked innocent and happy and healthy, and Sophie's heart swelled. Whatever it is, if it is anything, it is only for me, she thought thankfully. Nothing has hurt them. Teresa didn't eat a morsel of the apricots. She put the lamp down on the dressing table and looked at herself in the mirror. Do the pupils of my eyes look big? She thought they did but she could not be sure. Perhaps they always looked like that. There were beads of sweat on her cheeks. She could have laughed hysterically, but she sobered herself. But—no one would do that to *me*, she thought. Nobody *hates* me, she thought again.

A year ago she would have panicked. Indeed, for a moment, crouched there by her dressing table, she thought how she and the children were alone, defenceless, ringed in by servants and villagers who had become suddenly hostile. We can't stay here tonight, thought Sophie hysterically, though how they could avoid it she did not know. "Shall I take the children and go—even if I have to walk?" She felt as if the top of her head were lifting; she could have screamed but forced the feeling down and swallowed it. "You have stayed here every night for months, safely," said Sophie to Sophie. "You can stay here now." "Shall I go for the water-works policeman?" the panic cried again. "The waterworks policeman is probably down in the village smoking with the barber, who is at the bottom of this trouble," said Sophie. She connected it with the barber from the start, just as any villager would have done.

I must think what I shall do, she thought, digging her nails into her palms to be calm. She would have sent for Little Lochinvar or gone to the Mission, but—After that scene I must keep away, she thought. She did not want to distress Dr. Glenister. In the end she decided that in the morning she must go to Sister Locke.

The thought of the dry little sister calmed her; the panic receded. I needn't even go, thought Sophie quietly. I can send in the apple and a specimen. In India dysentery troubles are so common that a lay person like Sophie is used to laboratory tests of excreta, and Sophie thought, I can ask her to have them tested without saying anything to anyone. If I have been given anything it will show, and that will be proof. "In the morning I shall send Mahomet to Sister Locke," she said. "Mahomet will be coming for his herb orders as usual, and no one will know. And I shall find I have dysentery and this was a carelessness of Sultan's tonight."

She was calm enough to go to bed and was so exhausted that, almost immediately, she fell asleep, but she woke early with a fit of retching and pain, and again she was sick. Then it is real, thought Sophie—or some of it is real. Dysentery does not make you sick. She dried her sweating hands and face and put on a coat and went downstairs, clinging to the banisters. I shall be better when I get into the air, she thought, and I shall wake the lazy Sultan and make him get me some tea.

On the veranda she rested, looking through the swinging vine where the grapes were big now and growing tender. The first light was in the garden; the lake glimmered; but the wicker doors of the fruit-pickers' huts were still closed. The scales and boxes were ready under a tree, but as yet nobody stirred.

Sophie called across the courtyard for Sultan. Sultan would not get out of his bed while the small Habib was there to answer calls, and Habib came, but Sophie's voice, as she asked where Sultan was, sounded so curt that Sultan decided to wake and appear.

"Bring tea," said Sophie, "and put your cap on straight and do up your collar." The words were peremptory, but she did not say them peremptorily; she spoke wearily, with her eyes closed as if she did not want to see Sultan.

There was a long pause. "Well? Bring me tea," said Sophie. She opened her eyes and saw Sultan looking at her with dismay.

"Do you—feel so ill?" asked Sultan.

"Never mind how I feel," said Sophie. "Bring tea."

She went into the garden. The first cows and goats were appearing on the hill; the herd children were bringing up the flocks; she heard whistles and cries. The children had not been in for their baskets for a long time. We need some picking done, thought Sophie; but what she needed picked she could not exactly remember. Thyme? King candle? With an effort she went to the wall to call.

The herd children, as they came by, did not seem to want to stop. Most of them hurried on or turned their heads away, but at last she saw Salim and Zooni and called them by name, and, reluctantly, they came. When she showed them the baskets they looked frightened and shook their heads, but she insisted. "Tell them," she said to Sultan, who had come to tell her that the tea was ready, "if they work for me at all, they must work when I want."

"These are Dārs. They do not want to work," said Sultan promptly. "Let me bring you Mustaph Sheikh. He will get you all the flowers you need."

"If Mustaph Sheikh comes near the garden I shall fine you," said Sophie. "I don't like that boy. He was cruel to his pony. Salima, come back," she called, and she spoke to Salim again, coaxing him, and finally, under the eyes of the Sheikhs, the Dār children took the baskets. Once again etiquette was broken. All day the Sheikh children hung round the house like a cloud of angry little hornets.

৵

Nabir knew how angry they were. In the night he had been troubled about Sophie; he had lain awake—an unprecedented thing for him to do—turning over in his mind what he had guessed. Charras? Opium? What are they giving her? "That is wicked talk," she had said, "and foolish. I have a heatstroke, that is all. I didn't think you, Nabir Dār, would make mischief." But though she had been angry with him, he thought she had taken fright. Surely, thought Nabir, she will go to the doctor sahib; but he knew how obstinate Sophie was. He thought of fetching Dr. Lochinvar himself, but he had not the temerity. He thought of going to the pundit, but he had no proof. All night he pondered, but in the quiet and sense of the morning he decided to go up and work in the small high orchard where he had sat last night. It was his uncle's orchard, Nabir could go there. I shall go out of the way, thought Nabir. There is nothing I can do—and he shrugged. He felt he wanted to be quit of them—the villagers, Sultan, St. Nicholas, the children, Sophie, all of them—but his way up the mountain lay past Dhilkusha, and from habit, while he was so abstracted, he looked in Sophie's box for letters. He looked, and his face darkened. The box was full of faeces.

Is the feeling like that? thought Nabir, stunned. As bad as that? What ugliness had Sophie stirred up? His face hard, he took the box and smashed it and threw it into the bushes. That night he meant to see the bigger herd boys, Dārs as well as Sheikhs, and smack their heads for them—kick them. He stood on the path, weighing what he had seen. Perhaps I had better go to the pundit, he thought; but the pundit would have a fit of nerves. Nabir was still there, filled with ugly foreboding, when Mahomet came running down the path.

"Where are you going?" asked Nabir.

"To the Mission," said Mahomet. "If I hurry I can catch Aziz' tonga."

To the Mission! Then she had sent to the doctor. Nabir felt infinitely relieved and he went on up to the orchard with his spade and shawl and bundle of food.

༄

When she had packed Mahomet off, seen to the children, and done the house tasks, Sophie made herself go into the stillroom and work at her herb orders, but she was very slow and stupid. In this hot weather

162

everyone slept in the middle of the day; Sophie had been so slow that she had to stay awake and work again.

It was so hot that Teresa and Moo slept heavily. Everyone was asleep. House, garden, fields, the mountain, lay quiet. The herd children slept under the rocks; the field-workers had gone into the orchards; in the garden the fruit-pickers lay under the trees, their caps pulled over their eyes to keep off the flies; the servants slept in the servants' house; even the cats, even Louis and Bliss, lay curled and limp, and the lambs, big now, lay stretched in the shade with the little grey goat. Only Sophie toiled, her face clammy with sweat, though she was in the cool stillroom; her shirt stuck to her back, she felt unutterably tired and ill.

At three o'clock the postman came, grumbling because there was no box on the tree. "Of course there is a box," said Sophie.

"Your honour, there is not—and in this hot sun! My legs!" said the postman.

With the newspapers and a postcard for Teresa from the aunts was a letter from Toby and one from Profit David, enclosing his bill. "Seven hundred rupees," wrote Profit David, "and one hundred and eight rupees, annas six, owing from before."

Eight hundred and eight rupees. Sophie had worked all day, packing, mixing, and perhaps she had earned ten or twelve rupees from herbs that had already cost her their picking and drying. How can I pay? she thought with a catch in her breath. How can I pay?

On the table, with the letters and Sophie's bill forms and writing paper, was a little packet of loose papers written in Sultan's familiar hand. Every week he wrote the house bills, sometimes calling in the village letter-writer to help when they became too complicated. Sophie had seen the two of them that day, writing and calculating outside the kitchen door, with a stone as a table. She read:

Bred	4 annas
Mikl	12 annas
Saltspis	2 annas

Salt and spice used to be one anna, thought Sophie quickly and crossed it out. Then she had to laugh, though it was a laugh without funniness. Here she was, worrying about annas, when she had spent eight hundred rupees. Her fingers played a moment with the pieces of paper, and then her head went down on them. "I have made such a terrible, terrible mess of everything," sobbed Sophie. Nothing, not even last winter, had been such a mess as this. Her fingers closed on Toby's letter. She had an overwhelming longing for Toby, his strength, the comfort of his presence. He seemed unutterably dear. "When will there be a chance of seeing you?" Toby's letter said. "My dear one, when are you coming home?"

"Oh, Toby! Toby!" sobbed Sophie. Toby had always rescued her. With a shaking hand she picked up her pen, and, almost without thinking, she began to write. Panic and sickness overwhelmed her, and "Toby, I'm frightened," she wrote. "Frightened. Oh, please come. Please come and take us away."

She had another attack of sickness and hat to run to the bathroom, leaving the letter on the table.

※

When Teresa and Moo woke, Teresa dressed herself and washed Moo's face and hands, sticky with heat, and put him in clean dungarees. He ran downstairs to find Rahim, and she came thoughtfully down after him, carrying her hat. She had meant to take Pussy Maria for an airing in the garden, but now not only was the pucker on her forehead, but her face was ugly with worry and thinking.

She could hear Sophie in the bathroom. Sophie was getting ill again—ill again, thought Teresa, and for a moment she had to lean against the banisters and shut her eyes.

"But sometimes she is unkind to you," Sister Locke said afterwards, trying to probe Teresa's love for Sophie. "She is unkind."

"She isn't," said Teresa loyally, and then she said, her voice warm, "If she is she doesn't mean to be." She tried to find words for Sophie's love and kindness. "You don't know how kind she is. Why once everyone used to laugh at Pussy Maria. They said there wasn't any such name. They *laughed*," said Teresa, hurt. "Then one day Sophie found in the newspaper that a Miss Pussy Maria Pereira was going to be married. She cut out what it said and gave it to me. Then I could show there was such a name."

Now Teresa went down the last steps and into the stillroom, and there on the table she saw what Sophie had written—"I'm frightened." Teresa looked at the words until they seemed to be cut into her. Never, never had she known Sophie to be frightened. For a moment Teresa stood there as if she were mesmerized; then she ran upstairs to the bedroom. Sophie was lying on the bed, her eyes closed.

"Mother," said Teresa, her throat dry.

"Terry, could you give me a glass of water?" Sophie hardly ever called Teresa "Terry"—only in moments of great trouble. Teresa's heart began to beat hard. She brought the water, not spilling it even in her anxiety.

She took a handkerchief and dipped it in and wiped Sophie's face. "Lie still," she said authoritatively.

"I shall be—better in a moment," said Sophie and shut her eyes.

Teresa took the glass of water away and went back downstairs. In the stillroom she paused, looking at the letter.

After a moment she took an envelope and, copying the address from Toby's letter, she addressed it. She did not know his surname, so put "Dr. Toby." Sophie had not begun or ended her letter, and Teresa did that for her. "Dear Toby," she wrote in her round hand that was a little like Toby's own—she could spell "dear" now. Then came Sophie's writing. Teresa did not know how grown people ended their letters to one another but she was aware that they did not put "With love from" as she did herself. She copied one of the letters on the herb table. It was from a chemist in Bombay. "Yours faithfully, Sophie," wrote Teresa and put the letter into the envelope and closed it. There were stamps on the table and airmail labels. Teresa had often stamped Sophie's letters and she knew very well what to put. She stamped it and went out. The postman had just come out from the kitchen, where he had been lingering over tea. "A letter from the mem," said Teresa and gave it to him. She watched him go down the path, and, well content, went to look for Moo and Rahim.

᠄ᴥ

"Mother, where is Moo?" Teresa, as she ran into the stillroom, was so worried that she forgot to ask if Sophie was better. "Where is Moo? Where is he?" she said.

"Isn't he in the garden?" asked Sophie, wiping her forehead.

"No. I am sure he is out with Rahim."

"Then he is playing."

"But they have gone *out*. He is with the herd children. I know he is! Oh, *Mother!*" The panic in Teresa's voice irritated Sophie, and she gave Teresa a good scolding.

"The herd children are *children*, children like you," she said. "It's absurd, this fear—a big girl like you. It's morbid. It's unhealthy. Don't be such a little coward." In her own upset she spoke very sharply. "I won't have it. You make Moo into a baby."

"He is a baby," said Teresa desperately, but Sophie would not have that either. "The worst thing you can to for Moo is to fuss over him like this," said Sophie. "If you go on about the herd children I shall buy a cow and send you up on the mountain to keep it with them." She saw Teresa turn pale and swallow, and she softened. "How can you be so silly, Terry?" she said. She had called Teresa "Terry" twice. That shook Teresa's nerves still more.

"Terry, how can you be so silly?" Sophie came to her and put an arm round her and began, "When you were born they brought you in to me. You had a little feather of red-gold hair on your forehead . . ." The tale went on, but Teresa was suddenly too familiar with that little red-gold, sparrow-speaking child, and she knew that she detested her. Tears pricked her throat and her eyes, but she would not speak or move. She stood proudly in the circle of Sophie's arm, looking over Sophie's head, until at last Sophie let her go. "I'm disappointed in you," said Sophie. "I had hoped you were a brave girl."

"I'm not," said Teresa, her voice shaking.

"You must teach yourself to be brave," said Sophie. "You think Moo has gone out on the mountain with the herd children. Well, go straight up and look for him."

Teresa stood very still. She gave a frightened little squeak. The little timid noise made Sophie angry.

"Go at once!" said Sophie.

Teresa went out of the stillroom and across the courtyard. Through the window Sophie could see her go. At the bend in the path she did not turn to wave. Sophie could see her toiling up through the orchards, disappearing in and out of the trees, a small figure in a blue pinafore dress and one of the big cheap hats of chip straw, tied under the chin, that they both wore in the sun. She grew smaller and smaller, until Sophie lost sight of her. "I almost called her back," said Sophie afterwards.

After Teresa had gone, it was very quiet in the stillroom. Fruit-boys with heavy baskets passed through the courtyard, filling the market boxes with apricots, and the tally-keeper sat under a tree with his scales; Sophie could hear his monotonous counting. The last order was done, but a heap of rose-petals lay on a sheet on the table where St. Nicholas had laid them. They had to be pounded with sugar in the mortar to make rose-jam, but the scent of the petals was overpowering. Sophie lifted the heavy mortar onto the table, but weakness and drowsiness filled her. She pounded up some of the petals; then, exhausted, she sat down at the table where she had sobbed. She was too tired to move, to go on working, almost too tired to feel. The scent of the roses seemed to rise up all about her, filling the air. A fly buzzed, and its noise, near at hand, seemed to shut out the whole world. She put her head down on the table and went to sleep.

≈

She was roused by the rattle of teacups. For a moment she was dazed and then she knew that it was Sultan getting the tea. It must be late, thought Sophie. She sat up, stiff and aching, pushing her hair back.

I have slept a long time, she thought. She looked out. The apricot-pickers, the tally clerk had gone. The shadows were beginning to stretch under the trees; Sultan came through the hall and went upstairs with the tray. He is late himself, thought Sophie, looking at the light. It must be long after five o'clock. I must find the children. Then, all at once—Where are the children? thought Sophie.

But I have seen Moo, she thought suddenly. Yes, in her sleep she had seen Moo. He had gone into the kitchen and presently come back with a jam-jar tied with string, and she had known vaguely that he had some project. She stood stiffly up. Outside the sun lay on the garden; it was growing rich and deep in its light. It really is late, thought Sophie. They should have come in by now. She went out and listened. There was no human sound except from Sultan, who had come down to the kitchen— no sounds from the mountain, no voices on the clear air that would carry a sound for a mile. As she thought of that Sophie wondered again. Had she, in her sleep, heard a clamour that afternoon? But there were so many clamours—boys fighting, rolling one another among the stones, field-women quarrelling, men arguing and bargaining over the price of the crops. She had grown used to quarrelling, and fighting had been plentiful of late; now this silence felt odd. Then she saw several small baskets of herbs near the steps; the herd children had come and quietly put their baskets down and chalked their marks on the blackboard. They are learning manners at last, she thought, pleased.

She went through the courtyard, up to the back orchard terraces, and came out on the canal path under the poplar trees, where she had been last night, and there was Moo, down in the bed of the canal, which was dried now to a shallow stream and pools. Moo was breathing hard and holding a fish in his two hands, trying to put it into his jam-jar. The fish gave a wriggle, there was a small plop, and it was in the stream, swimming away as fast as it could go. Moo with his empty jar gazed after it.

"Where have you been?" said Sophie, climbing down beside him. "How dirty you are, and where are all your buttons?" She tried to do up his dungaree straps, which were trailing in the water. "Where is Teresa?"

Moo did not answer any of these questions. He gazed after his little fish; he still could not believe, after these hours of trying to catch it, he had lost it.

"Moo, where is Teresa?"

Vaguely Moo jerked his head towards the mountain. Sophie climbed up, out of the canal bed, and looked. On the mountain there was no sign of anyone.

"Moo, where is she?"

Sophie called. She went farther along the path and called. She took Moo and went back through the orchards; she went through the garden and the house. She began to be annoyed. Is she sulking? thought Sophie; but it was not like Teresa to sulk. Has she gone to someone's house? Down the village? To Nishat? I wonder, thought Sophie, if she has gone to Nishat to get me a surprise because I was cross. She might ask Amdhoo to give her a violet or a daisy in a pot . . .

At last she sent Sultan down to the village and St. Nicholas to Nishat while she gave Moo his tea. She got up continually and went to the window, or out on the veranda to call. "Teresa, Teresa." There was no answer.

Sultan came back quickly—Sultan was quite nimble—but "Miss Teresa not in the village," said Sultan. "Not on the road."

A long while after, St. Nicholas came in, shambling and puffing. "No. No baba."

She couldn't be hiding all this time, thought Sophie. She went onto the canal path again and called. Only the paradise flycatchers flew out of the poplars, surprised. She crossed the canal and walked along the mountain, looking, shading her eyes because the sun, low now, sent powerful rays over the rocks. She walked and looked, and looked and walked, and could see nothing.

Surely by now she has come in, thought Sophie, turning back. I expect this minute she is with Moo. Probably that idiot Sultan missed her in the village, if he ever went there. I won't scold her much, thought Sophie. I was a little too sharp this afternoon.

She was so tired that she saw what was not there. She thought she saw a figure and started towards it, but it was a rock. She saw someone move under a poplar tree, but it was a shadow. All round her the mountain rose, vast and silent. I think I dislike this mountain, she thought with a little shiver and crossed back over the bridge. Presently she was walking quickly through the orchards to the house.

"Teresa? Teresa?" She had been certain Teresa would answer, but only Sultan's voice came back. Sophie's heart seemed to turn over. Sultan and Moo were in the sitting room. There was still a little light outside, but it was dark in the house. Sultan had not lighted the lamp, and Moo was miserable and sleepy.

"Where is St. Nicholas?"

"Gone home."

"And you let him go? We might need him. Where is Habib?"

"He went to his mother."

Sophie was silent.

"Miss Teresa been gone many hours. I think she met with accident," said Sultan. His eyes were big with importance. "Many bad peoples are here."

"Don't be silly," said Sophie, cross in her fear. She stood there, thinking. Could she—might she—because I was cross—have gone to Sister Locke? She did not think Teresa could go all those miles, but a longing to hear the sister's voice, anyone's voice, filled her, and she told Sultan to get the house lights and put Moo into bed, and she took herself out of Moo's grasp. "No. You must be good. I'm looking for Teresa. I'm going to the waterworks shed to telephone." Moo howled bitterly, but Sophie went.

The shed lay about half a mile away in the direction of Srinagar. Sophie was very tired and she stumbled as she went along the canal path towards it.

Down below, across the lake, the far ranges of the mountains were tinged with red, but the lake itself was dark except for a reflected path of gold; a few last lonely little boats were going home across it. Up here trees and earth and stones were reddened, but already the shadows in the ravines were grey. Sophie did not like this dusk. She grew more and more frightened.

The policeman was at the shed. He had come on duty at six o'clock. No, he had not seen Teresa. He willingly let Sophie telephone; he knew he would get a rupee. It was an antiquated instrument, and it was only after what seemed like hours of winding and buzzing that Sophie heard the hospital clerk. She asked for Sister Locke. "Sister on day-leave. Away all day," said the clerk. "Back tonight."

Sophie asked for Dr. Glenister, but she, it seemed, had gone with Sister Locke. In the end Sophie had to wait while they fetched Little Lochinvar.

"Doctor Lochinvar?"

"*Sophie!*" There was none of the constraint she had expected in his voice. Instead it came back full of concern. "Sophie! Are you all right? Thank God! They brought me the package you sent in for Sister, and as it was marked 'Specimen' I opened it and sent it down. I have had the report from the laboratory, and I was coming out. Good heavens, Sophie! What—"

"Yes. Yes," said Sophie, interrupting him, "but—"

"This is a case for the police," cried Little Lochinvar, but Sophie broke in.

"Doctor Lochinvar, I know it's absurd, but is Teresa with you?"

He was checked. "Teresa?"

"I have lost her," said Sophie.

There was a shocked pause. Then his voice, level and medical—as when anyone was ill, thought Sophie—came back. "How long have you missed her?"

"She has been gone about six hours."

"I will come right away."

Sophie heard the seriousness of his voice. Was her trouble as bad as that? As she came out of the shed, after tipping the policeman, her legs felt so weak that she had to lean against the wall.

She has probably fallen and hurt herself, thought Sophie, broken a leg and can't move. Panic came up, but she pushed it down. "Concussion or a broken leg, nothing worse," said Sophie firmly to Sophie.

She crossed the canal again by a log bridge and came out on the mountain. The huge flank rolled away from her, the bare earth and rocks and iris clumps, dim now with shapes of rock-roses and stones and furze. She called, "Teresa, Teresa! Te-r-e-sa!" How could she find anyone here? A little speck of a child? "Teresa. Teresa." Her call came back to her, echoing back from the rocks, and nothing moved.

She walked on, looking, calling, and the rocks, only the rocks, gave her back her cry. She saw fresh goat droppings and some thrown-down handfuls of thyme; the herd children had been here, where she stood, this afternoon.

"Teresa. Teresa!"

She stopped. Something blue had caught her eyes. It lay among the stones; in the twilight its colour seemed to burn into Sophie. She went slowly forward and picked it up. It was the cuff of Teresa's dress, torn off.

Now she looked among the stones. She saw blood, and than a last gleam of sun shone on a wisp, a torn-out handful of hair; it was red. "Teresa!" said Sophie. "Teresa!"

Chapter 17

W hen Teresa had come out on the path beside the canal that afternoon she had seen a knot of boys up on the mountain, away on the right, on the other side of the canal. The herds were scattered, no one was looking after them, and she heard a shrill voice raised in argument, then another, then a scream, and a figure detached itself from the knot of boys and ran away. A stone hurtled after it. The figure fell and rolled among the stones, and she heard its shrill outcry. Then it got up and ran; by its smallness and its olive robe and the bright coral colour of its new cap she knew that it was Rahim.

He came running towards the place where she stood, and she ran over the log bridge, fearless in her fear, and caught him. His face was distorted with crying, and his nose was swollen and bleeding down his robe. He hardly recognized Teresa until she shook him. Then he gulped, "Moo Baba," and "Mustaph," and "Salim."

Teresa understood. The herd children had found Moo playing incautiously outside the garden with Rahim, probably up the mountain, and now they had got him.

Teresa's shoulders and legs turned cold. Here by the canal it was sunny and still, with only the dry sound of the poplar leaves and the sound of the shallow canal stream; there they were fighting. She turned to call Sophie, Sultan, St. Nicholas, all the powerful adult band, but she was a good way from the house, and now, from all over the mountain, boys were running—little boys in robes, big boys in coats, pink caps, white caps. The cows and goats were left to wander as after the boys came the girls, clutching their veils, their bracelets rattling; they stood on the fringe of the fight, hurling pebbles and stones and shouting abuse. "*Zinahook!* Bastard! Your mother was a donkey. *Zinahook!*" The knot grew thicker, and then Teresa heard an indignant screaming. It was Moo's voice, and the sound plummeted into her as if a bullet had shot her.

"Rahima, call the mem. Go and call the mem," she shouted to Rahim and began to run. Rahim scurried over the bridge to safety and then sat down on the path and sobbed. He had no intention of calling the mem, because she would probably scold. Rahim did not care for scolding, and he sat and sobbed and wiped his bleeding nose on his sleeve.

As Teresa ran the mountain seemed to run in front of her so that, no matter how fast she ran, there was always more. She slipped on the stones, she hit rocks and was caught in furze; her breath hurt in her chest and made a surprisingly loud noise. She could not make her legs go quickly enough, and the stones slipped under her shoes.

The knot of boys was in front of her. Now and again Moo appeared, jerked from one to another, his blue legs waving. They were not fighting Moo, they were fighting each other, but a girl threw a stone deliberately at Teresa; it hit her on the shoulder and made a sharp pain.

When she reached the boys, for a moment she stood still. They were jostling and fighting; she heard two heads crack together. Two boys fell, fighting and clawing, and fought on the ground like wildcats. Teresa hesitated; there were very many boys, and some of them were big. Then she heard Moo's furious howling, and all in a moment she grew hard and hot and she was not afraid. White with anger, she tore her way through the boys. She did not know how she could be so strong, nor did she care what she did. She stamped with her shoes on their bare feet—for the first time she was glad she wore shoes. She kicked and stamped and hit. They were so surprised by her onslaught that they let her through, and she reached Moo; he fell against her, holding her and sobbing. "Badmashes!" cried Teresa, which is to say, "Villains!" "Devils! Pigs! Dirty pigs! Children of pigs! Bastards. Shaitans!"

For a moment they did nothing. Then there was a loud angry murmur. Teresa, in spite of her fierceness and her command of language, was small; she had hurt them and insulted them, she was in the middle of them, and they began to bait her. The girls came crowding up; the girls were against Teresa, and the egged on the boys. Sophie and Moo were popular, but Teresa was unpopular. The herd children had always sensed she did not like them, and the schoolmaster was always holding her, a girl, up as an example to the boys.

Mustaph Sheikh put his hand round behind her and twitched off her hat from the other side so that she thought Salim Dār, with whom he had just been fighting, had done it. When she turned her head Mustaph pinged her neck with his nail. It was such a sharp little ping that it brought tears to Teresa's eyes.

"She's crying! Crying!" jeered Mustaph.

"I'm *not* crying."

The fact of having touched Teresa excited Mustaph. "Come with us," he jeered and pulled her as he had Moo.

"No, with us," cried Salim, pulling her back.

They all wanted to touch her, to feel this strange white flesh that they had so often looked at. Daveed pinched her. Sharp fingers held her arms and legs, and they pulled her backwards and forwards and sideways. Zooni darted in and pulled her hair.

"Don't," cried Teresa, and Mustaph pulled it harder. It was more fun to bait the aloof Teresa than to fight over the baby Moo.

Now Teresa began to be frightened. She had lost her hat. She was pulled and pushed, and almost at once it grew serious. The boys fell to fighting again, the Sheikhs with the Dārs, and now they began to fight over Teresa; and she became a rag doll, an Aunt Sally, a bone between angry dogs. Her feet would not balance on the rocks as the boys pulled her. She felt Moo's hold loosen and slip away. She shrieked, "Moo! Moo!" but the sound was lost. The fastenings of her dress tore open, and it was dragged off her shoulders. She saw the sky, then Salim's and Mustaph's faces, snarling as they fought each other. She fell, and the bad smell of a boy's coat was against her face. She was pulled up and pushed, stretched and shaken; fingers dug into her arm, and someone tore her ear so that she shrieked. Someone else tore out her hair, a big piece this time. The fighting grew fiercer; her mouth was pressed against wool, against flesh, against fern; she was thrown against rocks, bleeding, but still she struggled to keep her feet. Then someone hit her between the shoulders, and she went down. She saw a rock come up at her; it crashed black in her face, and she lay still.

⁊❧

Like a ball rolling out from a football scrum, Moo had come out of the crowd. Clutching his dungarees and sobbing loudly, he ran down the hill. No one was going to leave the fight or chase him, and they let him go.

When he reached the stream he stopped. He had seen something.

There was a pool, left when the canal dried to the small stream it was now, and in the pool was a marooned fish; it was a tiny trout escaped from the hatcheries at Harwan. Sobbing, his straps trailing from his broken buttons, Moo made his way down into the canal and squatted beside it.

The sun beat warmly on his shoulders; the stream ran peacefully; the little fish wriggled. Moo was always a detached child. Now the tears dried on his cheeks as he watched.

⁊❧

"Why doesn't she move?" asked Salim.

A strange silence had fallen on the herd children. They stood round Teresa in a silent throng.

Salim and Mustaph had seen, as they lifted her and swung her, that they were holding something still and heavy. She slumped between them, and, both together, they took their hands away. Teresa sagged and dropped on the ground and lay there. The fight was suddenly over.

They stood silent. Zooni crept forward and twitched down Teresa's skirts.

"Why doesn't she move?"

Her face had always looked strange to them, but now it looked stranger than they had ever seen it—white and purple and blue. One of her eyes had swelled so that it could not close; it gave her a strange fixed look of looking. "Aie!" cried a little Sheikh girl, Rahti, to Salim. "Aie! She is looking at you."

For a moment Salim hoped she was. He bent down and snapped his fingers and made encouraging noises, while Mustaph leaned over his shoulder to see, but Teresa did not move. Her eye did not blink, though the swelling slowly came up and hid it. Salim took a step backwards from her and clutched Mustaph's coat.

"Aie!" cried Mustaph, his cheeks paling. "Aie!" He backed away from Teresa, clutching Salim with him, and then, with one accord, the herd children turned and ran back to their flocks.

⁊❧

Late in the afternoon Nabir finished his work at the orchard. He had mended the walls with stones and cleaned the scrub away. The trees stood clear in dug ground with furze piled up against them for the winter. No one need touch them until the spring.

When he stood up he noticed it was strangely quiet on the mountain. It had not been quiet in the afternoon; he had heard the boys making an unholy din, but he was tired of their fighting and he had gone on working. Now he saw that the herds had gone down. Puzzled, he looked at the sun. It was no later than he had thought. He wondered what had sent them in. Has there been a real fight? thought Nabir. He picked up his spade and put it on his shoulder, took his sickle and bundle, and began to go down. He was halfway down when he almost stepped on Teresa.

Just as Teresa had been smitten with cold, by the canal, when she knew what had happened to Moo, now Nabir turned cold. His cap seemed to lift away from his head; the mountain seemed to run away from him in dizziness. He stood very still with Teresa at his feet.

Slowly he made himself bend down and look at her. Insects were running all over her, and a trickle of blood, coming from her ear, had dried on her cheek and on the stones, though it was still running. As Nabir bent down flies rose up from her. She has been there some time, thought Nabir. He, no more than Rahti, liked that swollen eye. Then his blood began suddenly to pound with relief; he saw that she was breathing.

He looked at her again and slowly stood up. Down below was Dhilkusha in the sun. Nabir knew quite well that he ought to take Teresa in to Sophie or fetch Sophie to Teresa; but for all his sense he was a village boy, and he did not dare.

He began to make excuses. I must get her out of the sun, thought Nabir; he knew the sun was dangerous to sick people. Carefully he slid his folded shawl underneath Teresa, without jerking her, and lifted her from the blood and the stones and carried her to the canal. I must wash the blood away before the memsahib sees her.

He had half an idea, half a hope, that the water in some miraculous way would heal Teresa, but even when her whole chest was wet the blood only ran faster, and her head rolled in a way he did not like. Nabir saw that he was making matters worse, and he began to panic. He thought he would hide her and go get his mother, who was clever with hurt things.

Nabir's mother had often mended a goat's leg, netting it with twigs and strings so that it was held in a stiff splint, and she sometimes cured abscesses. His mother or the barber, thought Nabir; the barber was very clever, even more clever than his mother. If they could make Teresa better before the memsahib saw her it would be a good thing. Nabir did not know what had happened, but he guessed, and he knew it meant trouble for everyone. I shall hide Teresa Baba and fetch help, thought Nabir. That will be best, and when she is better we can take her in. She is a good child. She wouldn't make trouble. She will be better soon.

In the high ravine, almost at the top, was the kiln that he had found. It was half tumbled down, unremarkable among the other stones. Nabir still slept in it sometimes and kept the bed of furze there fresh. Bending down, he carried Teresa in and carefully laid her down and pulled his shawl away from her. Why he took his shawl when he meant to come back, he did not know. He backed out and stood up, panting and shivering. In the whole might of the mountain the kiln looked a stone among its stones; it was very unlikely that anyone would find her there.

It was getting to be evening. A cool snow wind blew down the ravine; it touched Nabir and seemed to calm him. After a moment he bent down and looked into the kiln.

Teresa lay as if asleep. He could see the redness of her hair against the stones, and suddenly he hoped he had not hurt her as he pushed her in. Her dress was rucked up, and, like Zooni, he put out his hand and pulled it decently down. "I will be back soon," said Nabir, as if she could hear him, but the sound of his own voice frightened him and he quickly went away.

On the way down he began to feel he had done wrong. At the canal he stopped and wondered if he should not, after all, go to the house—but if he went to the house he would have, first of all, to go back and take Teresa out of the kiln. He was frightened to go to the house; he was even frightened to go down to the village. He knew how he had been frightened since last night, when Sophie was ill, more frightened since this morning. "Trouble. Trouble. Bad trouble," said Nabir. He hovered and waited. He went a little way back up the mountain, then came down again. His skin was wet and cold with sweat; the inside of his hands had marked the handle of his spade. He wished he could put on his shawl, but it had been under Teresa and he could not bring himself to put it on. At last, seeing it was almost dusk, he went home.

෩

"But *why* didn't you take her in? Why did you hide her?" asked his mother. "Why? Why? Why?"

"I don't know why," shouted Nabir. It made him feel better to shout. It made him feel a man again. He, who should have despised women, had gone straight to his mother like a child. He could not help it, he was frightened, but his mother only confirmed his fright. When he had told her what had happened she had gone livid and clutched the lobes of her ears to ward off evil; but they both knew the evil was here. "Why didn't you take her to the memsahib?" wailed his mother.

"You don't know the memsahib," said Nabir, surly with misery. His mother's scolding fell almost with happiness about his ears; Sophie's scolding rankled in his stomach. "She would have been angry," said Nabir simply.

"And won't she be angry now?"

"But if you and the barber—"

"The *barber!*" said his mother. "We should pay him to keep quiet the rest of our lives!"

"Then you come. You," said Nabir like a frightened little boy.

"And if they find us there with her?" asked his mother. Her eyes darted this way and that as she tried to think of something.

"I will go back and take her out," said Nabir, shivering.

"They will be all over the mountain themselves now," said his mother. Nabir had never heard her speak in this dull way; all the shrillness, the knife-edge of her voice was gone. "Aie!" said his mother in a long-drawn-out whisper. "Sultan Mahomet was here in the village asking for her. The memsahib knows she is lost. You stay here," said Nabir's mother, clutching him by the coat as he stood up. "You sit down. You know nothing about this. Nothing!" said his mother.

No one knew anything about it. As night came down Dr. Lochinvar's car drove out from Srinagar. He left it in the village. Soon they saw a light go to the waterworks shed. Lanterns bobbed backwards and forwards. Sultan came running to the village to fetch men. Lights went over the mountain, and then, as the moon rose, a lorry drove through the village and bumped to a standstill on the track below Dhilkusha, and soon the garden was alive with scarlet-peaked police turbans, which shone oddly in the moonlight. Policemen were beating the bushes with staves and searching along the canal. A police officer with a fringed end to his turban and a leather and brass belt and tall boots rode into the village on a motor bicycle. There was another at Dhilkusha in charge of the search, and a third, a chief inspector, in the blue and red turban of the Criminal Investigation Department, had set up a table in the courtyard under a petrol light and was having people up for cross-questioning.

The inspector questioned the children. "When did you last see her? And you? And you?"

"On the mountain." They all said that.

"Is she often on the mountain?"

A dozen voices assured him that she was often on the mountain.

"Can you think where she is?"

Quite truthfully they could assure him they could not. None of the herd children could think what had happened to Teresa. Had a devil or an ogre taken her? Had she turned into a ghost? Had the memsahib taken her into the house and hidden her and called the police to punish them? The children knew nothing, but on all their faces was the same wary look, and the Sheikhs and Dārs banded together in an odd way.

The mothers eyed their children thoughtfully. "You brought the herds down early."

"It was cold."

It was not cold, but the mothers accepted that it was cold. They took refuge in the fact that Nabir Dār had gone up this day to work at the orchard on the mountain, and Nabir Dār had been angry since the memsahib sent him away.

Now Nabir had gone up to join in the search with the other men; to stay away would have looked suspicious. Some of the women went up to watch, but Nabir's mother stayed down in the village with the more timid ones. Why, when she was not timid? There she was, standing in her doorway. When anyone passed she looked at them scornfully with furious eyes.

A few Sheikhs asked her, "Did your son finish his work at the orchard?"

"He did," said his mother.

"He was up there a long time."

"A place is not cleaned in five minutes," said Nabir's mother as if she wished the words would blister them.

The women in the village crowded the square, watching the lights. They were all terribly uneasy, and, in their way, they were sorry for Sophie. Their jewellery moved and clinked as they whispered.

"How did your Karim get that black eye?"

"He fell."

"And Raschid that cut lip?" "Torn coat?" "Rahti?" "Fathia?" "Abdul?" "He fell." "She fell." All these mysterious falls, and the herds had come down early! Once again the women fastened on Nabir Dār.

"Where is your son?" they asked his mother.

"Helping to look for the baba up on the mountain," said Nabir's mother.

They did not say he should know where to look, but that opinion was in the air.

Nabir felt it. He was very conscious of being watched, of the whispers.

All over the mountain were men with lanterns and flares; the glinting brass, the scarlet puggarees had a nightmare macabre look. When Sophie had first led the inspector and officers to the spot where she had found the cuff and Teresa's hair they had fixed a searchlight to a battery in a wooden box. Now the searchlight looked like another, whiter, ghastly moon under the moon.

"There has been a struggle," the inspector had pronounced. The herd children had looked at one another; it seemed as if he were reading things out of the ground with a horrible power.

"Here is more hair, but short black hair." Several eyes turned to Nabir. "A man's hair?" asked the inspector, looking up. "Here the earth is torn up," said the inspector, going on. "Here is blood." He had found a shred of woollen cloth, but it was the village homespun tweed, the same as any of them wore. If Nabir wore it there were a hundred others who wore it as well, but this time everyone looked at him. More and more clearly Nabir began to see what he had done.

The police asked Sophie, "Could anyone have a grudge against you? Have you had trouble with anyone? Was anyone dismissed?"

They had already been told the story of Nabir's beating and dismissal. Breathlessly eager, to anyone who would listen, Sultan, St. Nicholas, the Sheikhs told tales of him.

Nabir knew all this, but he did not know there was one worse question that the inspector had put to Sophie. "Was there anyone of whom the little girl seemed especially fond?"

Nabir was too simple to think of that. Teresa had had an exalted position, but to him she had always been a child like his own little niece. Everyone knew Teresa was fond of him and now that was added to the fact that Sophie had shamed him, that Nabir himself was stiff-necked and proud, and everyone in the village knew he had been up on the mountain that day.

"This, of the child, is of course connected with the other crime," the inspector said to Sophie.

"What crime?" asked Sophie. She had forgotten.

"Doctor Lochinvar has informed me," said the inspector. "In the laboratory they have found presence of charras, belladonna, and glass. At least your enemies were thorough!" said the inspector.

"*Belladonna!*" Even in this moment, that riveted Sophie's attention. "But that is—deadly nightshade. Poison!"

"And both are aphrodisiacs." Little Lochinvar's lips folded themselves into a thin line.

"An aphro—" Sophie's knees gave way, and she sat down at the table while the room swung round her. "Oh, no!" she said in a long whisper. "Oh, no! That is too hideous."

"It is hideous!" Little Lochinvar's voice was tense and cold with disapproval and disgust. "It's a mercy you found out in time."

"I am shocked! Shocked!" said the inspector.

Sophie supposed that she was shocked too, too shocked to feel. She had vomited again on the mountain, but now she scarcely thought of that, and as they looked hopelessly for Teresa even the shock was wiped from her mind.

It's strange, she was to think afterwards, that things that seem big are often, in the outcome, little; the little, big. Poison, that dreadful word, became almost nothing, a quarrel among children everything. Everything! Why talk about the crime? she thought impatiently. Why think of anything else but this? Teresa—Teresa. She watched the men's faces. Little Lochinvar's was impossible to read; it was set, completely medical, thought Sophie. The inspector talked with his officers. What does he *think?* cried Sophie silently. He gave no sign of what he thought; he went on with his work carefully and methodically—too methodically for Sophie's agonized impatience.

After an hour and a half he withdrew his men from the search and asked for tea.

"Tea?" said Sophie, bewildered.

"If my men are to search they must be comforted," said the inspector with asperity, and Sophie remembered that always, under any circumstances, etiquette demanded that there must be tea. "I will order trays for you," she said.

"No! No thank you!" said the inspector hastily. "We will make our own." And he said, half laughing, "I am afraid to take tea in this house."

All the same, the men took hot water from the kitchen, and tea and sugar and salt. Sophie told Sultan to ask the village bakers for kulchas, but already, in an intense propitiation, the villagers had brought food for the policemen. Sophie's quiet courtyard looked like a bivouac; the men had built a fire, their staves rested against a tree, the villagers ran backwards and forwards with tea, with rice and chupattis and luchis and fruit and sweets. Recklessly Sultan heaped Sophie's wood on the fire and gave out her salt, her cooking pans, her butter, sugar, and bread.

Sultan knew the police; if they wanted a confession they used their staves for beatings, they stamped on bare feet with their boots. Naturally anyone would confess anything in those circumstances—particularly Sultan, who was not brave. If they put anyone in prison it took much money to get him out, and Sultan had no money. All Sultan's importance and self-consequence were gone. He tried to make himself as small as he could. "I wish I had never seen the mem," moaned Sultan.

While the men had tea Sophie left Little Lochinvar in the sitting room and wandered into the bedroom where Moo lay asleep. He was made so pale by the moonlight that he looked like a child ghost. His hair shone silver, but when Sophie touched him his flesh was warm, and he breathed warmly and sweetly. He made movements with his hands as if he still caught the little fish, and for the hundredth time Sophie saw Teresa as she had gone up through the trees in her blue pinafore and big hat. She went so slowly because she did not want to go, thought Sophie; because she was afraid, and I sent her—out to what?

She could not bear to be still and she came downstairs and went out on the veranda. This waiting, this doing nothing while the tea-drinking went on, was one of the hardest things she had to do that night; it seemed interminable. Somewhere, out in the moonlight, was Teresa— Teresa lost, hurt. Sophie caught her breath if she thought further than that. And they drank tea and gossiped, even made jokes and laughed. When she heard the laughter Sophie had to dig her nails into her palms.

She saw that Nabir was standing at the foot of the steps; he kept looking behind him, his face quite senseless with terror. She had never seen Nabir look afraid before. She called, "Nabira," and he looked up at her. It was a long look, and now his face was filled not with terror but with—pity? asked Sophie, shrinking. No more than she had seen him look afraid had she seen Nabir pity anyone; it frightened her. What does he know? she thought in panic. He took a step towards her. He is going to tell me something, thought Sophie, shrinking, but the peaked turban of a policeman showed in the bushes; Nabir saw it and abruptly turned and went away, and Sophie heard the inspector's voice behind her. "Madam, we resume to search."

"That man, Nabir Dār, knows where she is," said Sophie. I have to say that, she thought, but she felt as if she were giving him away. "He knows." But the inspector was not excited.

"I think so too," said the inspector.

"Then ask him. Ask him. Make him tell! *Force* him," cried Sophie.

"Wait," said the inspector. "Wait. He will tell."

The search began again. Sophie watched from the canal path. Her hair was sticking to her forehead; her face was clammy; her dress was stained with dew and mud and her feet bruised with stumbling on the stones.

Searchers had gone as far away as Harwan. Nishat had been opened. They had gone to every village along the lake, looked in every house, questioned every person.

The inspector had asked Nabir two questions. When Nabir came in front of him he had looked at Nabir for a long time. "What is that on your shawl?" he asked.

Nabir looked at his shawl and saw that it had dark stains on it. He had never seen them before. Puzzled, he stared down at them, and then he knew that when Teresa had bled so copiously down by the canal she had bled on it. He put out a finger and touched the spots. They were quite dry. Of course, it was a long time ago, thought Nabir dizzily. He felt as if the moment was still here. "What is that?" asked the inspector hectoringly.

"Blood," said Nabir. He could not deny it.

"How did it get there?"

Nabir saw he must say something—but not that, thought Nabir. Not how the blood got there. Desperately he searched his mind for something to say. Then, "From this," he said and held out his wrist; there was a mark on it where a sharp end of wood had glanced off his axe a few days before and cut him. The flesh was still seared and swollen, only half healed. He hoped that it would do, though until that moment he had forgotten it. The inspector looked at it.

"That is old," said the inspector.

"So is the blood on the shawl," said Nabir.

The inspector let him go; nor did he ask him any more questions.

That frightened Nabir more than anything. He knew the inspector had examined Sultan, St. Nicholas, Habib, the pir, the barber, the schoolmaster. All the Sheikhs and Dārs had been seen, every villager, and still he, Nabir, had not been sent for again; but he knew that he was watched. A special little group of nimble policemen followed him unostentatiously everywhere he moved.

He began to move and talk to people with elaborate unconcern, but the inspector's eye was always on him, the scarlet puggarees and staves were always nonchalantly near him. His fear was beating in his head, and his mind began to behave like a little animal, darting this way and that to find a hole and escape. Soon he chose the wrong hole, as the inspector knew he would.

He went to one of the policemen. "There is a place," he said. "I have just remembered. It is higher still."

"Would she go as high as that?"

"What place?" That was his enemy, Guffar Sheikh, jeering.

"Nobody knows it but I," said the simple Nabir, and, with the beating becoming suffocating in his head, he led them to the kiln.

Chapter 18

Sophie did not resist when Little Lochinvar took them to the Mission. They went in his car. Moo had objected violently to being woken, but soon he was wide awake, sitting in front, while Sophie and the inspector were behind with Teresa, who was strapped and bandaged and wrapped in blankets, lying on the board they had made into a stretcher across their knees. Sophie found Teresa's hand under the blankets; the other, with the fingers broken, was strapped across Teresa's chest. The chill and limpness of the small hand she knew so well, that she had often held so carelessly or shaken off, seemed to creep slowly over Sophie and into her heart.

"Is she much hurt?" she had asked Little Lochinvar.

"Yes," said Little Lochinvar.

It was terrible to Sophie that it was such a violent going; a police car went in front, and behind, swaying in a lorry where they were made to stand, shackled together, were Nabir and Sultan. The procession had driven quickly through the moonlight to the city. The drivers, catching the excitement, had made great play on their horns, and in the villages along the road people who had been asleep ran out, shocked by the din; goats, sleeping in the road, started up and were scattered; the sound of crying from frightened children followed the car. In the moonlight it all had a nightmare brightness; for the rest of her life Sophie could not see moonlight again except as horror.

A young missionary and his wife had been staying in the familiar rooms of the Hutchinson Wing, but they moved out into camp. "That is good of them," said Sophie numbly as she and the children moved in.

"At a time like this they could do no less," said Dr. Glenister, and again Sophie felt, through her dazedness, the fear that she had felt when Little Lochinvar had answered her on the telephone. Is this as bad as that? she had thought. It was a little time before she realized how bad it was.

For the first few days she could think only of Teresa. "The baba has that look on her face," said Ayah. Ayah was back, grumbling, scolding, and predicting, but it was now Sophie who had to listen to her tales. "Sunset is the dangerous time," said Ayah with relish, and when five or six sunsets had come and gone—Sophie had lost count of time—and Teresa, though unconscious, still lived, Ayah changed and said, "Even if she doesn't die, with a knock on the head like that she will be simple. My cousin's wife's brother was hit on the head by a rice-boat paddle when he was young. Now he never speaks, and his face is all on one side."

Teresa looked now as if her face were all on one side. She lay, her eye and ear swaddled in bandages; the other eye, when they lifted the lid, seemed lifeless, without movement. "It's only because she is concussed," said Little Lochinvar, but Sophie could not look at it. Teresa's whole body was bruised and cut; two ribs and the fingers of her right hand were broken. Her arm was strapped to her chest, with the fingers splayed on a board. She had not recovered consciousness. "There is surgical emphysema and haemothorax from the fractured ribs," said Little Lochinvar. "We must wait and see."

Sophie and Sister Locke nursed her.

"But you yourself must go to bed," Dr. Glenister told Sophie.

"No," said Sophie. Her lips shut.

"We have to get rid of all this stuff in you, dearie. There is danger of perforation. I can't treat you while you are up and about."

"You must," said Sophie.

"I can't be responsible—" began Dr. Glenister.

"I am responsible," said Sophie, interrupting. Then her voice broke. "Responsible for everything," she said. As the numbing effects of the drugs wore off, she began to understand the full implication of what had happened.

"You will have to appear in court," Dr. Glenister told her gently. In these days it was Dr. Glenister who broke news to Sophie; it seemed as if Little Lochinvar could not bear the sight of her.

"In court?" asked Sophie. "But—I haven't charged anyone."

"You don't have to," said Dr. Glenister. "The state charges them."

"The state?" asked Sophie, startled. Slowly she became aware that in this she was not only herself, nor was Teresa; they were citizens, part of a sate, a country, a law. They, equally with Nabir and Sultan and the villagers, were caught in what had happened.

There was no escape.

"Who will be charged? With what?" asked Sophie, but she had really no need to ask; she knew. Sultan and Nabir were in prison, waiting for trial; Dhilkusha was closed; the whole village was under cross-examination. The barber and the schoolmaster had been brought in for questioning—even the pundit.

"*Not* the pundit!" said Sophie, shocked.

"Most certainly," said the inspector. "You had put the house in repair. It was finished, and you were living there for very little rent. He had every reason for wishing you gone."

"But he *didn't* wish us gone. He liked us," cried Sophie. The inspector shrugged, and Sophie, white and sick, imagined how outraged the pundit would be, the fits of nerves he would suffer, and how he would twitch and pale and tremble. "Oh, no!" she said. "Oh, *no!*" He will never get over it, never, and all because of me! *Not* the Pundit Sahib," she pleaded with the inspector.

"Madam, I must remind you that this is a case of attempted murder," said the inspector. "It is a grave thing. It may be graver. If your child dies it will be murder."

Sophie was silent, too sick to speak.

One of the most terrible things to her was the publicity of the case. She had to see the English resident and the assistant resident, Mr. Pye; the Kashmiri officials, the chief of police, the state chief medical officer. She could have borne that—they were, after all, doing their duty—but she could not bear the talk, and there was talk all over Srinagar and Gulmarg, especially among the European residents and visitors. It was not that they were not kind. Inquiries flowed into the Mission, offers of help, even gifts. "But—I don't know these people now," said Sophie, bewildered. She might have added that when she had known them she had not been very polite to them, she had kept away from them and despised them; the kindness brought that sharply back to her, and it did not hide the division she had made between them. There was a feeling of

"I told you so" in the air. Sophie was very proud and she could imagine everyone saying, "Well, she was always odd. There *is* something odd about anyone who lives away like that." There was curiosity too. "Did you live out there in native fashion?" asked Mr. Pye. Sophie felt he would have said "Live like a wog" to anyone else.

"I lived in my own fashion," she said stiffly.

"Hm!" said Mr. Pye. "In a strange country it's better to conform, no doubt about that. People ought to hang together in a place like this; there is always trouble if they don't. We don't want trouble. Our position is difficult enough in a Native State." He made it clear that people thought Sophie had "let them down." After all, you *are* English, Mr. Pye would have said.

"Then why don't they ostracize me?" Sophie cried. "Why, why are they so kind?" she said, smarting, to Dr. Glenister.

"At a time like this," said Dr. Glenister, "we white people should band together. We know we are only a handful in an alien place."

There was something so fanatical in the way she said this that Sophie stared at her. "But it isn't a question of white people against dark," she said slowly. "And Kashmiris are not dark anyway. They are as fair as we are. It isn't that."

"We don't know what it is," said Dr. Glenister. Her voice had risen, and her eyes behind her glasses glittered. This was wise, tolerant Dr. Glenister, and Sophie remembered how the gentle Sister Pilkington had said as she undressed Teresa, "They ought to be shot like dogs! Like dogs!"

She knew that Ayah had been telling hideous tales. "Ayah, nothing, *nothing* was done to the baba—except her wound-injuries," said Sophie. She did not know what else to call them. "You know the doctor sahibs made a careful examination."

"Doctor sahibs!" said Ayah scornfully. She knew better than a hundred doctor sahibs. Sophie expected tales of Ayah—but "We don't know what might have happened," said Dr. Glenister, and she said in a sinister voice, "We don't know what did."

"If it had been a sexual crime," said Sophie (she called things by their proper names, she hated the cloaking and whispering, but she could hardly bring herself to say this) "—a crime like they say, I should have felt it. I—" she began indignantly. Then she was suddenly silent. She was remembering those hot summer nights, the singing, the lotus dream. Could there have been something actual behind it? "Oh—no!" said Sophie again but in a whisper. "No!" But she had to say, "There might have been."

She hid her face in her hands, and Dr. Glenister came and put a hand on her shoulder. "Dearie, don't, don't dwell on it." Sophie did not know what made her answer, "I have to dwell on it," and take her hands down from her face and sit upright.

Through all the speculations and questions and exclamations she had increasingly the feeling that this was not as people said. She seemed to see Nabir's face as it had been when he looked at her in the bivouac fire-light. He would have told me, she thought, if he had not been afraid. She saw the silly, clumsy, vainglorious little Sultan, the pundit, the villagers. Like the eyes of the cows, Portia and Mamie in the picture, they seemed to follow her, puzzled, asking, while Nabir, like Aunt Rose, looked disdainfully away. If only my head didn't feel so stupid, she thought. If I could only think. And "I *must* dwell on it," she told Dr. Glenister, and she said slowly, "It is my duty."

"But, dearie, they hurt you terribly."

Have you a duty to those who hurt you? Surprisingly the answer seemed to be that you had. If Sophie shrank from that answer, that did not take the duty away.

"Who is at the bottom of this noxious crime?" the inspector said. He came every day; his smart uniform, the polished boots, the handsome peaked turban with its long hanging scarf had become familiar. He was very zealous; this was the first case he had been given to handle on his own, and it promised to be sensational. "This noxious crime," he said, but "Is it noxious?" asked Sophie slowly.

"*Madam!*" The inspector looked shocked. He plainly thought her lacking in feeling.

It was strange for Sophie, who always made the ordinary extraordinary, to be entering on a battle to make the extraordinary ordinary, but a feeling of truth came to her each time she tried. She could not put this feeling into words but she knew this was one time when her mind must not be coloured, not give way to panic.

It was hard not to. The very words were melodramatic—charras, ground glass, aphrodisiac, assault, prison, victim, manslaughter, murder. Sophie heard them all, and Teresa lay hour after hour, with no change, no sign of life but the bare breathing. For herself Sophie could think temperately, but for Teresa she felt such fear and anger and remorse that she was lost. "But I did it, I—I," she insisted to herself. "I brought it on her."

"Sophie omits the effect," Aunt Rose had said. This time Sophie could not omit it; she was caught in the effect.

"And the worst of the punishment is," Aunt Rose had said, "that you punish someone else."

&

Even with all the publicity, Sophie was not prepared when Dr. Glenister said one day, "Dearie, I think you should cable your people at home, your aunts."

"I—I was waiting to see how Teresa—" began Sophie.

"I know," said Dr. Glenister. "But you don't want them to read it in the papers."

"The papers?" asked Sophie, bewildered. "How would the paper know?"

"There are press reporters in Srinagar like everywhere else," said Dr. Glenister. "They have been here. One came yesterday. Doctor Lochinvar tried to put them off, but it must come out."

It had come out; before Sophie had time to cable the aunts, Ayah brought her a cable. It was a cable of distress and alarm, signed by all three of them, even Aunt Rose. Aunt Rose! thought Sophie. That impressed her. The cable ended with five words that were, to Sophie, cryptic. "Thank God Toby has left."

"Has left"? Sophie puzzled over that. Were the aunts trying to spare him—concern? she thought. Left Finstead? That thought was impossible. Suppose, she thought suddenly and wildly, he has left for here? Suppose, at this moment, Toby should come? Toby was big, solid, and immovable. He had always protected her. He would stand between her and the inspector and Mr. Pye. *Mr. Pye!* thought Sophie, with clenched teeth. Mr. Pye would be more respectful if Toby were here. Toby would keep her, shelter her, settle everything. "But would he settle it as you wish?" said her own clear little voice, a voice that was beginning to remind her more and more of Aunt Rose. Sophie refused to notice it. She shut her eyes and sat, lulled for a moment, luxurious in the very thought of Toby's being near. "Toby," she whispered, "Toby dear." She had, of course, to open her eyes. Toby was far away, in England if not in Finstead, and she was here in Srinagar. He would be worried and sorry when he heard, but he could be no more than that. He was in England, and she was alone.

۰

In the days that followed she began to know how much alone that was. She found that when she tried to defend—even reasonably, thought Sophie—Nabir or Sultan, the pundit or the villagers, she become oddly unpopular, even suspect.

"Leave it to us," "Do what we tell you," said the inspector, the chief of police, the doctors, Mr. Pye, and when she said, "I can't," they looked at her as if she had offended them.

"These people have got hold of you," said Mr. Pye with distaste.

"They gave you poison, they assaulted your child," said the inspector.

"I know they did," said Sophie wearily.

"Is not that a crime?" demanded the inspector.

Sophie shook her head.

"What is it then?"

"It's a muddle," said Sophie, "an accident. Not a crime. I—I'm sure of that. It's a hideous accident."

"Bah!" said the inspector—or a sound very like it.

Little Lochinvar avoided her; she had denunciatory letters from the pundit; but once again there was one person who was in accord with her, and strangely enough she had tried to avoid seeing him. Profit David had called again and again and asked for her. Each time the missionaries sent him away.

Then he wrote Sophie a letter. "Honestly all my sympathies are with you. Bible David was always anxious to get trouble as he believed that

193

after it one gets a very good time for long future. Madam, it needs a heart to get worries, you have pluck I know and will show the courage in everything. I shall have the happiness to come tomorrow and present my bill, rupees eight hundred and eight, annas six."

"Yes, I owe him money," said Sophie with a sigh. "He has a right to see me." And she asked Little Lochinvar to let him in.

His first question was, "Where is the rug?"

"The—the rug?" Sophie had forgotten all about it.

"You have left it in the house! A valuable rug like that!" cried Profit David. "You must go back at once."

"When Teresa, my child, is so ill?"

Profit David did not say it, but it was plain he thought that one could get another child but not another rug like that.

"The police are in the house," said Sophie.

"The police are worse than the villagers," said Profit David. "Do you suppose the police don't know the worth of a carpet?" And he snapped, "The value of things doesn't alter because there is a crime."

"No," said Sophie slowly. She needed to remember that and she was glad that she had seen him; and he was not quite unsympathetic. He had brought something for Sophie. He unwrapped from a piece of silk a small figure of Kwan Yin; it was perhaps four inches high, carved of coral, and exquisite. "This is for you," he said.

"Oh—oh!" said Sophie.

"She is not for sale," said Profit David. "She is for lend. Presently you must give her back. She belongs to me; she is priceless." Sophie knew very well that, with Profit David, everything had its price, but she was touched. "She is to stay with you till Miss Teresa is better, and there is nothing to pay." He could not say anything more handsome than that. "As for the crime," said Profit David, "don't grieve for it. It is in character. I told you you were like the emperors. The emperors suffered many things like this—poison and glass and influential drugs—and their children were always suffering too."

"Don't," said Sophie sharply.

"They had to expect it *because* they were emperors' children," said Profit David firmly. "And the emperors had to expect it too, because they were emperors." He looked at the Kwan Yin. "I thought this would be a good time to show her to you. She is Chinese goddess of children," said Profit David.

"She is the goddess of mercy too," said Sophie, her voice shaking, and she put out a hand and touched the little figure with her finger.

"And now, about my bill . . ." said Profit David.

"How could you see him?" said Sister Locke afterwards. "He only came here for money. He is the worst rogue in Srinagar."

"He is a rogue and a Persian humbug and he only came here for money," said Sophie. "But he has put more sense into me than any of you," and she asked to see Sultan in prison. When she said Sultan she also meant Nabir, but she flinched in a way she did not understand from saying Nabir's name.

"Dearie, don't go," said Dr. Glenister. "You will distress yourself for nothing. These things are cruel but they must take their course."

"I must go," said Sophie.

"How you dare!" said Sister Pilkington.

"How you can!" said Sister Locke.

"It isn't fit for a woman," said Mr. Pye. "You are only meddling with what you don't understand."

"I must meddle," said Sophie.

The decision did not rest with Mr. Pye, or she could not have gone. It rested with the chief of police, and at last permission was given.

"But I must go with you," said the inspector.

"I want to see Sultan alone," said Sophie.

"But madam, he is criminal. He might injure you."

This is Sultan, stupid little Sultan! Sophie wanted to cry, and she had a sudden and accurate vision. It was as if mists had cleared in her head. She knew it was accurate. A crime! thought Sophie. A crime! It wasn't a crime. It was Sultan making his love drink. I see it all now. His love drink, to make me kind to him. She began to laugh. "It wasn't for Katiji, it was for me," she said. "For me, and I gave it to him." It was too much; her laughing grew hysterical. She saw the inspector start towards her, but before he could reach her she had fainted.

❧

When she came round she was with Little Lochinvar. "Keep still," he said. "Sip this." He gave her a draught that took her breath away. "Sip it slowly," said Little Lochinvar. "Wipe your face with this," and he gave her a wetted handkerchief. "Keep your head down." He went on giving her these orders, without looking at her, even after Sophie was able to sit up. "Doctor Glenister is out," he said.

Or you wouldn't have touched me, thought Sophie. She looked at his resolutely turned back and thought, He will marry Sister Pilkington. She felt a pang, but not as much for herself as for him. She thought of Sister Pilkington's bright cheeks and bright uncomprehending smile, of her indigo curtains, her texts. The end of romance, of violets, rubies, snow—and foolishness—thought Sophie mistily. He touched my heart, and she remembered how she had looked up "cockles" in the dictionary.

"I'm sorry," said Sophie humbly. "I didn't mean to trouble you. It was—thinking about Sultan."

"And you think you are fit to go to that prison," said Little Lochinvar.

"I must," said Sophie and she struggled to explain. Little Lochinvar listened with a cold stiff face and at the end did not seem convinced.

"You say he used your herbs, but you had no poisonous herbs; if it was Sultan he gave you poison," said Little Lochinvar. "Well, where did he get it from? Not from you. You had no poison. Belladonna is deadly nightshade," said Little Lochinvar coldly, "alkaloid atropin—poisoning by atropin, and there was ground glass as well."

"I found the glass, only I couldn't believe it," said Sophie, and she asked, "Why didn't it kill me?"

"Because like most criminals, they ground it too small."

"Then it was Sultan," said Sophie positively. "He never could do anything properly."

Little Lochinvar seemed to think this remark in poor taste. "It was attempted murder," he said flatly.

"It was not!" cried Sophie, but her cry fell on deaf ears—worse than deaf, antagonistic ears. After that she did not attempt to tell anyone else, Mr. Pye or the police. I must work on my own, thought Sophie, and she went with the inspector to the prison.

❧

The interview was infinitely distressing. Nabir and Sultan had been taken to a small prison, earth-walled, outside the city. The inspector took Sophie in through a small door in a big wooden gate, into a courtyard of baked earth; it looked sunny and curiously innocent for a prison; a cock and hens were walking about, and there were pumpkins ripening on the roof. Sophie was shown into a little room next to the guardroom, and Sultan was brought to her there.

"I shall be next door if you want me," said the inspector.

When Sultan saw Sophie he burst into tears. He fell down on his knees and clutched her dress and hid his face in her skirt. "Take me away from here, memsahib. Take me away," sobbed Sultan. "Take me *away.*" He sobbed it over and over again. He looked very thin and dirty and derelict; his small paunch had gone, he had not shaved, the coat of which he had ben so proud was soiled and torn, and there was a bruise on his face. "Get me out, memsahib! Get me out."

"I can't get you out," said Sophie, and she tried to make him understand. "It wasn't I, it was you, yourself, who put yourself in prison."

That was too subtle for Sultan and he cried, "Why did you send for the police?"

"Sultana, don't be so *silly!*" said Sophie. "If you do such bad things I have to send for the police."

"Nabir did it," said Sultan. Sophie shook her head.

"Why did you give me those things?" asked Sophie directly. "They say you wanted to kill me."

"I *never* killed you," said Sultan indignantly. He began to cry again. "I only wanted you to do as I wanted, and you never would." And he burst out in English wrathfully, "English ladies are too much difficult."

"You gave me a love drink," said Sophie.

"No," said Sultan, but he knew it was no use pretending with Sophie, and he said, "Yes," sulkily. "And what was the good?" he asked with tears running down his face. "You didn't love me. Nobody loves me. They twist my arms," he said, breaking into sobs. "I asked you, I asked the barber. I asked everyone. The barber said, 'Don't make it too strong.' Guffar Sheikh said, 'Don't make it too weak.' Everyone said something different. I took so much trouble. I put in everything I could think of," wailed Sultan.

"You put in glass," said Sophie.

"Glass is imitation jewels. You said jewels," said Sultan sulkily.

Sophie tried to remember what she had said.

"I said pearls—pearls dissolved," said Sophie.

"I ground the glass."

"'Dissolved' means 'melted.' Glass is sharp," said Sophie feelingly.

"I ground it," said Sultan virtuously, "but the barber said things to mix me. Why did you make him hate you? Why did you take away his fees? I was afraid I had killed you. I meant to be careful but I forgot how much he said. You know how I forget," he wailed. "I only put in a *little*, but you got too ill," he said accusingly.

"Didn't you think I should get ill?" asked Sophie.

"I didn't think at all," said Sultan and he wept bitterly. "I was only trying to make you do as I said, and you never would. Never! Never! Never!"

Even then Sophie thought it a strange way for a prisoner to talk to his victim—but it confirmed what she knew.

"Try and find out who was behind him," the inspector had said.

"No one was behind him," said Sophie, but it was too simple for them to believe. Sultan had confessed to everything and anything they wanted, but he had implicated too many people—Nabir, the pundit, the barber, the Dārs, the Sheikhs. "He is useless," said the inspector in disgust.

By the end of the interview Sultan was sodden with tears, and when they came to take him away he shrieked and flung himself on the ground and clung to Sophie's feet. They had to lift him and carry him away.

"As you are here, please to see Nabir Dār," said the inspector. Sophie was already white and sick. She dreaded it, but she saw Nabir.

He was brought in and stood in front of her. She knew now that there was a quality in Nabir that made her feel, if not afraid, very respectful. He was in prison, remanded in custody, because he was suspected of doing them a great injury—and I feel as if I had injured him unspeakably, thought Sophie. From the moment she had seen him taken away she had had an unspeakable sense of wrong. He had walked quite silently between two policemen with his wrists handcuffed behind him. Sophie knew that all his life, if nothing worse came of this, he would feel those handcuffs. His silence had been all the more marked because of the sobbing and shrieking of Sultan. Now the silence was here again, and it unnerved her. "Nabira," she began, but the words died in her throat. He too looked thin. His coat was torn, and he had lost his pink cap; to be bareheaded was an indignity, and he had twisted up a piece of rag into a small turban. I must get the inspector to get him a cap, thought Sophie. At least I can do that.

"Nabira, I—Teresa Baba is still—sleeping." She did not know how to say "unconscious." "She can't tell us what happened," said Sophie. "You must tell us, Nabira." There was a long silence; she thought he was not going to answer. Then, "You have heard what they say," said Nabir.

"But I haven't heard what you say," said Sophie. He shrugged. It was the same insolent shrug that Sophie had seen him give so often, and it always enraged her. "*Why* can't you *speak?*" she said sharply.

He looked away over her head, and it came to her that he was offended. Offended? thought Sophie. That was a little word, but it was true. He was bitterly offended—and for that he may be hung, she thought, and shivered. She tried to frighten him. "If anything happens to—to Teresa Baba, things may go badly with you."

"The memsahib says so," said Nabir in his old insolent way.

"Nabira, I'm trying to help you!" cried Sophie. He looked over her head again, and her helpful words fell to the ground.

"It was a bad day for us when you came," said Nabir. He said it quietly, as a fact, not as bitterness. "It was a bad day." Sophie was silent, staring at the courtyard outside, the cocks and the hens, the pumpkins, but now it did not seem innocent and sunny. A shadow was creeping over them all, over Nabir, and it was her shadow. What can I do? thought Sophie in despair.

"May I go now?" asked Nabir, as he might ask, Have you finished with me?

"Go! Go! Go!" cried Sophie almost hysterically. He called, and a policeman came and took him away.

❧

"Well, did you find out anything?" asked the inspector as they drove away.

"He wouldn't speak," said Sophie and, thoroughly unnerved, she began to tremble.

"We will try another beating. That will make him speak," said the inspector, trying to soothe her.

"I wish that you could let him go," said Sophie.

"But madam, he is the king-pin," said the inspector, deeply pained.

"I think you are wrong," said Sophie, but the inspector already had everything arranged in his mind. If he called Nabir the king-pin, he called Sultan the accomplice.

"But if Nabir wanted an accomplice," said Sophie, "he would never take Sultan. Never."

"You do not know these people, madam," said the inspector.

"I know Nabir," said Sophie. It was true. She knew him now.

"If only we could stop the case," she said to Sister Locke.

"*Stop* the case?"

"Yes. It's wrong. I know it's wrong."

"You owe it to Teresa to carry it through," said Sister Locke indignantly.

"Teresa would hate it," said Sophie. "If only she could speak!" And she bent down by the bed. "Teresa," she called urgently. "Teresa. It's Mother—Sophie. Do you hear me? Terry. Terry! Do you hear me?" But Teresa lay without a flicker of recognition or life, and after a little while Sophie turned hopelessly away.

Chapter 19

"Would it be safe for me to leave Teresa for a few hours?"
Sophie asked Sister Locke.

"Her pulse is stronger," said the sister. "I don't think any
change will come while you are away." She gave Sophie a long searching
look and said, "You are going to Dhilkusha."

"Yes," said Sophie. "I must."

Tossing and turning at night, unable to sleep, she seemed to hear not
the wakeful hospital sounds but the sounds of Dhilkusha, the house
sounds, the stream, the poplar trees moving in the wind, the calls of the
herd children, the singing in the fields, the far sounds from the lake,
and—How did it all come to this? she thought. Thinking back, she knew
there was much she could have controlled and stopped if she had tried. If
I had not let things run on—she was thinking of those days in early
spring when she had been rapt away. Then she swung to the opposite—
If I had simply let them run on—and she thought of her interference, her
efforts with the people, with the servants, her sewing circle, her favours
among the Sheikhs and Dārs. I understand about the Sheikhs and Dārs
now, when it is too late, she thought bitterly, and she thought, No matter what I had known I expect I should have been wrong! Yet, still, I am
sure I can make things right, thought Sophie, obstinate.

"Do you have to go?" asked Sister Locke.

"I have to," said Sophie.

Sister Locke said slowly, "These people can be nasty."

"I know," said Sophie, and she said, "I ought to know."

She also knew quite well what the wise people would say—Little
Lochinvar, for instance, the inspector, Mr. Pye; at the thought of Mr.
Pye she tightened her lips. She herself did not know how unwise her
going might be but she could measure the feeling in the village by
Nabir's resentment. There were police at Dhilkusha, but she did not

mean to use them; she was not sure what it was she had to do, but she knew that, to get the village confidence, she must go unprotected and alone. "I have to go," she said. "There has been a mistake." It was the first time she had said that aloud, and as soon as she heard it she knew it was true.

"What mistake?" said Sister Locke sharply.

"I know part of it," said Sophie. "The rest I have to find out."

If Sister Locke thought Sophie foolish she did not say it. Instead she made a surprising offer. "It's my afternoon off," she said. "I will stay with Teresa, but if you are not back by dusk I shall send after you."

୬

The nearer she came to Dhilkusha, the more afraid Sophie grew. All the way, in the tonga, she had felt as if she were retracing the violence of that night rush to the city. I can't undo it, she thought, but to retrace it was like a pilgrimage of expiation. As she drove back, quietly, insignificantly, in the daytime, with the feet of the pony clopping so quietly on the road that hardly anyone looked up as they passed, a little of the horror was undone.

I was right to come, thought Sophie.

When the tonga passed Nishat she remember Amdhoo and thought of Nabir's four brothers, the *shaitans*. Would they come out in a pack against her? As she passed the place on the lake where the fishing boats were tied she thought of the day she had wanted to buy the fish and of the abuse the fishermen had shouted when Nabir stopped her. She thought of the fights between the milkmen, woodmen, eggmen, tonga-men, between Nabir and St. Nicholas, and—I was silly to come, thought Sophie. I ought to go back. But she went on.

When the tonga-man had driven off the road and up the track she stopped the tonga, within sight of Dhilkusha, but before the village. "Wait here," she said. She tried to sound calm. "I shall be a few hours," she said. "Go into the village and get tea if you like," and she added, "Please take the horse out of the shafts."

"I will look after my own horse," said the tonga-man, scowling.

"There you go," said Sophie to Sophie, "interfering again."

She walked slowly up to the house. The first time she had come to it, it had been winter; now it was late summer, almost autumn. Everything was green, lush, the trees bowed down with apples, the melons and pumpkins ripe. A smell of sun and flowers was in the air, but it was spoiled by the smell of dust and of decay; wasps rose up from the rotting fruit on the ground as she passed; there were flies, even here in the lane, and the leaves were drying. This end of summer is my least favourite time of the year, thought Sophie; she did not like the smells. She passed some herd children. She saw Zooni, a Dār, sitting with a child she recognized by her cross-eyes as Rahti, one of the Sheikhs. A Dār to sit with a Sheikh! Sophie knew now how unusual that was. Then had the whole village banded together? she wondered. Sophie greeted the children, and they did not answer; they looked at her with stony faces. That was as she had known it would be, but it hurt.

Two policemen had been left in charge of the house. The rooms upstairs were sealed, but the policemen had been living in the kitchen; her pretty little kitchen and the hall and veranda were filthy with spittle, and they had squatted down just outside the door. Sophie could have cried, but they were the police and she had to do as the common people did and swallow her wrath and disgust: she had to ask politely if she could come into her own house. It all looked neglected, dirty, deserted. The cats came running to meet her; the obese Louis looked thin, and Bliss was a skeleton. Their meowing seemed to tear her heart.

She gave them milk and tried half-heartedly to tidy the rooms, but all the time she kept an ear, and eye strained towards the garden. If no one from the village itself had seen her, Zooni and Rahti had. Would the people come? She thought once or twice that she saw heads peep over the wall; she heard voices whispering, but when she looked no one was there. If I am quiet they will come, she thought; but the afternoon passed and nobody came. Then she became aware that a knot of herd children was at the back door. She was in the stillroom and she carefully went on with her pretence of working.

"Memsahib—"

Sophie had picked up an account book. Deliberately she turned a page and frowned down at it.

"Memsahib."

"*Heo*, Salima," she said carelessly, giving him the Kashmiri greeting. All the Dār children were there, and again, as with Zooni, there were Sheikh children with them. Salim had the blackboard.

"We picked the flowers. We were not paid the last time," he said.

That's why they have come, thought Sophie. Nothing but money would have brought them! It was a bitter thought.

She fetched her purse and, going out into the courtyard, counted their marks and paid them in annas. "It's too much," she said, "but I haven't any cakes or pice."

Their eyes gleamed when they saw the silver. The Sheikhs looked longingly but restrained themselves and behaved.

Rahim sidled through to the front. "Moo Baba?" he said.

"Tell him Moo Baba is in Srinagar," Sophie told Salim. Salim translated, and Rahim answered volubly, wiping his running nose with his sleeve. "He says Moo Baba should come back," said Salim.

Sophie shook her head. "My babas were hurt," she said. "How can I let them come back?"

They looked at her, then at their feet. They sidled their feet in the dust for a moment and then, with one accord, as if she had been an evil spirit, they turned and ran away.

When they had gone she went back into the stillroom and sat miserably at the table. No one came. The whole mountain was silent. No one is going to come; I shall find out nothing, thought Sophie miserably. She drummed her fingers on the table, wondering what to do. She sensed antagonism and fear all round her.

All at once she knew she was being watched. She could hear breathing, with a little snuffling sound as if the someone who watched her had adenoids. Then a pair of eyes under a dirty veil came round the door. Sophie did not move, and the whole face slowly showed. It was Rahti, the ugly little cross-eyed Sheikh girl who had been with Zooni.

Sophie called, "Rahti." The head vanished. There was a silence, but she knew that Rahti had not gone away. She called again, "Rahti!" Presently, very timidly, Rahti came round the door.

"Come," said Sophie.

Rahti came fearfully. Like the others, she seemed terrified of Sophie. She was a dirty little girl with sores and flies on her face, a running nose, and the open mouth of bad adenoids. She had big dark eyes like most Kashmiri children, but here were so crossed that Sophie could hardly tell which way they were looking. She could see, though, that they were bright with curiosity.

Rahti, a Sheikh child, had never been in the stillroom, though she had heard of its wonders. She looked round her with awe. On the table was the mortar of sugared roses that Sophie had been pounding that fatal afternoon; they had crystallized, and the sticky mass smelled of sugar and scent. Rahti's nose twitched. She seemed to be looking at the wall, but Sophie saw she was really looking at the roses. The jam had been dirtied and it was covered with flies, but Rahti was used to dirt and flies. She came to the table, and Sophie saw a trickle of saliva run out of her mouth, but the little girl had manners. Without looking at the wall—which meant the roses—again, she asked, "Is Teresa Baba better?"

"What does she say?" Sophie asked one of the policemen, who was in the doorway watching her. Rahti shied away when she saw him, but when he translated for her and Sophie answered she came back.

"Teresa Baba isn't better yet," said Sophie through the policeman, and Rahti nodded as if she had not expected any other news.

"She had a very bad eye," said Rahti. "Aie, but her eye was bad! It looked at us. I thought she was dead." She looked at Sophie fearfully, but Sophie was carefully not looking at her. The policeman translated, and Rahti jumped at his voice. Sophie felt as if she had a bird on a twig and was hoping it would take her crumb. She stirred the rose-jam with a spoon. "Taste," she said to Rahti, holding out the spoon.

"Taste," said the policeman encouragingly in Kashmiri.

Rahti tasted. She had never imagined anything could taste like that. "Teresa Baba had a bad eye," said Sophie conversationally. "But the hit on her head was worse, where she hit the stones."

"We all hit the stones," said Rahti cheerfully, her mind on the jam. "Taji had a burst ear and she was nothing to do with the fight. Aie! When I saw Mustaph pull off the baba's hat I was afraid."

"Don't be absurd, Teresa. They are only children. A child should be happy and confident." The room seemed to spin in front of Sophie, but she held out another spoonful of jam.

"The baba hurt her ear too," said Sophie. Now Rahti's idea was only to stay. She would have told Sophie anything to get more rose-jam, and she began to tell all about the fight, not noticing that the policeman translated. Rahti's little torrent of words went on, the policeman murmured the translation to Sophie, Sophie gave jam to Rahti. When Rahti came to the end and told how Teresa would not move and they had all been afraid and run away, Sophie only said, "No more jam now, Rahti, or you will be ill. Run away home."

Rahti looked up. The greed and unconsciousness left her eyes. She saw Sophie and the policeman looking at her, and she clapped her veil over her mouth and scuttled on her hard little bare feet out of the room.

There was a silence after she left, but Sophie had not done with diplomacy yet. "You speak English very well," she said to the policeman. He smiled and showed his teeth, pleased. "And you can read and write English, too, I expect," she said admiringly.

"I can write English and Urdu—big long words," he boasted.

"You know, of course," said Sophie, "that what that little girl was saying was a very important statement?"

"Very important," he said gravely. "What did she say?"

"You can remember," said Sophie. "Your officer will be pleased that you heard it. He would be more pleased," said Sophie in a silky voice, "if you could write it down—in Urdu and in English."

He hesitated. "How can I remember what she said?"

"I will tell you," said Sophie, "and I will give you paper and pens." An Urdu pen is reed-shaped and cut like a quill. Sophie had had some for lessons, and she cut one for him; for the English she lent him her fountain pen, which pleased him. He breathed hard as he wrote, and his tongue came in and out, licking his lips; she could only hope his writing was intelligible. He was very slow, and when he had done the afternoon was late.

"Now you must sign it," said Sophie, and she took his finger prints in the ink.

"The memsahib is like a vakil," he said, a little cross because he was tired.

"I have learned to be like a vakil in Kashmir," said Sophie severely, afraid he would retract, and she said, "What you have done will save a fellow Kashmiri."

The policeman was disappointed. Fellow Kashmiris were not remu- nerative, and he had hoped it was done for her. "I should like some tea," he said sulkily; he was sweating.

"You deserve some," said Sophie, and his sulks changed to smiles as she gave him two rupees.

She had the paper, but when she was alone such a wave of sickness went through her over Rahti's story that she had to sit down, powerless. Her own voice echoed in her head, and the words she had said last time she was here in the stillroom echoed too. "Don't be such a little coward. They are *children*. They can't hurt you." Her voice seemed to go on and on, and she knew she would hear it forever. "Children. They can't hurt you." She sat, sick and shivering, until she heard steps behind her, the steps of feet in boots. The other policeman was standing at her elbow.

"Memsahib. The people have all gone home. Hari says they are gath- ering in the village. The memsahib should go back to the city."

"What did you say?" Sophie raised her head, dazed.

"Go back, memsahib," said the policeman.

On the table were a few things she had collected to take back to the Mission; among them were the rug and the cow picture. Now she seemed to hear Profit David's tart remark. "Values don't change because there is a crime." Sophie picked up the picture and looked at it. The two white cows, the aunts, looked back. If Aunt Portia and Aunt Mamie had a dif- ference with anyone in the village, or out of it, they dealt with it. They immediately wrote to the person, or made a journey, or put on their hats and gloves and sallied out into the village to see him. There is something brave and immediate about the words "to sally," thought Sophie. She looked at the brown cow, Aunt Rose. Is it your business? Aunt Rose seemed to say. I think it is, thought Sophie.

"If memsahib doesn't go I must send for the inspector sahib," said the policeman.

"I am going," said Sophie, and slowly she got up.

≈

"What is that on your mouth?" Zooni asked Rahti.

Rahti had not thought there was anything on her mouth. She had put out her tongue and licked as far as she could, but Zooni stabbed her cheek with a finger and, from among the flies and sores, brought away some rose-jam. Zooni sniffed it, tasted it, and "You have been with the mem!" she said.

"No," said Rahti glibly, but it was no use. In a minute they were swarming round her. She was pulled and pushed down, and soon the jam was mixed in a smear with dust and tears.

"Memsahib's pet! Memsahib's pet!" they jeered.

"I hate the mem," sobbed Rahti. That was true. At the moment she disliked and feared Sophie more than anyone else in the world. She knew that in some way she had been tricked and fooled. The memsahib had tricked and fooled her, and Rahti was afraid for what she had told. No one else, not the smallest boy in the village, had given anything away; now she, Rahti, had done it.

"Memsahib's pet!" cried Salim Dār, and he punched Rahti. Her own relation, Mustaph Sheikh, punched her too. "Run to your mem," they jeered as Sophie came down the path. "Run! Run!"

"I hate the mem," said Rahti, and, sobbing blindly as they ran away and left her, she picked up a stone.

❧

The first thing that Sophie noticed in the village was that nobody was working. No tap was running; the grain poles lay idle against the wooden mortars; the shifting baskets were still. The cobbler's shop, the breadshop were empty. They had hoped to find the schoolmaster, but the veranda of his house was deserted. There were the barber's tin mug and his towel on his pitch, but the barber was not there. He was in the square; everyone was in the square; Sophie could see his dark coat and violet turban in the crowd.

There was a loud crowd; it was not talking, it was waiting. Waiting for what? thought Sophie, but she need not have asked. The herd children had said she was coming. They are waiting for me, thought Sophie.

But what sort of me? she thought. She seemed to have turned into some sort of monster. That made her both miserable and afraid. I'm afraid because they are afraid of me, thought Sophie. People are hurtful when they are afraid. The stillness of he crowd was frightening. For a moment she quailed. This is what Teresa felt, she thought. It's only just that I should feel it too. And, looking at the people as they looked at her, she went towards them, with Rahti stalking after her.

She tried to walk naturally. When she came to the first knot of people she stopped casually and asked, "Which is Nabir Dār's house?"

Nobody answered until the barber came from behind them. He stood directly in her path and said, "Memsahib, you shouldn't come here. Please to go away."

"Which is Nabir Dār's house?" repeated Sophie.

"If you come there will be more trouble," said the barber loudly. "If anything happens the police will come. We have had the police. We don't want them again." As he said that a chorus of angry voices broke out; some of the men were shouting. "They came in our houses," they shouted.

"They see the things you gave us and say we stole them," said one.

"Why did you give them?" cried another.

"The police take our wood."

"Our tea."

"Rice."

"Eggs."

Bruises were shown Sophie, cuts, a torn coat. She still said steadily, "Which is Nabir Dār's house?"

"Memsahib, go away," said the barber. "Go away!"

"Which is Nabir Dār's house?"

"Go away!"

"Which is Nabir Dār's house?" asked Sophie.

Her steadiness won. She and the barber had been like two principals with different themes, each speaking a part without acknowledging the other and with the villagers as chorus; but suddenly the barber abandoned this and spoke to her directly. "Nabir Dār is in prison," he said.

"I know," said Sophie. "That is why I have come."

"They nearly took me to prison," said the barber. His eyes were black with anger, but Sophie did not flinch.

"If they took Sultan Mahomet, they should have taken you," she said, and those villagers who understood gave a little gasp. Everyone was in awe of the barber, and soon Sophie heard what she had said being repeated in the crowd. "You gave Sultan Mahomet those bad things," said Sophie, and she asked flatly, "Didn't you?"

"Yes, and what did he do?" shouted the barber. "Is it my fault that you have a servant like that? That is what you made them think with your work-factory—that in a few weeks they could do what it has taken me years to learn. Memsahibs and servants!" He hissed. It was as if he said "amateurs," but Sophie held her ground.

"And what do you do?" she asked in return. "Didn't he put ink on your baby for a burn?" she called to Suroya, whom she could see in the crowd. "And charged you eight annas? Eight annas for ink! He put dung on Salim Dār's cut, and Salim had to go to hospital, and his father had to pay for that. Dung that you pick up in the road!"

"Dung is expensive," said Raschid gravely, but nobody listened. They were enthralled and astonished at the temerity of both Sophie and the barber.

"You gave Sultan those dangerous things," said Sophie boldly.

"He should have given them like this," said the barber, and he showed Sophie an infinitesimal measure on the tip of his finger. "It would not have hurt you at all. It would have made you nice and quiet and peaceful," he said, as if it were an accepted fact that she was neither nice and quiet nor peaceful.

"And the glass?" said Sophie.

"I don't believe in the glass," said the barber.

"I saw it," said Sophie.

"Then it was his own idea, not mine; God is my witness," shouted the barber. Sophie believed him. She knew Sultan's ideas. "In God's name!" the barber said. "Once he gave you ten doses together!"

"Ten doses?" said Sophie faintly.

"Yes, you might have been dead!" said the barber. "And all those things you had to mix it with up there!"

"I had no poisons," said Sophie.

"God knows what you had!" said the barber. "You don't know yourself what you had. Didn't you sell sooji as issufgool?"

Do they know everything? thought Sophie, and she said hotly, "That was before I had learned—"

"Aha! So you were selling before you had learned," said the barber. "And now you come here!" said the barber. "Something will happen again, and you will call the police."

"Ahh!" said the crowd in agreement. For all the sport—and they had liked to hear the mem beard the barber, the barber beard the mem—they knew Sophie was dangerous.

"Memsahib, please go away," said Raschid. "Please go away at once." He was an elder, but no more than anyone else did Sophie listen to him.

"I want to go to Nabir Dār's house," said Sophie, "I want to see his mother and his brother."

"I am his brother."

"Then take me to his house. When I have talked with you I will go away." As Raschid still hesitated, she said, "Nothing will happen."

There was an uncertain silence. "Nothing will happen," said Sophie. They looked at her as if they might believe her. The feeling was beginning to change when Rahti threw her stone.

Rahti was a very bad thrower. She did not mean to hit Sophie, she meant the stone to go wide; but she was always last at teenka and at the game they played up on the mountain, toppling over targets with stones. It was her cross-eyes, the children said. The stone hit Sophie on the cheek, on the bone just below the eye. It was a large, sharp stone and it gashed Sophie's cheek open and made her nose bleed. She clapped her hand up. Blood came through her fingers, and there was a horrified moan from the crowd as she reeled.

No one quite liked to touch her, but it was a hard blow, and she reeled again. The barber had to catch her by the arm.

He did it gingerly, almost reverently, commanding Raschid to hold her at the other side. Sophie did not know what happened. The square seemed to go in circles round her; blood came up in her throat, and she choked. But they took her where she had wanted to go, to Nabir's house, and presently she found herself sitting on a string bed, with a woman timidly touching her face with a dirty wet cloth, while another held a bucket.

"Give me a clean towel," said Sophie, but no one had a clean towel. After a moment Mahomet came running from the schoolmaster's house with a clean checked duster.

Sophie sat bleeding into the bucket, her head whirling. "Aie!" said the barber, and the frightened women echoed, "Aie!" To Sophie the nose-bleeding was ignominious, but to the villagers it was impressive; they measured a wound by the amount of blood. News was relayed from the house to the crowd outside. "Bad bleeding. Much, much blood." "There will be trouble for this," the men told one another, and the word "Police . . . police . . . police" went from mouth to mouth.

Besides being afraid, the elders were ashamed. "Such a thing has never happened in our village," they said in shocked whispers. They called Raschid out to speak to them and then sent him back in to Sophie. "Memsahib, it was a child who threw the stone," said Raschid.

"I know," said Sophie, bringing down the duster for a moment. "It was Rahti."

There was a stunned silence. They had not thought she knew Rahti's name. She was instantly assured by everyone that it could not have been Rahti. Rahti was up on the mountain. She had gone to her grandfather's house. She was out on the lake gathering weeds. But the whispers died away. The memsahib said firmly, "It was Rahti," but she was not angry. It seemed also she was not making a fuss. The blood had no sooner stopped than she washed her face as clean as she could with the wrung-out duster, looked at the cut and her quickly blackening eye in the little mirror she kept in her bag, put the mirror away, and asked, "Which is Nabir Dār's mother?"

It was the same calmness that had made Nabir respect her when they had talked about wild animals and avalanches the first day at Dhilkusha. The villagers respected her now; like Nabir, they did not know how strong she was when her will was set on anything.

"Which is Nabir's mother?" asked Sophie. There was a long, long pause.

This was the lower room of the house, where the cattle were kept in winter. It had been cleaned out, but the floor was littered with dried dung. There were bundles of hay in the corner; hoes and baskets lay along the wall. A flight of rough wooden steps went up to the room above, from which smoke—the fire had been lit for the evening meal— eddied down the stairs. The room seemed full of women, and Sophie became aware that one of them was looking at her with eyes more hostile than any she had yet seen. It was Nabir's mother.

She was like Nabir, tall and a little insolent. She had the same way of standing as he; her black hair streamed over an olive-green pheran, and she had a hawk nose and angry black eyes.

Sophie's head was throbbing, but she knew that now she must fight another battle, a fiercer battle even than with the barber. Instinctively she knew she must give no quarter. She stood up and found she could stay on her feet, and she went up to the woman and said, "I must speak to you."

To her surprise Nabir's mother answered in Urdu, but she spoke looking straight past Sophie, like Aunt Rose, and said, "I will not speak with the *mem!*"

"If you don't," said Sophie promptly, "I shall say what I have to say about your son aloud in the village street."

Nabir's mother did not know what it was Sophie had to say, but this sounded derogatory. There was a pause; then she angrily jerked her head to the other women to go outside.

When they were alone Sophie said, "I know what the herd children did."

Nabir's mother stood very still. "Will you tell the police?"

"Yes," said Sophie. Nabir's mother flinched. "The police can't punish thirty or forty children," said Sophie. "They may beat a few of the older boys, but they can't hurt them."

"Mahomet—" The word hardly came through the woman's lips.

"Nabir," said Sophie in return. "Mahomet may get a beating, but if—my baba dies, and she is very, very, ill," said Sophie, her voice trembling, "they may hang Nabir."

Nabir's mother searched Sophie's face with her eyes as if she would rake out her meaning. "They may hang him," repeated Sophie.

"And because of that you came?" asked Nabir's mother.

"Because of that I came." And Sophie said, "Nabir didn't hurt my baba that afternoon, but what did he do? You know, and you must say."

Nabir's mother looked at Sophie, Sophie looked back at her, and after a minute Nabir's mother began to tell what had happened on that dread day. She wept, her Urdu broke down, and Sophie called Raschid to translate. At the end Sophie made them say it again more slowly while she wrote it down. Nabir's mother put her mark and fingerprints on the paper, then she said. "What will the mem do now?"

Sophie saw this was no time for vacillating. "I shall stop the case." And she pledged herself, "The police will go away."

"And they won't take the children?"

"They won't take the children," said Sophie and hoped that she was right.

As she took the second precious paper from Raschid and put it with Rahti's, a new sound seemed to fill the whole room. It was the putt-putt of a motorcycle coming nearer. "The police!" cried Nabir's mother. She and Raschid and Sophie ran to the doorway. The other women streamed in and crowded round them as the people broke and scattered; some ran into their houses, some made for the orchards and the fields. But now the two policemen from Dhilkusha came running down and they met the people and drove them back to the square as a motorcycle, ridden by a policeman, swept into the village. Behind it came a car, and before the car had stopped its doors were open and the inspector jumped out with more police. Sophie heard quick orders given, and she called out peremptorily, "Stop! Don't do anything. I am quite all right."

The inspector came striding towards her, his polished boots scattering hens and children, his turban-end swinging. He looked very angry and perturbed.

Sophie had the papers in her hand. She had triumphed, but now she felt suddenly very tired, too tired to deal with the inspector. Her head was hurting; she felt giddy; and when he cried "Madam, you are hurt," she could only say again, "I am quite all right. I am quite all right."

"You are hurt! Who did it?" cried the inspector, and he swung on his heel and looked menacingly at the crowd. The crowd stood silent. Sophie felt their eyes looking at her, expectant eyes. There was a terrible pause until, with an effort, she rallied herself.

"I am hurt," she said. "I fell by the lake and—spiked my cheek on a tree. The Dār family have been helping me."

It was weak, and for a moment Sophie thought it would not do. The inspector stood in front of her, looking at her eye, the split cheek, the blood soaked into her dress. "What tree?" he asked.

"A—a willow," said Sophie.

"Willow trees, I think, are not so sharp," said the inspector.

His voice roused all the opposition in Sophie. "It was a willow," she said flatly, and she appealed to the barber who was standing just below her. "Ask them all. Wasn't it a willow?" A hundred voices assured the inspector that it was.

"In that case," he began angrily, but Sophie was looking past him. A second car had driven up, and who was this getting out of it? Sophie put out her hand to hold the wall and found the inspector's sleeve. It was someone tall and burly and big, dressed in khaki. Then Sophie's breath seemed to leave her body in wonder, and her fingers tightened on the inspector's arm so that he winced. It was Toby. "How—*how?*" she whispered.

She wanted to run into his arms like a child, but something held her in the doorway, looking. She saw the width of his shoulders, his short-cut hair. Toby always did cut his hair too short, she thought. She could see his blue eyes, the red-brown of his face, and she thought, Toby always did burn red. Then these two little cold criticisms were stilled. "Toby! Toby!" she called out brokenly, and, for the first time in all those long days, she burst into tears.

Chapter 20

I thought it was going to end in weepings," cried the pundit, "and it hasn't. No, not at all."

For a long time the pundit had been too shocked and shamed to come near them. "They said such things," he told Sophie. "Such *things!* I thought I was ruined. I and all my family members. At one time it was very ignoble," he said, and Sophie thought that was a good word for it. "Now you have made it noble again." A tear ran down his cheek beside his nose, and Sophie was stung by that tear. The pundit had grown even smaller and thinner; his face was lined, and he twitched more than ever. "Was there anyone I didn't make suffer?" cried Sophie.

"It's all over now," said Toby and took her hand in his.

It was strange how everything had come right together.

"You needed a man to settle things, that is all," said Toby. It was on the tip of Sophie's tongue to point out that she had settled it all herself before he came, but she was too happy and grateful to quibble.

They were back at Dhilkusha, with Toby in a houseboat down on the lake to guard them. "But we don't need guarding now," said Sophie.

"You will always need guarding," said Toby, and Sophie looked down from the veranda across the terrace to where Teresa, able to walk now a little, able to play sedately, sat on the lawn with Pussy Maria under the apple trees, and, "Yes," said Sophie with a deep breath.

While she had been with the villagers that day, Sister Locke, sewing by Teresa's bed, had looked up and seen that Teresa's eyes were open. They were fixed on her.

"Where is Moo?" Teresa's voice was a little croak, but the words were plain.

"Moo is in the garden, playing, safe and happy," Sister Locke said, trying to keep her own voice even.

Teresa shut her eyes; they were still puffy and discoloured, though the bandages had been taken off. It was difficult to open one eye, but after a moment she opened them both, wide. For Teresa, the room had unaccustomed angles and planes that seemed to slide together in the light; her head ached, and something else ached too—my hand? thought Teresa, surprised. Why did it ache? The pucker came between her eyes. "Where is Mother?" she asked and whimpered.

"Gone out, but she will soon be back," said Sister Locke soothingly.

"Where did she go?"

"Only to Dhilkusha, to tidy up the house." But, for all her carefulness, the old acid came into the sister's voice. "She went, and the—the gentleman went after her." Sister Locke's voice seemed to say, *Another man!* But Teresa did not understand and she whimpered again.

Then the pucker went away, and Teresa smiled at Sister Locke; it was a stiff, crooked smile, but there was a look of excitement in her eyes. "I fought the herd children," she croaked. "I fought Zooni and Salim and Mustaph and Taji—all of them. I—" She stopped. "Did they hurt me?" she asked.

"They did—a little," said Sister Locke.

"Well, I hurt them," said Teresa in deep contentment and fell asleep.

Teresa, playing now, was taller and thinner, a Teresa with cropped hair, a different Teresa. It was as if she had broken the sheath of her last self and emerged—as I did, thought Sophie, like the snake from its skin. Yes, Teresa had changed. If anyone said, "When the herd children got you," Teresa corrected them with dignity. "They didn't 'get' me. I fought them," she said. If she spoke with the herd children now, it was with friendly authority, and they answered her with respect. I could say, It's done her good, thought Sophie, marvelling, and the thought came into her mind: She needed guarding before, but not now, not now.

The village was itself again. The police had gone. Nabir had been released. After Sophie's new evidence, brought with the statements from Nabir's mother and Rahti, the case against him was stopped. "We can't prosecute *children*," said the inspector, "and the little miss is better." Sophie thought he said this almost regretfully. "It should have been a sensational case," he said and sighed.

He had no better luck with Sultan. Sultan was given four months' imprisonment, of which six weeks had already been served. When the case came on he had been so palpably muddled and misled that no more than Sophie could the court take him seriously as a criminal. "They could find no malice," said the inspector and sighed again.

Profit David too thought a little malice would have made it much more interesting. "The emperors had crimes," he said reproachfully.

"I told you I wasn't an emperor," said Sophie.

"No—but you might have been," said Profit David. Sophie felt he was disappointed in her.

He was the only one. Since Toby came, Sophie had lived in a warm glow of approval from everyone.

"This is what I have prayed for," said Dr. Glenister fervently.

"And little Teresa sent that letter! It's so romantic!" said Sister Pilkington, marvelling.

"He is an M.R.C.P. and M.D. Edinburgh," said Little Lochinvar. "There is no better training than that."

"Another husband, at your age! What luck!" said Ayah.

"I must say you deserved some luck," said Sister Locke surprisingly. She added, "'Unto everyone that hath shall be given.' That's in the Bible, so it must be just."

Even Mr. Pye seemed to like Toby, while the pundit revered him. "A noble, virtuous man," said the pundit. "Noble" and "virtuous" had become his two favourite words.

Aunt Portia wrote a long happy letter. "It is what Mamie and I have always wanted," she wrote. The letter was interspersed with loving messages from Aunt Mamie—but Aunt Rose was silent. "Well, she never had much to say," said Toby.

"And yet she said—everything," said Sophie.

It was autumn, and the days were almost as beautiful as in the spring. There were sharp mornings clear with sun; the dew was frosty, and the colours were clear and pale with a pale blue sky. There was a blond dry stubble on the fields, and the poplars were turning gold. The lake was pale and still, and the mountains looked many-sided, many-humped, with the chasing of the sun and cloud shadows; the crevices of the rocks were orange with sorrel. The village lambs were grown now, and Sophie's own lambs and kid were up on the mountain with the flocks. In her garden only the aubergines were left, heavy and glossy and purple on their plants—they and a few tomatoes and late melons, pumpkins and persimmons tied carefully in muslin bags; but the flowerbeds were still brilliant with zinnias, marigolds, petunias, and bright balls of dahlias.

It was the last of colour, of heat, of sun, as these were the last flowers, vegetables, fruit, and crops. The reapers had come to the last high fields; the mirror flash of the sickles sent back reflections from Dhilkusha's very windows, and the reaping songs sounded as if they were in the garden.

"How monotonous they are," said Toby.

"Monotonous!" Sophie was startled. To her they were so beautiful they made her heart ache.

In these halcyon days her heart had strangely begun to ache. It was not all quite as halcyon as it seemed.

Sophie had asked Nabir to come back. "The memsahib wants you," said the pundit. "You should go back." Nabir shook his head.

"It will give you face," said his mother.

"I don't want face," growled Nabir.

"If you go back Dārs, not Sheikhs, will be there again," said Amdhoo. The old rivalry was creeping back. But Nabir was silent.

"Guffar Sheikh," taunted Amdhoo, but Nabir was still silent.

"Perhaps he doesn't want to go," said Raschid, but nobody heard him.

When Nabir would not come, Sophie told the pundit to offer him double pay. "That would be foolish," said the pundit. Sophie knew it was foolish, but she had a desperate feeling that if Nabir would not come back nothing would be healed. "Double pay," she insisted. Nabir's answer was to go and find himself work in one of the remote market gardens at Harwan.

When the pundit came back with the news Sophie was so upset that she burst into tears and ran upstairs and threw herself on her bed.

Toby followed her, astonished and uncomfortable. "In front of the *pundit*, an *Indian!*" he said.

"The pundit knows how I feel," said Sophie and, though Toby disapproved, she wept.

She had tried to pretend to herself that everything had come right—though Teresa was changed, the pundit was marked, and Sultan was in prison. "But Sultan deserved to be punished," she said.

"Deserved to be punished!" said Toby. "Kicking was too good for him."

"He was often kicked," said Sophie sadly.

"How you ever came to employ a mean, lickspittle little bearer like that!" said Toby wrathfully.

"He wanted me to love him, and I never did," said Sophie, still sad.

"Love him! Good God!" said Toby.

The barber had been fined in lieu of imprisonment. "That won't hurt him very much," said Sophie. "He has plenty of money."

"You sound as if you didn't want him to be punished," said Toby.

"I—I don't," said Sophie.

"These people have got hold of you," said Toby.

"You sound like Mr. Pye."

"Pye is a very decent chap," said Toby.

"I know," said Sophie curtly. That was true, and it was true that these people had got hold of her—but in a way that you don't understand, said Sophie silently. No one could understand unless he too had lived here and lived through this, she thought. There was a new feeling of mutual understanding and respect between Dhilkusha and the village; each kept its distance because each now knew its place. "I could live here now," said Sophie. "I know now how to live here." It was ironical that now she must not stay. Apart from anything else, the resident had settled it with the state that she must go. "If there were any more trouble . . ." said Mr. Pye.

"There won't be," said Sophie, but for all the notice Mr. Pye took of that she might have been a fly.

Now the compass points on the veranda seemed to mock her. To be taken on when you did not want to go was a new experience for Sophie, though she had done it to everyone else. She felt as if the sailor were ruthless, with his uncaring stars. "But of course stars don't care," said Sophie. She must go, as Nabir had already gone. It was ended. "Nabir is wiser than I am," she said aloud. "He always was."

"A village boy?" asked Toby.

"Nabir has made me see—what no one before has ever made me see," said Sophie.

She thought of Nabir, his height, the new thinness he had seen in prison. She saw his tilted eyes that gave him his look of aloofness, his pink cap and homespun coat, his independent shrug, and she thought of his gentleness, the proud isolation of his heart. "You have to be fit, to qualify, to live in lonely places," she said, "to be with lonely people." There were a very few in Sophie's life who had those proud lonely hearts—people who won't bend, she thought; perhaps only Nabir, that unknown sailor. Sophie smiled at herself. And Aunt Rose—though Aunt Rose has given in, she can't make herself bend. Aunt Rose and Vennie, Aunt Rose's runaway son? thought Sophie. For a little while she, Sophie, had been of their company. Now—her eyes blurred with tears again, and she said, "I wasn't fit to be with Nabir."

"Good God!" said Toby.

Toby had been saying "Good God!" ever since he came. It made Sophie angry.

"You don't understand!" said Sophie.

"I certainly don't understand all this fuss about a village boy."

"Stop saying 'a village boy' as if that were a kind of—animal!" said Sophie hotly.

"Really, Sophie!" said Toby. "I hate to say it, but you make me wonder if there isn't something in what people say."

"What do they say?" asked Sophie challengingly.

"You know quite well," said Toby.

There was a pause. Then, "They said I was given—something to make me loving, to take my will away," said Sophie softly.

She sat up and looked out of the window. High over Toby's head she could see the tip of one tall poplar tree, standing by itself. She had not noticed it specially before; now its leaves were yellow against the sky. Through the window the smell of dried leaves and of hay and of flowers in the sun, all the scents of the garden and mountain, blew in to her. She could hear the streams, the distant lowing and bleating, the doves on the roof, Moo's voice in the garden, and faint, from far away, the sound of paddles on the lake.

"What they say is true," said Sophie. "I am loving." Her voice hardened and grew certain. "They have had their way. I love these people and this place."

222

It was that evening that she had a letter from Mr. Kirkpatrick. "Kirkpatrick?" asked Toby. "Who is he?"

"A—a man," said Sophie dreamily. "I thought he had forgotten us. He said he would find work for me. How funny if he has found it now."

"Has he?" asked Toby, holding out his hand for the letter.

"Yes," said Sophie, but she did not give the letter to Toby. She looked up from it, far away, beyond the lake, to the line of the far mountains where a first star was glimmering.

Mr. Kirkpatrick's post was mundane enough—to teach in the company welfare centre at Beirut. Sophie read the letter aloud. "With your knowledge of Urdu you should find Arabic fairly easy, and you know French," Mr. Kirkpatrick had written, and "Crafts and music and dancing will help."

"I can do all those," said Sophie. "He says he has heard I run a cottage industry here."

"But you don't," said Toby, "and you are not qualified to teach."

"No," said Sophie, unperturbed, "but I can teach—except Teresa," she said. *The Wise Teacher* had gone on the bonfire. "The letter says, 'Free house, servant allowance, medical care, educational facilities, passages every three years, pension scheme, double benefits as Denzil's widow...'"

"It's a wonderful offer," said Toby. "Too wonderful. It seems to me this Kirkpatrick it too interested in you. Still, you needn't think of it now."

"No," said Sophie, but she did not put the letter away. "I have never been to Lebanon," she said slowly. "In Beirut there are orange groves and wisteria, and white houses standing in the sun, and mountains and— Tuaregs," said Sophie, entranced.

"Not Tuaregs, Arabs and Lebanese," said Toby, and he said, "Give me that letter. You are not going to Lebanon. You are coming home to Finstead with me."

The last days came, and everything was settled. The pundit was to take over Dhilkusha again.

"Take care of it," said Sophie.

"I will try," said the pundit gloomily. "But the Sheikhs and the Dārs—" He broke off in agitation. Sophie gave him her furniture except the desk and the kingfisher lamp, which she gave to Sister Locke in gratitude for nursing Teresa. "And nursing me," said Sophie.

"It was a pleasure to nurse Teresa," said Sister Locke.

The lambs and kid went back to the flocks of their original owners. Louis and Bliss were given to Sister Pilkington. Sophie arranged with Little Lochinvar that he should see Sultan when Sultan came out of prison and give him a new coat and some money to start off with again.

The packing was soon done. There was a box of clothes, a box of books, and a special box holding the Chinese teapot and the carriage clock. Teresa had a little trunk painted green with a rose on it, which she had bought in the bazaar for Pussy Maria. The rug was to go in a long roll. "I shall carry that under my arm," said Sophie. "It is my bankroll."

"But you haven't paid for it," said Toby.

"No-o," said Sophie.

There had been a little tension between Toby and Sophie over the rug. "But you mean you bought it when you couldn't pay for it?" he had asked, and he said seriously, "Dearest, you *mustn't* do things like that."

"I know I mustn't but I did," said Sophie.

Toby had taken out his wallet when she stopped him. "No, don't, Toby. I must pay for it myself."

"How can you?" He knew all the story of Sophie's poverty by now.

"I don't know," said Sophie slowly. "But wait and see. Something will happen."

"Don't be silly," said Toby. Sophie could not explain, but she felt it would be fatal to let Toby pay for the rug. It would be the end of me, as a person, she thought. It would break my faith, my power in myself. But she did not say this to Toby; she only said, "No—please!"

"Well then, how—?"

"Something will come," said Sophie. "It always does."

"Does it?" asked Toby. "Look what has just happened." And he asked, "Have you ever thought what it was like for me to have your Aunt Portia's news? To travel with it for days, and then to arrive and find you gone to that village?"

"But—I made it right," said Sophie.

"Right! You were cut and hurt, with a black eye, and covered in blood, and that rabble was all round you."

"But—I must do as I must," said Sophie.

Toby shook his head. He took her in his arms and kissed her lips and eyes until they had to shut, and she leaned against him, breathless. "That rabble!" said Toby savagely.

They are not rabble, they are people, Sophie wanted to cry, but Toby's kisses took her breath away; the strength and comfort of his arms were round her. All at once the people seemed rabble, ugly and menacing, and she shuddered. "Yes, hold me tight," she said. "Keep me, keep me safe."

"When I get you home," said Toby, "I shall never let you go again."

❧

"Portia says you shall have the Rockingham china," wrote Aunt Mamie—"That is a beautiful tea set in grey and white and gold," Sophie told Teresa—"and Toby's mother left a silver service, which would go with it. I *think* it had a tray." "Toby's mother died when he was a boy," Sophie said. "Will you bring your cats home?" wrote Aunt Portia. "If not, you shall have one of Bessie's kittens." "Bessie is a blue Persian," said Sophie, skirting hastily away from the question of Louis and Bliss. "Toby's Mrs. Hurst won't stay, but Deborah's niece would come to you." "Mrs. Hurst is Toby's housekeeper. Deborah is Aunt Rose's cook," explained Sophie. Aunt Portia and Aunt Mamie wrote endlessly. But there is never any word from Aunt Rose, thought Sophie. It was strange how badly she wanted that word.

To her infinite surprise she had presents. The pundit gave her a samovar of good metal, its base and cover fretted and ornamented with gilt. "But samovars are expensive!" said Sophie, bewildered.

"Well, see what he got from you," said Toby.

"But for a samowar he must have had to pay down *money!*" said Sophie; but of course Toby did not now what it was to the pundit to spend money.

Profit David brought toys, a boat and a little lamp, and trinket boxes made of turquoise and brass. They were trash, and Sophie was confirmed in her feeling that Profit David was disappointed in her.

"Of course he hasn't been paid for the rug," said Toby.

"No-o," said Sophie, but she knew the disappointment was not that.

"He will have to be paid," said Toby.

"He will be," said Sophie and shut her lips.

Every morning shy and absurd presents were laid on the back doorstep, bunches of herbs, a crystal, some beautiful pebbles, a tiny basket of grass stems—presents for the children from the herd children. The barber brought a bowl of red honey; the pir, a goose; St. Nicholas, apples; and Raschid, eggs laid out on vine leaves.

"Eggs are an especially honourable present," said Sophie. "They mean the highest respect," and she turned away with a catch in her breath.

"But we can't travel with a goose and apples and a great bowl of honey," said Toby.

"We must," said Sophie, and Teresa agreed. "The *pir* gave the goose," she said reverently. She looked at Toby with alarmed eyes. "You won't make us leave the pir's goose behind?" she asked.

"We are going to take them all the way to Finstead," said Sophie and she picked up the samowar. "We'll teach Deborah's niece to make the tea in this."

They laughed, but Sophie was suddenly silent. She was seeing herself in Toby's house—at teatime. She saw the room, with the curtains drawn against the winter dark, the tea-table with a lace cloth, the plates set out with cakes and scones and crumpets. She saw the valuable china, the silver spoons, and Deborah's niece coming in, not with the samowar but with the silver teapot from Toby's mother on a silver tray. As she saw that, she saw the samowar, as she had used one at picnics or in Dhilkusha—lit in a moment with dried leaves and set down on the grass; the tea drunk from bowls so valueless that when they were used they were broken and thrown away.

The stream by Dhilkusha was running quickly now, helter-skelter, as if it knew that soon the ice would come. The pale clear colours had gone; the lake reflected the mountain's powdering of snow; for the rest it was dark blue, barred with yellow from the reflections of the poplar trees. The willow leaves were falling too, and the boats were out, the people gathering leaves for compost before winter. The caravans of rough little ponies were bringing down the winter's wood; everywhere the charcoal-burners were busy, the smoke from their fires curled far up the mountain. In the village the downstairs rooms were being cleared for the cattle and fodder was being stacked in bundles up on the roofs; the firepot baskets were mended, and straw sandals made against the coming cold. The year was running out, moving quickly toward its end—like us, thought Sophie. Only two things remained to be done. She had not made her peace with Nabir, and she had not paid for the rug.

❧

She had a letter from Aunt Rose.

"Aunt Rose? But she is the one that never writes," said Teresa. Aunt Rose had not written much now, only one line and a postscript. "I have an idea you may need this," said the one line. "This," was a draft for a hundred pounds. "What is it?" asked Teresa, and Sophie answered in a dazed voice, looking at it—"It's the—the money for the rug."

But how did she know? thought Sophie, marvelling. How did she? She couldn't have known, and yet—Aunt Rose always knew everything. Now Sophie was able to say to Toby, "You see! You see!" She was triumphant, but Toby was a little put out. "Lady Munthe means it for the hospital bill and for warm clothes for the voyage," he said.

"No, she doesn't," said Sophie and she read out the post-script. "It's not for bills," wrote Aunt Rose. "Anyone can pay bills."

"She means me, I suppose," said Toby resentfully.

"If you have no especial need of it," wrote Aunt Rose, "buy something of beauty for yourself out of this place you love." Sophie had to break off; her eyes were full of tears. "Out of this place you love." "Aunt Rose knows," said Sophie. Then—"A hundred pounds. That's more than seven hundred rupees. Much more! It's thirteen hundred. Toby, I believe I could get the little Kwan Yin!"

"Good God!" said Toby.

"Mother loves the little Kwan Yin," said Teresa to Toby, her voice stiff.

The stiffness seemed familiar. Teresa's voice is always stiff now when she speaks to Toby, thought Sophie.

"Don't you like Toby?" Sophie asked when they were alone.

"I do," said Teresa, "but Moo doesn't."

"Moo?" Sophie had not thought of him. "Moo is a baby," said Sophie. "He doesn't matter."

Teresa was silent. Since the herd children, Sophie had taken more notice of Teresa's silences.

But Teresa wants to go with Toby, thought Sophie. He is a doctor. There is a niche of her there. Then Sophie remembered how once, after a particularly difficult bout of lessons, she had asked Teresa, "Wouldn't you like me to send you to Finstead, to the aunts?" She had drawn the delights of all Teresa would have, how the aunts would love her and look after her, how she could go to school at Forteviot House, go to the sea- side, to parties—"Like Margaret Robinson," Sophie had said, and she asked, "Wouldn't you like to go?"

"Away from Moo?" Teresa had said. She sounded appalled. "Away from you?" And she had burst into loud heartbroken sobs.

"Finstead is a little like Camberley," Sophie had reminded her.

"I want to stay with you," sobbed Teresa.

Now—"Toby calls Moo 'Tommy'!" said Teresa. Sophie had said herself that Moo should not be called by his silly baby name, but she had to admit that "Tommy" did not suit him. "Wouldn't Thomas be bet- ter?" she asked.

"Tommy," said Toby firmly.

"Don't do that," said Toby sharply and often to Moo, and Moo looked at him and went on with what he was doing. There were scenes. "He must learn to do as he is told," said Toby. "I shall teach him." But after two hours of struggle Toby was usually bathed in sweat, Moo in tears, and still Moo had not done what he was told. Sophie could make him obey, but not in the way Toby wanted, not in that peremptory way. There are some people who won't bend, remembered Sophie; and she thought, Vennie ran away.

228

"Tommy will be more sensible when he is older," said Toby.

"Will he?" asked Sophie.

"Yes. I shall teach him to hold a bat and use a rifle," said Toby. "He must learn to box."

"But I don't think Moo is that sort of little boy."

"There is only one sort of little boy—Boy," said Toby.

"You don't know what people are like," said Sophie.

"Well, you think all your geese are swans," Toby retorted with reason.

"I find out my mistake," said Sophie.

"You do indeed," said Toby.

No one, thought Sophie, ever made as many mistakes as I—but, if I am often wrong, at least I apprehend there *is* a truth. Even in Moo there is truth, thought Sophie, and it should be respected.

She remembered how she had felt that with the patients in the Mission. The missionaries worked for the people but did not respect them. For all their love and zeal they wanted to bend them, bend them out of their own truth, and—I left the Mission, thought Sophie.

*

At one time she used to carry round Toby's letters as talismans; now she carried Aunt Rose's letter. She did not take it out and look at it, she kept it with her. Now, once again, she opened it. The brief lines seemed to hearten her. Aunt Rose feels what I feel—often, thought Sophie. She looked at the letter and she saw what she had not noticed in the excitement of its news. In the corner there were three words in Aunt Rose's small, clear, acrid writing. As she read them it was, for Sophie, as if the brown cow in the picture had ceased to look away and had turned its head and looked directly at her.

"Don't do it," wrote Aunt Rose.

*

It was, after all, a little thing that decided it. On their last evening Toby came upstairs to the sitting room.

"By the way," he said, "I forgot to tell you. That fellow Nabir Dār was here to see you."

"Nabir!" Sophie spun round. "Nabir! Where is he? Where?" She was running downstairs when Toby caught her.

"He's gone," said Toby. "I sent him away."

"You—sent him away?"

"No point in seeing him," said Toby. "I didn't want you to distress yourself."

"You—didn't—want—me—to—distress—myself—and—you—sent—him away?" asked Sophie.

"Yes, dear," said Toby firmly, and he bent down and kissed her. "Go to bed and sleep well," he said cheerfully. "You have a long day tomorrow."

As he left he said, "I shall be here in the morning." But Sophie was not.

Chapter 21

In the very early morning Aziz the tonga-man bumped his tonga as far as he could up the track to Dhilkusha. It might have been the symbol of Sophie's wagon.

The whole village had turned out to see it go. The pir, the schoolmaster, the elders, with Raschid, the barber, the tailor, Nabir's mother—all the men who had sold so much to Sophie, all the women who had watched her, the babies she had doctored, all the herd children: Salim, Zooni, Rahim, Daveed, Taji, Mustaph, Rahti, and the others, waited.

Sophie had telephoned from the waterworks shed for places in a car to Rawalpindi, and had sent a telegram to Mr. Kirkpatrick. Now, in the first light, she came out, with the children, dressed for travelling. Moo carried the little turquoise boat from Profit David; Teresa carried Pussy Maria, and the trunk with the rose; Raschid and Nabir followed with the boxes, the goose with its feet tied together, and a basket of apples. Mahomet carried the bowl of honey on his head, steadying it with one hand; in the other hand he had the samowar. Sophie carried her bag and the rug in a long roll under her arm.

On the veranda she paused. She looked up at the mountain, then out over the gardens and down to the lake. There, in the houseboat, Toby lay, she hoped, fast asleep.

"It isn't very polite to go without saying good-bye to Toby," said Teresa.

"If we talk we won't go," said Sophie, and Teresa, catching her fearfulness, cried to Moo, "Hurry! Hurry!" But Sophie had not moved. She was looking at the compass.

"The sailor is better for you," said Sophie to Sophie. "Even if he is cold comfort, even if you never see him or catch his star. Take him for yours," said Sophie sternly, and Sophie said, "I will."

"What are you doing?" asked Teresa, coming back.

Sophie might have said, "Wedding myself," but she only took Teresa's hand.

Nabir shifted his feet and waited. Late last night Sophie had sent for Nabir. She had been afraid he would not come, but he came. Now, looking at the compass too, "Which way," he asked, "will the memsahib go?"

Sophie sketched it for him with her finger between the north and the west star, and told him the name. "Lebanon," he said, trying it on his tongue, and his eyes grew alarmed at its unfamiliarity. "Aie! The memsahib is brave."

"Not brave," said Sophie. "I have to go. It's not brave to do as you must do."

"Memsahib, Moo Baba has his feet in the mud," cried Mahomet.

"In his clean shoes!" said Teresa and flew.

Sophie gave a long sigh. "Yes, we must go," she said.

"Better! Better!" urged Nabir.

Teresa had caught Moo. The procession formed itself again, and with Nabir and the others, the boxes and strange bundles, the goose, the samowar, the apples, the rug under her arm, Sophie with Teresa and Moo went down the path.

❧

Down in the houseboat Toby slept. Beside it, in the willows, the kingfishers glinted in the morning sun as they flew in and out of the willow trees, quite close to his head.

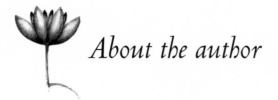

About the author

Rumer Godden was born in Sussex, England, but at six months old she was taken out to India, where her father worked for Inland Navigation. She and her three sisters spent most of their childhood on the banks of the rivers of Assam and Bengal—now Bangladesh—where they lived in a jute trading town called Narayangunj.

When Rumer was twelve years old and her older sister Jon was fourteen, they were sent back to England for schooling. Rumer returned to India as soon as possible, and, at the age of twenty, she ran a dancing school in Calcutta, married, and parted from her husband. During the war, she took her two small daughters to Kashmir, where, as she had no money, she rented a little Kashmiri house far in the country where they could live as cheaply as peasants. It had no electricity, no running water, no road up to it. She looked after and taught her children, and she earned a living by writing and by running an herb farm. Rumer Godden describes those years as "years of beauty and content." In 1946 she was repatriated to England, where she married again.

Rumer Godden has written more than sixty well-loved and enduring books for both adults and children, nine of which have been made into films.

Designed by Don Leeper
Art by R. W. Scholes
Typeset in Centaur
by Stanton Publication Services
Printed on acid-free Liberty Antique paper
by Arcata Graphics.

More fiction from Milkweed Editions: